UNTAMED

Dark Moon Shifters Book Two

BELLA JACOBS

UNTAMED

A Dark Moon Shifters Novel

By Bella Jacobs

�֎ Created with Vellum

ABOUT THE BOOK

Once upon a time there was a very good girl, who followed all the rules.

That girl is dead.

I am no longer Wren Frame, the bird with the broken wing. I am Wren Wander, a rare shapeshifter determined to take back everything the cult stole from me—my health, my hope, and most importantly, my family.

My sister is still out there somewhere. **Alive.**

And with the help of the four brave, formidable, sexy-as-hell alphas destined to be my mates, I intend to keep her that way.

All I have to do is gain control of my unpredictable new powers, learn hand-to-hand combat, avoid capture by a mad scientist out to rid the world of shifters, and stay ten steps ahead of a Big Bad Evil hungry for my blood.

And that's not the worst of it.

In order to fully control my powers, I have to form bonds with all four of my mates. But for a woman who's been betrayed by every person she's ever loved, trust doesn't come easy, no matter how much I'm coming to adore these incredible men.

Can I win this battle of the heart in time? Or will the enemies closing in end our fight for the future before it even gets started?

UNTAMED is part two of the Dark Moon Shifters series, a red-hot reverse harem paranormal and urban fantasy romance. Expect pulse-pounding action, suspense, swoon-worthy romance, and four sexy shifter men who will make you wish you had a bear, wolf, lynx, and griffin of your own.

*To all the brave women who inspire
me daily. Thank you for your big, beautiful,
fearless hearts.*

CHAPTER 1

DR. MARTIN HIGHBORN

The lights are dim in the operating theater, so dim the students watching from the back of the bleachers won't be able to observe the finer points of the procedure.

All they'll see is red and white.

Blood and sheets.

Flash of silver as my scalpel darts into the open cavity, flutter of gloved hands and glowing metal wands as my assistants rush to cauterize the wounds.

But sometimes shadows are necessary.

Tilting my head, I raise my voice to be heard through my surgical mask, "Feline shifters have highly sensitive eyesight. By keeping the lights low, we reduce the risk of a fight or flight response should the subject regain consciousness during the procedure." I draw my hands away, motioning toward the abdomen as I add to my team, "Suction. Keep that area clear."

"Why not increase the dose of anesthesia, doctor?" a trembling voice asks from the darkness.

I encourage questions, but first-year apprentices are often timid about speaking up. It takes time for these former med school students to adjust to the reality that no hospital board or government agency is going to rush in and shut us down for coloring outside the lines. It takes even more time for them to accept that our patients aren't people—not really, no matter how much they resemble our species in their bipedal forms.

They aren't fellow humans deserving of compassionate care. They're apex predators poised to wipe our species from the earth, and we at Elysium are on the front lines, fighting to save humanity from certain annihilation.

Our work is sanctioned by the government and assisted by the Department of Homeland Preservation. Without their support and funding none of this—not the reassignment we're completing today, or any of our more classified projects—would be possible.

But so many of my students are still naïve young people. They think the big bad wolf is a character from a fairytale, that the monster under the bed becomes a harmless pile of clothes once the lights are flicked on.

So, we go slow, each dose of reality cloaked in soothing half-truths to make the pills easier to swallow.

"We're administering the maximum dose of intravenous drugs recommended for an organism of this size," I reply, returning to work as the blood pooling near the remaining ovary is suctioned away. "A higher dose would increase the risk of heart failure and compromise the subject's ability to survive the procedure. Forceps."

I hold out my hand, palm open, waiting until my scalpel is replaced with the clamps to continue. "Ideally, we work to slow the subject's metabolism in the days before surgery with fasting and the addition of nightshade to the diet. But with subjects who are apprehended, rather than recruited, we often aren't able to obtain that level of cooperation."

In other words, this little beast fought capture with every mutated cell in its body, wrecking a containment van and nearly killing two men before it was tranquilized into submission. If my students were ready, I could explain that the subject's DNA has already been altered with IV therapies and that the procedure they're watching today is simply a garden variety hysterectomy, the old-fashioned kind performed before surgeons developed more sophisticated techniques to avoid cutting through the abdominal wall.

But there's no need to be gentle with this creature. It will recover quickly enough. Even with most of its shifter genes disabled, it will continue to heal at an accelerated rate. We've honed the therapies needed to shut down the ability to transition into animal form and to access the telepathic powers possessed by so many of their kind, but we've yet to fine-tune the suppression of their superior immune systems.

We're getting closer every day.

If only I could concentrate fully on the work...

Soon. Only one obstacle still stands in the way, and her days are numbered. The girl escaped capture, but we learned so much about her in the process. She believes she has a soul. She values kindness and imagines herself capable of mercy, love, and a host of other emotions only humans can fully experience.

Which reminds me...

"Rilke once wrote that perhaps everything terrible is, in its deepest, truest being, something helpless in need of aid," I say as I transfer the last of the reproductive organs to the stainless-steel basin, ensuring this monster won't be able to breed again.

Leaving my assistants to finish and close, I strip off my gloves and step away from the table, tugging my mask down as I address the faces floating in the darkness, "After you've completed the assigned reading for the day, I'd like you to meditate on Rilke's thoughts and come prepared to offer insight at the start of class tomorrow." I smile. "And if you signed up to bring coffee or donuts, please don't shirk your responsibilities, First Years. Especially the coffee. I can't be expected to talk philosophy without caffeine."

Laughter murmurs softly through the group of eighteen or twenty as they rise to file out of the operating theater.

I can't remember how many we have left this semester. We've lost several. Even with our rigorous vetting system, some students prove unfit for the work.

It can be distressing to watch a subject go into seizures during IV therapy or come out of sedation too early, weeping, begging to be allowed to go home to a partner or child. The pre-pubescent subjects are especially challenging for the more tender-hearted students.

The little ones do such an excellent job of playing human, of hugging their stuffed toys and crying for their parents the way a real child would.

It can make it hard to remember that it's all a smoke-screen, an adaptation for survival.

Shifters instinctively mimic human behavior. For thousands of years, their existence depended on passing as human. Their "emotions" are plumage allowing them to hide in plain sight, blending in with their prey. In evolutionary biologist circles, it's called aggressive mimicry. Creation is rife with spiders camouflaged as ants, beetles pretending to be fireflies, and serpents with tails adapted to resemble the insects the birds in their habitat love to eat.

The one thing they have in common?

Mimicry makes it easier for them to kill.

Shifters are no different. The very young and those who have been raised in human homes may not realize they aren't experiencing love or fear the way a human would. They may not consciously understand that they are predators, but biology always betrays them in the end.

Nature wins over nurture. Every. Single. Time.

This girl will be no different. Her savage side *will* win out, sooner or later.

In the meantime, we'll use her delusions to our advantage.

After washing up and changing into clean scrubs, I leave the operating theater antechamber, making my way to the restricted wing at the far edge of the facility. Pressing my palm to the sensor on the door, I push inside, bound for the decontamination rooms and the cellblock beyond.

It's quiet as a tomb in this corner of the Institute, without the curses and cries for mercy so common in the other wings. Here, we've taken full control of our subjects. They don't eat, sleep, shift, or shit without guidance from the handlers controlling their biological cues. They are perfectly docile in their cells and ruthlessly vicious when our occasion calls for it.

They are abominations, weapons destined to be destroyed as soon as every shifter has been sterilized and reassigned, but they are also...magnificent.

I would be lying if I said I wasn't proud of our beautiful monsters, these beasts who will help reclaim the world from the things that go bump in the night.

I step out of the lab into the decontamination area and suit up. A compromised immune system is one of the unfortunate side effects of our work with these subjects. They sicken easily and struggle to fight off even the mildest infections. We lost one to strep throat in December and another to complications from a staph infection last month.

And the bears killed their share in the raid last week.

Even the girl killed one. *Almost* killed one. According to the footage obtained from the subject's corneal implant, she was prepared to show it mercy once it shifted into its human form. Someone else pulled the trigger, someone out of our subject's line of sight, who I'd like to have strapped to my table, prepared to pay for the damage he's caused.

The subject he destroyed shouldn't have been able to shift until the transformation was triggered by his handler. It was a glitch, one I would have been able to fix if the subject had been returned to the lab with the rest of the deployed. Instead, his body was lost to us, presumably burned with the rest of the bear shifters' dead.

Burned.

Such a waste. Not only of the knowledge to be gained from study of the corpse, but of the tech that could have been recycled for use in another subject.

Reduce, reuse, recycle—if humanity had taken the mantra to heart earlier, we might not be where we are today, pushed inland by rising tides and fearing the super storms sweeping across the skies the way our ancestors feared their gods.

Though there are upsides to living at this point in history.

Now, men can *be* gods, bending the building blocks of creation to their will.

"Dr. Highborn. Glad you're here." Dr. Monroe, my lead on the Apex experiment, greets me inside the cell-block, his brown eyes troubled behind the plastic visor of his full body suit. "I wanted to touch base. Be sure I was reading your directions correctly before I started the therapy on Subject Seven."

"You read them correctly." I lead the way down the quiet hall toward the last cell on the left. In the rooms on either side, the subjects are sleeping off their daily infusion, curled quietly on their bunks, as docile as any well-trained animal. "I want the subject isolated in a biohazard-secure cell in C block and infected with Devour virus."

Monroe makes a note on his clipboard. "Might I ask why, sir? It's a strong specimen, in perfect physical condition. With proper modification, it could be a valuable asset now that we've lost Subjects Four, Eleven, and Sixteen."

I stop beside the last cell, where Subject 7 is proving her mettle, the only subject still upright after her daily infusion of nutrients, immune-system-boosting drugs, and heavy sedatives.

I meet her pale eyes, not surprised when her expression remains sluggishly hostile. "Tell me, Dr. Monroe, what do you see when you look at Subject Seven?"

He shifts beside me. "Subject Seven appears to be female. Of Irish or Germanic heritage, perhaps both."

I smile. "You're cheating. You've seen her chart. Use your eyes, doctor."

Monroe clears his throat, falling silent for a long moment before he offers, "She's a young woman, no more than twenty, maybe still in adolescence. She's petite but strong, with good muscle tone. Attractive. Pretty when she smiles." He pauses, cocking his head to one side. "And her eyes are striking. They draw you in, make you want to know what she's feeling."

"Good," I murmur. "It's the eyes I want. Those big blue eyes. Think how much bigger they'll seem when she's wasted away to practically nothing, so frail and helpless it will hurt to look at her." I step closer to the bars, gaze fixed on 7's heart-shaped face. "What have we learned about the young Fata Morgana, Alex?"

"That she's coming into her powers quickly, and that she's surrounded herself with potential consorts who will make her even more dangerous once they've formed power-sharing bonds."

"What else? What do we know about her human life? About who Wren Frame thinks she is?" I ask, lips curving as Subject 7 drags first one leg and then the other across her cot, letting each fall heavily to the floor.

"She's been sheltered," Alex says. "She was a Church of Humanity rescue who spent most of her life on shifter suppression drugs. She only recently learned of her true nature and likely still identifies as human. At least in her own mind. She's a rare shifter with challenging powers and no willing mentors, which means we likely still have time before she becomes a serious threat."

Subject 7 scoots forward on the mattress.

Monroe steps away from the bars; I stay where I am, watching the girl rock back and forth as I ask, "And what else? What about her weaknesses? What makes her different than the man she was born to challenge?"

Monroe pulls in a breath, holding it before he lets it out soft and low. "I see. At least, I think I do."

"Tell me," I encourage, as Subject 7 braces a hand on the concrete block wall, her jaw clenching with the effort.

"Mercy," he murmurs. "She has mercy. Even on Subject Eleven, after the attack on the bear settlement. She wasn't going to kill him."

"And how do we use mercy to our advantage? Do we

send in predators the girl will be on her guard against now that she knows of their existence?" I loop my fingers around the bars. "Or do we send in a creature so deliciously broken Wren won't hesitate to offer it aid?"

Subject 7 lurches to her feet, her blue eyes blazing.

"You don't think she'll suspect something?" Monroe asks. "During the debrief, Subject Seven said the girl had no idea there was a tracking device on the vehicle. As far as Wren knows, her friend Carrie Ann is an ally who sent us down the wrong path. How do we explain her sudden appearance at the camp?"

"Leave that to me." I watch Subject 7, Carrie Ann, one of my most precocious creations, shuffle toward me, exerting Herculean amounts of will to keep from succumbing to the sedatives coursing through her bloodstream. "I have a few tricks up my sleeve still, Monroe."

"Of course, sir," Monroe says. "Though, I can't help but wonder…"

"What do you wonder, my friend?" I murmur.

"If there's even a chance Wren might be able to…remove him…"

Him. We don't say his name—he's the villain of a children's book, too terrible to be spoken of aloud—but we all know it. Atlas. The reigning Fata Morgana. The man with a thousand forms, an army of supernatural defenders, and a fortress no satellite can locate, no matter how hard we've tried.

Atlas, the ally and taskmaster we've embraced because that's what you do with enemies who are too powerful to destroy—you make them friends.

"We'll never have the weapons or tech to take him out," Monroe whispers tightly as Carrie Ann weaves closer. "But that's what Wren Frame was born to do. Shouldn't we let her try? If she fails, nothing changes. But if she succeeds..."

If she succeeds, we'd finally have a shot at wiping out every shifter on the planet—including the all-powerful Atlas. Wren kills Atlas, then we kill her, a much easier target than a monster who's had millennia to fine-tune his defenses.

But the fact remains that the monster has had *millennia* to prepare.

And the monster has a knack for being everywhere, all at once.

And the monster isn't stupid enough to leave any vital corner of his kingdom unguarded.

Monroe should have known better than to say such dangerous things. He should have known better than to *think* them.

For a moment, I'm filled with a sharp, sudden sadness.

There are few people in my world who have proven their loyalty and commitment to the cause the way he has.

I'm going to miss Monroe.

"No." I lean into the space between the bars, my gaze tangled with Carrie Ann's. "We are loyal to Atlas. We keep our promises to him, he keeps his promises to us, and we all live happily ever after."

"Sir?" Monroe's voice cracks in the middle of the word.

We all know the self-termination trigger. It's the final protocol, the last chance to go out on your own terms, to reach for whatever lies on the other side of this life with dignity before it's too late. Not a traditional "happily ever after," for damned sure, but better than the alternative.

So much better…

"No, sir." Monroe lifts shaking hands in supplication. "Please, I was just talking. I'm loyal. You know that." He swallows hard "Please, Martin. Lacey's having the baby in a month. She needs me. My daughter needs me. Please, God, I'm begging you…"

But God has no skin in this game, and no one, god or mortal, can grant Monroe's prayer. I know that, but when his breath catches and his hands fly to his mask, I can't help but flinch.

Behind his fumbling fingers, something small and black scuttles from his dark hair, down his sweat-beaded forehead. It's followed by another creature, no bigger than the tip of a ball-point pen, and then another.

And another.

Soon the insects—ticks maybe, or one of those flesh-eating African fleas my college roommate studied our sophomore year—are pooled in the corners of his eyes, churning, burrowing as Monroe begins to scream. Within moments there's a faint pop as the insects break through, swarming into his sockets. Blood splatters the plastic visor from the inside, obscuring my view as Monroe falls to his knees, shrieking in agony as he claws at the hood of the suit that's become his death shroud.

It is mercifully quick—less than a minute between penetration and annihilation—but not fast enough. Carrie Ann reaches the bars while I'm distracted by the corpse twitching at my feet. I'm reminded of her presence by a sharp pressure on the knuckle of my middle finger, followed quickly by pain as her teeth break through the thick fabric of my suit, finding skin and bone.

Howling through gritted teeth, I snatch a handful of her filthy blond hair, shoving her head back before slamming it forward into the bars—once, twice, three times. On the fourth, the skin on her forehead bursts, and her jaw loosens. I rip my hand from her filthy mouth before introducing her forehead to the cold iron again and again, only stopping when her eyes roll back and her knees buckle.

I release her with a grunt, breathing heavily as she crumples to the floor against the bars.

Once again, the cellblock is eerily still, no sound but the snoring of one of the subjects at the opposite end of the hall and the rustle of tiny legs as the insects abandon Dr. Monroe's corpse. I watch them stream from between the zipper that secures the hood to the hazmat suit, leaving bloody footprints behind them.

There are hundreds of them, I realize, enough to make a statement without saying a word.

The creatures separate into three groups—two forming large black dots on the polished concrete and the third, a curved line below them.

A smiley face.

Evidently, Atlas is still pleased with my contribution to our partnership.

I nod in response, and the smile dissolves as the insects lift into the air on previously invisible wings, climbing until they vanish into the ductwork in the ceiling.

Clutching my wounded hand to my chest, I hit the call button on the side of my helmet. "We need a cleaner in the Apex cell block, and tell Dr. Casey I'm headed to the infirmary for stitches and an antibiotic drip."

"Right away, Dr. Highborn," the voice on the other end of the com replies, knowing better than to ask questions.

There is a time for curiosity—in the lab, in the class-room, in the operating theater when discovering fasci-nating anomalies in the shifter reproductive system—and there is a time for following protocol.

Protocol is what keeps the people working here safe from the monster too big and bad to ever bring to heel.

Because Rilke was wrong. Not everything terrible is truly something helpless in need of aid. Some monsters are pure evil, through and through, and the only truth is that they will get their teeth into you—sooner or later.

It's just a matter of time.

CHAPTER 2
WREN

I have no idea what I'm doing.

Absolutely no clue.

As I sit in this cramped hotel room in the wilds outside Spokane, watching two of the four men in my life prowl the flowered carpet like caged animals, while the third seethes in a tattered wingback chair in the corner, and the fourth broods on the bed beside me with a still sadness that breaks my heart, I am struck by how utterly unqualified I am. I am not fit to be the glue that holds five people together in a relationship—*any* relationship, let alone a supernatural union that is the only shot at survival for ourselves, the planet, and everyone we love.

I've never had a steady boyfriend.

Aside from my adopted parents, I've never even *observed* a functional union up close. My girlfriends in high school were all wallflowers like me, or in intense, secretive, highly sexual relationships with other band nerds. In college, I was too busy volunteering at the shelter and trying not to die to have time to be part of a couple, and the few illicit liaisons I witnessed at work always ended badly.

My sister had one serious boyfriend when she was in high school, but Chad vanished from the picture pretty quickly once Scarlett was sent to rehab. He did show up to her memorial service with a bouquet of lilies, but we all knew that was more about assuaging guilt than expressing affection. He was the one who'd given Scarlett the drugs that landed her in rehab in the first place, and his offering only proved he hadn't known my sister at all.

Scarlett hated lilies. They made her sneeze.

They make *her sneeze*, I correct myself.

My sister is still alive. For now. And as long as there is breath in my body, I intend to keep her that way. Which means we have to decide our next move. Fast. Before our enemies catch up with us again.

I force my lips to part, and more uncomfortable words to come out. "I know this is hard, and that we're all tired and scared, but we have to decide on a place to settle. We can't keep running in circles."

"Agreed." Creedence's voice is a soft rumble, but I know he's still angry.

Enraged is a better word. His blood is running so hot I'm sure it's kicking up the temperature in the already warm room a couple degrees.

"A decision has to be made," he continues. "Preferably one that ends with all of us staying alive. Which would be easier if certain members of our happy family would quit lying every time they open their fucking mouths."

"Nastiness isn't productive," Kite says with a sigh.

"Oh, I'm sorry, Pooh-bie." Creedence presses a hand to his chest as he leans forward in his chair, his amber eyes blazing. "I apologize for not being as Zen as you and your old lady, but I figure we have enough enemies out there." He jabs a thumb at the window, where the trees droop in the summer rain, their heavy leaves looking as dejected as I feel. "Half of creation wants to take us out. If we can't trust and depend on each other, we might as well put a gun to our heads now and save the bad guys the trouble."

"Please don't talk that way," I beg, my stomach churning sickly as flashes from the attack on the reservation rush through my head. It's been a week since we fled east, but the memories of carnage are still way too fresh.

Every time I close my eyes, I see blood, tears streaming down terrified faces, and a hole exploding in the center of a man's forehead as he begs me for help.

A hole Luke put there with his gun.

A hole Luke doesn't regret for a second.

A hole that inspired Luke's everlasting contempt when I made it clear I'm serious about showing our enemies mercy, even when mercy feels impossible.

I peek at him beneath my lashes, but Luke's gaze remains fixed on the carpet as he paces from the sink to the silent television and back again, sticking to his side of the space by unspoken agreement with Dust, who paces a slower, shorter path between the bed and the door.

When I shift my attention Dust's way, his gray eyes are filled with equal parts frustration and a helplessness that worries me.

Dust is our captain. If he's lost, what does that mean for the rest of us?

It means no one is steering the ship. They're fighting over the wheel, and you'd better step in and take charge before you all end up smashed against the rocks.

But how do I take charge?

How do I lead, when I know for a fact that at least one of my potential mates doesn't want to follow me—or to be my mate at all? Luke's only in this for the fake ID he's been promised when we cross the border. And then there's Creedence, who thinks I'm a naïve child, Dust, who's having an existential crisis, and Kite, my first mate, first love, first *everything*, who is quietly slipping into depression in the wake of the deaths of his family and friends.

I tighten my grip on Kite's hand, wishing I could spare him this pain, that I could take it into myself somehow. But I can't. All I can do is hold his hand and be there for him when he wakes up crying out in the night and promise that I'll never give up on him or on our mission.

If I give up, if we fail, then all those deaths, all that suffering and loss, will have been for nothing.

"Dust has apologized," I say in my most soothing voice, "and explained why he made the decision he made. We may not agree with it, but I understand why he felt it was the right call at the time. He was trying to give us some stability, to keep us from being any more frightened than we were already."

"With all due respect, Slim," Creedence says, "I'm a grown man, not a child who needs to be sheltered from the big bad world. I'm also more than this mark on my ass. I have experience slipping by the authorities. I was helping my sister make fake IDs before I could ride a bike without training wheels."

"And those are skills we can put to use now," Dust says, speaking up for the first time in several minutes. "We're going to need—"

"I don't give a fuck what you need!" Creedence surges to his feet so fast his shaggy golden hair flies into his face, errant strands sticking to the beard he's grown while we've been living on the road. "I don't work for you, Captain." The last word is spoken in a sneer so cutting it makes me flinch. "You aren't calling the shots around here anymore."

"Then who is?" Dust shouts, clearly done apologizing. "You? You think you've got what it takes to run a mission I've trained two years to lead? Just because you hail from a family of thieves and con artists?"

"Thieves and con artists who got away with millions," Creedence pops back. "Most of it without getting anyone caught or killed. We both know you can't say the same. How many casualties have you chalked up so far? Fifteen? Twenty?"

Dust stiffens, his jaw clenching tight.

Creedence jerks his head toward Luke. "And if it hadn't been for Mister Paranoid Puppy over there, we'd be dead now, too. Just like those innocent people, those kids we might as well have slaughtered with our bare hands for all the—"

"Don't," Kite snaps, lifting his gaze from our tangled fingers. "Don't use the deaths of my people to make your point. We get it. We all understand what's at stake."

"I don't think you do," Luke offers in a silky voice so relaxed that, if it weren't for his endless pacing, I would think he didn't care about any of this. Any of us. "Someone put a tracking device on the Hummer. If we hadn't found it, the people hunting Wren would have found *us*. And the person who put them on our trail is someone we think we can trust." He pauses, glancing Cree's way. "I'm sure, if I weren't the one who suggested we do a sweep, I'd be a suspect."

"Maybe you still are," Creedence says with a dangerous smile. "Maybe you're playing a long game, pretending to be our buddy now so we'll relax our guard and give you the chance to really stick it to us later."

Luke smiles back. "If I wanted you dead, you wouldn't be breathing right now, brother."

"I'm not your brother. And I'm done with this conversation." Creedence snatches the keys from the table near his chair. "I need some fucking air."

"Please, stay." I swing my feet to the floor, standing between the two rumpled beds where we all slept poorly last night. "Please Cree," I plead as he starts for the door. "We need to be on the same page, and that won't happen if you leave. We need you here. *I* need you here."

He glances over his shoulder, his wild gaze soften-ing. But he doesn't move back into the room. "I'll bring back something to eat," he says, his shoulders hunching closer to his ears. "All of you assholes are getting too skinny."

He slips out the door, leaving silence filled only by the hum of the tiny refrigerator hidden beneath the television.

A part of me wants to go after him, but not to insist he come back and finish the discussion we've started.

I want to slam into the battered Mustang convertible we bought three towns back and go for a ride. I want to put the top down and go fast, until the wind rushing past my ears drowns out all the ugliness and fear and the terrifying possibilities I can't quit dreaming about every time I fall asleep.

But heroes, even ill-suited ones like me, don't get to run away.

It's not part of the job description.

I prop my hands on my hips and dig back in. "It could have been Carrie Ann. Or my parents." My voice catches on the last word, but I clear my throat and push on, "They all got close enough to the Hummer to slip the tracker under the bumper."

"Or it could have happened on the reservation," Kite says. "My sister knew we were planning to take the Hummer when we left. She could have told someone who told someone. I don't like to think about any of those people turning traitor, but it's possible."

"Or your sister could be the rat," Luke says, earning a

glare from Kite so intense I shift forward, positioning myself between the two men—just in case.

"It's not Leda," Kite snaps. "She's family."

"And Carrie Ann is like a sister to Wren," Luke says gently—for him—but I can tell Kite isn't taking it that way. "And her adopted parents raised her since she was four years old. It fucking sucks when people we love betray us, but it happens. Even with our ride-or-die crew."

"I don't like to think it could be someone *any* of us knows," I say, jumping in before Kite can explode. He's usually a peacemaker—so is Creedence, for that matter —but we're all on edge. "But I'm even less inclined to believe it's anyone in this room." I lift a hand toward the door. "Or anyone who recently left the room. You're all good at shielding, but you also all drop your guard every now and then, and I haven't felt a whiff of that kind of malice from any of you."

"Me, either," Kite seconds.

I gained access to and amplified Kite's empathic gifts when we mate-bonded last week. Now we're both capable of reading an average, unguarded person's intentions in about six seconds flat.

Luke, Creedence, and Dust have been working on psychic shielding in order to keep us out of their personal business, but I still catch my share of unchecked emotional responses.

Luke is angrier, and more hurt, than he lets on. Dust is tormented by guilt. And Creedence secretly wants comfort so badly, sometimes it's all I can do not to sneak up behind him and hug him until he can't breathe. But none of them seem to want to hurt me, or each other.

Even this morning, when Creedence came back from that trance he goes into when he's seeing the future. He'd been red-faced and so angry that he railed at Dust for five minutes straight before anyone could get a word in edgewise, but he didn't truly want to hurt him.

He just wanted to strangle him.

Lightly.

For a prolonged time...

"But you didn't pick up on Dust's secret," Luke says, always willing to play the devil's advocate—or just the devil, depending on his mood. "We might be better at hiding shit than you think."

"We can't read thoughts," Kite says wearily. "We pick up on emotional resonance. Dust feeling upset about our handlers being taken out blended in with Dust feeling upset that my people were murdered at a party. Both are very different than Dust meaning any of us harm."

Luke shrugs. "Maybe Dust is feeling upset about having to murder us in our beds tonight, too. Not everyone approaches homicide the same way."

"Enough," I say, my tone sharp. I'll tolerate a lot from Luke, but not kicking a man who's already down. Dust is swimming in regret. The last thing he needs is Creedence and Luke both on his ass. "That part of the discussion is over. Dust kept a secret he shouldn't have. He's sorry, and it won't happen again. It's time to move on. If you can't do that, then you can leave. We won't try to stop you."

"If I leave, you're down to three little helpers, Princess. Maybe two if the cat doesn't come back." Luke's dark eyes glitter as he faces me down across the room. "You sure that's what you want, chica?"

What I want is for Luke to go all in, to promise he'll be here today, tomorrow, and for as long as it takes to dethrone Atlas and shut down every other threat to the survival of our people and this planet. I want him to say that he respects my perspective and values—even if he doesn't agree with them—and that he's willing to work to find common ground between hopeless naïveté and ruthless cynicism.

Even more than all that, I want him to confess that he feels it, too, this super-powered pull that snatches at my chest every time we're breathing the same air.

I treasure Kite as my first love, I adore Dust as my oldest friend, and when I'm not too miserable and scared to access other emotions, I want to get close to Creedence—really close and really naked—and for him to do all those wicked things he promised to do the one time we kissed.

But with Luke...

With Luke there's something else, something primal and a little scary but that I desperately want to learn more about. I want to reach out and touch my fingertips to his flame, even if it burns me. But all he wants is a fresh start north of the border, and he doesn't even want *that* badly enough to fight for a place in this circle of five.

If I tell him to go, he will.

For a moment, I consider it. Because that's one of the things Luke does to me, too. He makes me crazy and inclined to do stupid, impulsive things.

Instead, I force myself to say, "No, I don't want you to go. I want you to stay, but I need to move on to the problem-solving portion of the discussion. Our handlers are dead, we can't be certain the safe house they arranged for us is safe, and we can no longer count on financial, logistical, or any other form of assistance from the outside. We're on our own, and it's time to sort out where we go from here."

Luke holds my gaze for a long beat. "All right. I vote no on the safe house. It's too much of a risk."

"I agree," Dust seconds softly. "Though, it might not be a completely lost cause. I could go in alone, bring back anything I find that might be useful."

"Useful like what?" Luke prompts. "Passports? Money?"

Dust nods. "Those things. There might also be medicine and gear for the crossing. Even in summer it can get below freezing in the mountains at night. We'll need to be prepared for the weather."

"We could cross in kin form instead." I recently added a fox to my repertoire of alternative shapes, and I've been practicing shifting into kin form at will. Without accessing my spirit world, where Atlas is waiting to take me out, it isn't easy, but I'm getting there.

Slowly, but surely.

"At least one of us will need to go over as human,"

Dust says. "To carry money, passports, any additional weapons we acquire between now and then."

I nibble my thumb, thoughts racing. "Okay, but I'm going with you to the safe house."

"Absolutely not," Dust says, at the same moment Luke grunts, "Hell, no."

"Hell, yes." I stand up straighter. "I'm the logical choice. My fox is the smallest kin form, so Dust can easily carry me on his back. But my fire form is danger-ous, so I'll be able to offer backup if our enemies are waiting for us."

"You're forgetting one important thing," Dust says. "I'm replaceable. You're not."

I feel warm fingers on my wrist and look up to find Kite standing beside me. "He's right. I know you prefer to think of the good of the group, but this is our reality now. If we lose you, we're all lost. You're the only one who can stop Atlas. Your safety has to come first. We all know that, and none of us resent you for it."

Glancing around the room, I see the truth of his words reflected in Dust's sober expression and even Luke's relatively calm eyes. "Okay," I say tightly, my breath rushing out. "But I have to do something. I can't just sit here, locked in a hotel room, trying not to get killed."

"We'll start your training tomorrow." Luke motions toward the woods outside our sleepy little motel. "We'll start with a two-mile run, get you warmed up while we're ditching civilization, and then I'll teach you how to suck less at kicking ass."

His tone makes me feel prickly all over, like one of

those cactuses that shoot spines when you get too close to them, but I nod and say, "Okay, sounds good,"

Because I am an adult.

I am a grown-up, I am a grown-up, I am a grown-up. It's a mantra I repeat a lot these days, when I'm wondering why *I'm* the one in charge of remaining rational all the time, when I am—

1. The youngest member of our five, aside from Kite, who is still light years ahead of me when it comes to life experience.

2. The least knowledgeable about shifter rules, limitations, powers, risks, customs, and—oh, yeah—*actually being able to shift* into one of my kin forms.

3. The newest recruit on this mission. Dust, Kite, and Cree have been plotting and planning together for months. And sure, Luke was kidnapped around the same time I was, but he's a former werewolf gang member who spent years in prison and is infinitely more prepared to fight a supernatural war than I'll ever be, even if we had a hundred years to whip me into shape.

4. Scared. I am so, so scared.

I'm as terrified as I am determined to see this through.

I want to save the world, I really do. I want to give all the innocent people out there struggling to survive on our increasingly hostile planet a shot at a brighter tomorrow, but I still feel so helpless and small.

I am one girl.

One *woman*, but just barely.

At twenty-four, I know I should feel like a full-fledged grown-up, but until Kite spirited me away from my house two weeks ago, I still lived with my parents. I have never lived by myself, never gone to bed without hugging my mother and father goodnight, never woken up in the morning without being greeted by the smells and sounds of people who love me cooking breakfast down the hall.

But the people who loved me are also the people who poisoned me, who nearly killed me and my sister. That ugly, undeniable fact worms into my heart, eating away at the organ I've always trusted to be my touchstone.

How can I follow my heart, when my heart has been a fool that couldn't tell the difference between unconditional love and absolute control? How can I lean into the bonds I'm supposed to form with these men—the one I've *already* formed with Kite—when a vicious new voice in my head constantly reminds me that I'm an idiot who shouldn't have the luxury of letting my guard down. I can care about other people, but I can't let myself need or depend on them. I can't allow myself to let go and become so horribly vulnerable ever again.

Just imagining it makes me feel like I'm suffocating, like I have to claw my way free of the bonds tightening around me, even though these bonds are my only shot at survival.

"Want to go for a walk?" Kite asks.

"It's raining," I murmur even as I decide I don't care and nod. "But yeah. I'll grab my poncho and meet you downstairs."

I snag my poncho from the closet and head for the

door without looking at Luke. I'm as frustrated with him as he is with me and that's not going to be resolved any time soon. Maybe ever. We might very well spend the next few months resenting each other and part ways at the end of the summer, never to cross paths again.

The thought makes me angry. And resentful.

And stupidly sad.

"Hang in there," Dust says as he opens the door to let me out. "It'll get better. We're going to be okay, I promise."

I reach out, squeezing his arm in what I hope is a reassuring way. But I don't say a word before stepping out onto the covered walkway and starting toward the concrete stairs leading to the ground floor.

I'm not sure we're going to be okay, and I refuse to tell lies—not to myself or to anyone else.

CHAPTER 3

KITE

I'm losing her.

As we walk through the persistent drizzle, down the path leading into the woods, up into the foothills of this part of the Rocky Mountain range, Wren's hand is warm in mine, but she might as well be a thousand miles away.

I can feel it, the way she's pulling back a little more every day.

I just found her, just told her how much I love her, just made her mine.

But she *isn't* mine. Not the way I thought she would be once we were bonded.

Yes, I can sense what emotional state she's in most of the time. And yes, I'm so connected to her that sometimes it's like her body is an extension of mine—I feel the texture of what she's touching, sense she's hungry before she realizes it herself—but there's a part of her I can't reach.

She's tucked it away and started work on a wall to keep everyone else on the other side.

Sometimes I find it comforting that she's pushing the others away, too, but mostly it scares me. My inner selfish idiot wants to keep her all to myself, but that path only leads one place—a funeral pyre, and a graveyard with matching his and hers headstones.

Wren has to bond with a marked member of each of the four kin groups—feline, canine, forest, and antiquity—or Atlas is going to kill her. It's that simple.

Even if she forges the bonds, harnesses the powers she'll gain from each of us, and gets a grip on her own hard-to-handle abilities as a Fata Morgana, she might still die.

We all might. These could be our final weeks, days, hours on earth. I don't want to spend them wallowing in misery or longing for things to go back the way they were before my people were killed, before Wren realized how dangerous this quest truly is, before falling in love started to feel irrelevant compared to everything else going on in our fractured world.

Because falling in love isn't stupid.

Love is what we're fighting for, and I'm not betraying the memory of the people I lost by enjoying what time I'm able to steal with my mate, my Wren, the Bird Girl who stole my heart the first time I laid eyes on her face.

I stop, holding tight to her hand as I draw her off the trail and onto the bed of brown pine needles blanketing the forest floor.

"What's up?" Her blue eyes blink up at me from

beneath the hood of the cheap yellow poncho we bought with the last of our cash back in Wilbur.

But I don't answer her with words. Words aren't getting us anywhere lately. Instead, I wrap an arm around her waist, cup her cheek, and kiss her, holding nothing back. I don't try to hide from her or spare her or give her only what I think she can handle. I tell her the truth, show her how much I need her, how much I've missed her, how lonely I am with her heart walled away and mine shivering on the other side.

After the briefest hesitation, she returns the kiss, wrapping her arms so tight around my neck that the hood of my jacket slides down. But I welcome the rain sliding down my neck. It's cold, but clean, washing away the fog of pain and confusion that's haunted my thoughts.

I may not know who killed our leaders or how close they are to killing us, but I know that I love this woman. I know I want to live for her, won't hesitate to die for her, and that she was woven into the fabric of my soul long before we met.

Most of all, I know I'm not going to let her slip away without a fight. Pulling back just long enough to strip off my jacket and spread it on the ground, I return to her with a moan as her mouth presses hungrily to mine.

"I'm sorry," she whispers as we tumble to the ground, her breath coming faster as I roll her beneath me. "I'm so sorry."

"Don't be sorry," I insist, pulling her poncho off and running one hand down her ribs to the curve of her waist. "I understand."

"I don't." She arches into my touch as I slip my fingers beneath her T-shirt to caress the hot skin beneath. "I don't know what's wrong with me."

"Your entire life has changed." I kiss her forehead, her temple. "Your past was rewritten, your present set on fire, and your future is one big question mark with a bunch of devils brandishing pitchforks dancing around it."

She makes a sound somewhere between a laugh and a sob. "Yeah. You get it. Of course you do." She cradles my face in her palms. "I know that, Kite. I do. In the moments when I'm truly myself. The fear and confusion just get so big sometimes…"

"And when they do, I'm here, baby," I remind her. "I'll come running. You don't even have to call my name."

She smiles, and her eyes begin to shine. "I love that song so much. That's all I want to do—put on a Carol King record and roll around in bed with you all day with nothing to worry about except whether or not we'll be able to find a cupcake place that delivers."

"We don't need store-bought cupcakes." I cup her breast in my hand, loving the way she shivers as I brush my thumb across her tight nipple through the thin fabric of her bra. "I know my way around a cupcake pan. I'll whip up a batch of homemade red velvet so fast you won't realize I've left the bed until you smell them cooking."

"No, I'd know you left." Her hands drift between us, tugging my belt through the loops of my jeans. "I always know when you're not as close as I want you to be."

"And how close is that?" I murmur, groaning as her hand slides into my boxers to grip my cock, her cool fingers erotic as hell against my burning length.

"Inside me," she whispers. "Where you belong."

I couldn't agree more, which I attempt to prove to the best of my ability, considering we're naked on the forest floor in the pouring rain. But I don't feel the cold. All I feel is bliss and love and the absolute certainty that I will always belong here, in Wren's arms.

I glide into where she's so wet, so tight, and it's so good I almost lose control in that first deep thrust. But then she sighs into my mouth, the relief in the sound giving me the strength I need to hold back. I want more than relief for my woman. I want her pleasure. I want her coming, crying out my name, her body pulsing around my cock, assuring me that we'll always find our way back to each other, no matter how hard things get.

"I love you," I breathe as her legs lock tight around my waist and her hands tangle in my hair.

She lifts into me, every shift of her hips assuring me that she loves me, too. That she needs me, needs *this*, every bit as much as I do. But the moment she comes, crying out as her body squeezes so tight around me I can't hold back another second, is still a revelation.

A miracle.

All I ever want, and all I'll ever need.

I come calling her name, grateful that shifter children can only be conceived with the focused intent of both the mother and the father. I love having nothing between us but skin and heat and love so intense I can't help but feel like the luckiest bastard in the world. Even now, when the sky is so dark I'm not sure there are any stars left to wish on.

After, I hold her close, covering us with her discarded poncho while she rests her head on my chest, fitting so perfectly against me we don't have to work to find a snuggle position.

Despite the rain and the cool breeze, I'm almost asleep when she whispers, "There's something I need to tell you. I have to trust someone with it, or I'm going to go crazy."

Instantly awake, I turn to face her as she shifts onto her side on the jacket beneath us. "You can trust me with anything. Always. I hope you know that."

"I know, and I do trust you," she says, nibbling the pad of her thumb. The sight of her nude and propped up on one arm, the position emphasizing the dramatic curve from her waist to her hip makes me wish I had charcoal and paper.

I haven't had much time for drawing the past few years, but now I ache for the tools to capture every elegant, sensual line of the woman I love.

"But?" I prompt after a moment.

"No buts. It's just…" She rolls onto her stomach, her chin propped on her fists, concealing most of her from my gaze, making it easier to focus as she says, "You remember the dream I told everyone about, the one where my birth mother came to me and told me that Scarlett is still alive?"

"Of course." I would call it a spirit visitation, not a dream, but it doesn't matter what Wren calls it, only that there's something she's been holding back. "So, your mother said something else, something you weren't ready to share before?"

Wren nods, her brow furrowing. "She said that one of my four knows where Scarlett is. That the answer is locked inside of him, but that he doesn't remember or know it's there. And that he won't until I set the secret free." She shakes her head. "But my gut said to keep that part to myself. At least for a little while."

I hum. "The secret part is odd. If he has the secret of where your sister is locked inside him, what else has he got hidden away? And why can't he remember it?"

"Exactly." Her eyes narrow the way they do when she's struggling to sort out a puzzle. "I've been rolling it over in my head, but all I can think of is a head injury, maybe? Something that caused him to lose access to some of his memories? But that wouldn't explain how he knew where Scarlett is in the first place."

"If the resistance was involved, Dust has that kind of clearance." I pause, throat going tight as I remember that the leaders of the resistance are dead. Celeste and Niles and all the people who took a chance on an angry, cage-fighting kid, when even my own family doubted I would ever get my shit together, are gone. "Or he did. Before."

"I thought about that." Wren tucks an increasingly damp lock of hair behind her ear. "And aside from you, Dust is the one I trust the most."

"So did the people in charge, which is a big deal. They vetted everyone who joined the resistance. Repeatedly. As he climbed the ranks, Dust would have been investigated several times, and that's not taking into account who his parents are."

"Royalty, right?" Wren's mouth quirks. "It's still strange to think of Dust as a prince. I remember him as a troublemaker with skinned knees and a chocolate milk mustache who got in trouble for telling stories that gave the rest of us nightmares."

I smile. "Strange or not, it's true. His parents have ruled the UK for over a thousand years. They've held onto the throne longer than any other royal family, and they've done it by being meticulous, tough, and transparent."

"They don't color outside the lines," she murmurs.

"They don't color at all. They don't believe in wasting time on fun."

Wren's forehead furrows. "Poor Dust."

I grunt in response.

"Seriously," she says. "It can't have been easy for him to go back to that after so many years with his adoptive parents. The Parsons weren't the most affectionate people, but I was always jealous of how much freedom they gave Dust. They let him run as wild as a kid that sick could run." She tilts her head on her fists, her eyes taking on a faraway look. "He could ride his bike anywhere in the neighborhood, and if he got too tired to make it home, they would come pick him up in their big station wagon. My parents made me stay on our street, right in front of the house. I couldn't even go down the hill to the marine barrier. I didn't have the strength to, really, but I always wanted to try, or to see if

I could make it across the neighborhood to the playground all by myself."

I reach out, smearing the raindrops beading on her cheek together until they drip off her perfectly pointed chin. "When this is all over, we'll go on an epic bike ride. We'll have to bring camping equipment, we'll be out so long."

She smiles that happy-sad smile of hers, the one I swear to God I'm going to turn one hundred percent joyful someday. "Sounds perfect. I'll bring the termite snacks."

I laugh, actually *laugh*, for the first time in this long, miserable, grief-filled week. It hurts a little, that puff of hope breaking through the weight heavy on my heart, but it's a good hurt. So good I can't resist leaning in to kiss Wren and whisper, "I love you," against her lips.

"I love you, too. So, we agree, then?" she asks as I pull back to catch her determined gaze. "We go to Dust with this and ask him if there's any way he might have secrets locked inside him that he's forgotten about?"

I nod. "Even if he doesn't, he has more background information on Creedence and Luke than we do. If either one of them could have been in a position to discover that kind of information, Dust will know about it."

"Or if someone suffered a head injury," Wren says, even as her lips slide to the side and the light in her eyes dims. "But that's naïve, isn't it? To think it's something as innocent as that? More likely one of us is a traitor."

"Your mother said the secret was *locked* inside," I remind her. "That doesn't sound like whoever it is has a choice about sharing it. You can't betray someone without free will. And, for what it's worth, I believe the others care about you. If any of them knew how to get a warning to your sister, they would tell you. Even Luke."

Wren studies me, rain collecting on her lashes, before she blinks and her smile returns, bigger and brighter than it was before.

"What?" I ask, laughing. "What's funny?"

She shakes her head. "Nothing, I just..." She shrugs. "Sometimes I want to punch Luke. Hard. Right in the face."

"Woman, I hear you." I roll onto my back, grinning as I study the evergreen limbs forming an asterisk against the sky. "Sounds like you'll get your chance at that tomorrow."

"I don't understand why *you* can't teach me how to fight," she grumbles, scooting over to lie on top of my chest again, the feel of her breasts bare against my cool skin making my blood pump faster. "You were a professional fighter. It was like your job."

"Right, it was my *job*. I fought in cage matches for money. Luke fought to stay alive. It's different." I gaze down at her, smiling as her nose wrinkles. "But I could teach you a few tricks. Give you something to pull out of your sleeve if he gets too bossy for his britches."

Wren's eyes light up. "Yes, please. Teach me smackdown tricks."

"I will." I urge her farther on top of me as I add in a thicker voice, "Right after I make you come for me again."

She straddles my hips, making a sexy sound low in

her throat as my erection brushes against where she's wet, hot. "That sounds like the best plan I've heard all day."

It isn't a plan, but it's important. And as I take my mate again, urging her on as she rides me with sensuous strokes of her hips, I make a solemn vow not to let anything keep me from this.

From her body.

From her pleasure.

From this love that is every bit as important as saving the world.

I want to stay forever in the woods, where things feel simple again.

But after multiple orgasms and a brief tutoring session in rudimentary self-defense techniques, it's getting dark and time to head in for the night.

By the time Kite and I get back to the room, Creedence has returned with two buckets of fried chicken and a wide variety of sides.

I scan the bureau near the television where the spread is laid out, my eyes going wide as I take in yeast rolls, mashed potatoes, sautéed kale, green beans, corn, and a pasta salad large enough to feed a small army.

"Where did you get the money for all this?" My mouth waters as I grab a paper plate and load up, snacking on a roll as I go. I can't seem to get enough to eat these days. Since the shifter suppression drugs left my system and my powers came online, I'm constantly ravenous. "I thought we were down to our last twenty bucks."

"I have my ways." Cree's lips curve in a lazy smile. He seems calmer after his drive, making me hope we'll be able to move on from the blow-up this afternoon without any further drama.

"Who did you rob?" Kite jokes.

"No one who will miss a hundred bucks." Creedence pulls a pair of expensive looking sunglasses from the pocket of his battered jean jacket. "Or his shades, the dickweed."

Kite goes still for a moment before nodding and continuing to spoon pasta onto his plate. I'm not a fan of stealing, either, but desperate times call for desperate measures, and I trust Creedence not to prey on the weak. And we can't save the world on an empty stomach. And if we don't save the world, then the dickweed with the fancy sunglasses won't have anywhere to spend his money or wear his glasses, so karma-wise it should all shake out in the end.

"Hopefully, our money problems will be over after tonight." Dust wipes the chicken grease from his fingers as he explains the plan to canvas the safe house for supplies to Creedence, who agrees to tag along for backup.

"Just to see you shift, if nothing else. I'm starting to think griffins are imaginary." Creedence tosses his empty plate into the trash with a loaded glance Luke's way. "Wolves, too. We haven't seen you furry yet, either, hombre."

Luke takes another bite of chicken leg and chews,

holding Creedence's gaze without a word until the strained moment drags on so long, I have to break the tension. "I just want you both to be careful. We don't know who might be waiting for us. Promise you'll get in, get out, and get back before morning."

"We'll do our best," Dust says, turning to Kite. "But if we're not back by tomorrow evening and we haven't made contact, get out of here. Go far and go fast and don't tell anyone where you're headed."

"How will you find us?" Kite asks.

"This." He reaches into the pocket of his smoothly pressed gray pants, drawing out a circle that flashes brightly in the muted hotel room light.

"My coin!" I bounce out of the corner chair, ditching my now-empty plate in the trash as I cross to Dust. "I thought I lost it at the reservation."

He presses it into my outstretched hand, his fingertips and the metal both warm on my palm. "You did. This is a new one. My last one."

I nod soberly. "I won't lose it, I swear." I wish I hadn't lost the first one. I'd held onto it since we were kids, when Dust had slipped what he promised was a magical coin into my sticky, eight-year-old fingers and promised he'd always look out for me.

"To help with that, I had a hole drilled at the top." Dust pulls a slim metal chain from his other pocket and pools it onto my palm next to the coin. "You can wear it as a necklace. It should stay in place, even when you shift. The chain is tempered to withstand extreme heat, as well."

In case I catch fire, remains unspoken.

I catch fire now sometimes. It's a thing.

It's all still so surreal, this new life of mine, that sometimes it feels like a game. A big pretend I'm playing until my real life picks up where it left off.

But of course, it isn't pretend, and the stakes are higher than any game I've ever played. These men could die tonight. None of our enemies are pulling punches, and for one reason or another, all of them want Dust and Creedence dead.

I stand on tiptoe, pressing an impulsive kiss to Dust's cheek. "Thank you. Be safe."

"You, too." Dust's hand settles on my waist, giving a light squeeze. Surprisingly, a current of awareness courses across my skin, making my breath catch. I glance up at Dust, wondering if he feels it, too, this more-than-friends energy thick in the air.

But before I can get a read on his always-composed features, Creedence says, "I would tell you two to get a room, but we have a room, and this is it."

He glides up behind me until his body heat warms my back and the current coursing through me becomes a sizzle, a rush of heat that makes my nipples pull tight beneath my T-shirt as Cree's hands settle possessively on my hips. "So, I'll just take my 'don't die' kiss, too, and we'll be on our way."

I glance over my shoulder, lips parting to insist no one is going to die, but Creedence doesn't give me the chance to speak.

His mouth slants across mine as his fingers drive into my still-damp hair. His tongue strokes deep into my mouth, kissing me like there's no one else in the room. No one else in the world. He claims my mouth like I'm his to possess, to ravage any way he sees fit, and my body responds the way it did the first time this usually laid-back man showed me a glimpse of his carnal side.

I go weak in the knees, hot and achy in all the places where Kite made my body sing just an hour ago. Creedence steals my breath away, his powerful chest becoming my anchor and his kiss the center of my world.

I want to push him back on the bed, strip off my clothes, and get him inside me—forget the consequences or how seriously an unbreakable mate bond should be considered before things go that far. I want to drown in him, to get lost and found in the primal escape he offers with every possessive sweep of his tongue against mine.

"Hold that thought, Slim." Creedence murmurs against my lips as he pulls away. "I want to explore that further when we get back. What about you Dust? You ready to go?" He shifts his dancing, heat-filled gaze Dust's way.

My focus follows, my breath hitching again as I witness the hunger clear in Dust's eyes. A sudden image —of Dust drawing my nipple into his mouth as Creedence slides into me from behind—explodes on my mental screen, followed by a nuclear rush of desire.

I want that, I realize. God help me, but I want them both. At the same time. I want Dust's hands *and* Cree's skimming across my bare skin, lighting me up like a sky filled with falling stars.

And maybe I want Kite there, too...

Kite's mouth on mine, Kite's big hands cupping my breasts, teasing my nipples as Dust spreads my legs and—

I swallow hard, firming up my shields like my life depends on it and praying no one else has sensed the supernova of lust that just lit my ovaries on fire.

But of course, they did, and when Dust speaks his voice is husky in a way I haven't heard before. "I can't help but feel the cat got the better 'don't die' kiss. Maybe I should try mine again?"

My lungs go still in my chest, but I bob my head "yes." I want to know what it feels like to kiss my friend, this brave man who would die for me in a heartbeat, even though we haven't formed a mate bond.

A heartbeat is all it takes for Dust's lips to press to mine and warmth like honey and bourbon mixed together to flood my veins. His kiss is campfire smoke and hot chocolate on a cool winter morning. It's the ancient stillness of the woods and the electrifying rush of standing at the edge of a cliff at the edge of the world, realizing there's so much to explore that the adventure could go on forever.

I could kiss him *forever*. I don't want to drown in him the way I do Creedence or melt into his safe, steady arms the way I do with Kite. I want to...dance with Dust. Explore with him. I want to see what new kind of magic we could make together now that we're all grown up.

We draw apart a long moment later, slow and easy, our auras still sticky and close. I see that he's smiling, that crooked, troublemaker grin from when we were little, and a rush of affection fills me to overflowing. I lift a hand to his face, tempted to tell him I absolutely adore him, but I don't want to rush into something like that.

And I suspect he knows.

"Time to suit up." Creedence slaps my ass as he circles around me, headed for the door.

I huff at the unexpected smack, but then he winks at me over his shoulder, and the flash of annoyance fades away. It's hard to get angry with Creedence. He's a mischief-maker, can have a temper at times, and definitely isn't shy about asserting himself sexually, but my pretty cat's primary mission in life is to make people smile.

I hope someday that will be his only mission, that there will come a time when our lives are so peaceful that none of us has to worry about what new danger looms on the horizon.

Creedence leads the way out of the room, followed by Dust and Kite, who squeezes my hand on his way by, gently assuring me that he's okay with me opening my heart—and maybe soon, my bed—to the other men. I'm about to follow him when I feel that sharp tug deep in my chest and glance back to see Luke leaning against the wall by the bureau.

His dark gaze crashes into mine, and I think I see longing in his eyes, but a beat later, it's gone, replaced by the unreadable calm I've become accustomed to from our wolf.

He nods toward the door, "Going to see them off?"

"Yes. You?"

"No. I'll stay here, grab a shower while it's free." He tips his head toward the bathroom. "But tell them good luck for me. I hope no one gets hurt."

I can tell he's sincere, but I can also see that he doesn't care the way the rest of us do. He doesn't want anyone killed, but he wouldn't shed any tears over us, either.

Maybe he wouldn't shed tears over anyone at all. Maybe he's incapable of that kind of emotion. Maybe he cried his last tear the day his brother was killed and he vowed to slaughter every last person who played a role in the murder.

I don't know, but I know that he makes me angry.

And sad.

And that a part of me wants to hug him as much as I want to punch him.

I don't do either. I nod and head out into the night behind the three men who want to be mine, ignoring the nagging feeling that I can't do this without Luke.

I can, and I will. And as soon as Dust gets back, we're going to have a long talk—about secrets and my sister and where to start looking for another marked canine shifter to take Luke's place.

CHAPTER 5

WREN

The rain has finally stopped falling and the moon is big and bright above the dark outline of the trees. The air is damp, but cool and soothing in my lungs as I jog between Creedence and Kite down the path.

It feels good to move fast through the shadows, but I can't help but wish I were able to shift more easily. I'd love to be in my fox form right now, feeling the living carpet of the forest floor beneath my feet, smelling the thousand secret smells a human nose can't catch or decipher.

The longing sharpens as we reach the same glen where Kite and I spent the afternoon. Creedence instantly ripples into his lynx form while Dust lifts his arms overhead, seeming to levitate in the air for a moment before blooming gracefully into a beast easily five times his human size.

I step back with a soft, "Woah," that makes Kite laugh beside me.

"Didn't expect a griffin to be that big, huh?" He takes my hand as my eyes dart from Dust's giant wings—a span as wide as a school bus, covered with gorgeous silver and gold feathers than glitter in the moonlight—to his powerful lion's body, curved beak, and bright yellow eyes.

"No." I smile. "But I like it. I like it when the big, scary things are on our side."

Dust's large head swivels my way in response, and my heart pounds faster. His face is unlike anything I've seen before—a mixture of feline and avian that's as striking as it is beautiful—but it's the look in those glowing eyes that makes my blood rush. He's not nearly as civilized as a griffin. There is no veneer of stuffy English manners in that look. There is only hunger and an eagerness to be gone so he can come back to me as soon as possible.

I lift a hand, blowing a kiss first to Dust and then to the cat with the tufted ears who leaps onto the griffin's back, settling between his wings for the ride. "See you soon," I whisper, and then they're gone, launching into the cloud-smeared sky with a powerful flex of Dust's lion haunches.

Kite and I watch them go, keeping them in our sights until they snuff out in a shower of sparks like shredded moonlight, hidden away by Dust's gift for concealing things he would rather not be seen.

It feels like there's a clue there, tucked in the pocket of that thought.

I make a mental note to mull it over later—when I'm lying awake in bed tonight, wrestling with the insomnia that's plagued me for the past week—and turn to Kite. "Ready to head back?"

"Let's go for a walk first. Give Luke some time to himself." Kite kisses my cheek before adding in a softer voice, "Dust's not the only one who gives a great piggyback ride, you know."

I turn my head, kissing his lips long and slow, because a piggyback ride sounds delightful. A few minutes later, my big teddy bear of a mate is literally a giant grizzly, his clothes are folded and tucked under my arm, and I'm on his furry back, soaking the hearth-and-family smell of him into my soul as he starts off through the forest.

Instinctively, I know he's going to take me to the top of the rise, to look down on the moonlit treetops and imagine what it will be like when the world is as peaceful as it seems right now.

And I know that I will let myself believe in happy endings.

At least for a little while.

CHAPTER 6
DR. MARTIN HIGHBORN

The study is warm. Too warm.

But that's the way Bea likes it just before bed, so that's the way it will stay.

And my team leader on this mission could stand to sweat a little.

"So, you've lost them?" I ask softly, refusing to lose my temper. Beatrice has been through enough. Sparring her further anxiety is the least I can do for my wife.

"They ditched the Hummer outside of Wilbur, sir," Gareth says, rolling his shoulders back and lifting his chin. "But we've got a lead on the location of the safe house. The team is working in shifts around the clock, sorting through the intel we gathered from the resistance compound. We're ninety percent sure we know where they're going."

"Ninety percent." Bea lifts expectant eyes to mine. "That sounds good."

"It is," I assure her with a smile.

"Wonderful," she says, hugging her knitting closer to her chest.

She's making a sweater for our granddaughter. Our only living grandchild. It will be too small. They always are, as if Bea can't bring herself to admit that Wendy has aged a day since the morning her mother and three older brothers were killed.

My daughter was the sweetest soul ever brought into this world, but she only got thirty-two years on the planet. Further proof that Fate is cruel and there is no such thing as karmic justice. If there were, Natalie would be here with her mother and I, sharing a port before bed, with all four of her little ones asleep upstairs.

Instead, there is only Wendy in her twin bed, sedated into a shallow rest because not even years of therapy have been able to ease her night terrors.

Seeing your mother's head ripped from her body by a pack of wolves isn't something that's easy to come back from. My granddaughter may always be damaged. She may never sleep easily, even on the day when I'm finally able to look into her frightened eyes and promise her that all the monsters are dead and gone.

Some wounds never heal. They stay open and raw, stinging every time something reminds you of the way they were made.

Gareth wasn't in his current position the day my daughter was attacked, but his arrogance reminds me of his predecessor, the man who assumed the threats against my family were just idle talk.

That man is now locked in a facility somewhere off

the coast of Thailand, a prisoner of the U.S. government, charged with criminal conspiracy.

He isn't guilty. It doesn't matter. Natalie, Benji, Rick, and Heath's blood is still on his hands, and my contact within the Department of Homeland Preservation has assured me he will never see daylight.

I want to remind Gareth of what happens to men who overestimate their abilities and underestimate the enemy. But I settle for meeting his eyes across the study and letting the silence stretch on too long.

The way his throat works assures me the message has been received.

"We'll have everything ready in time, sir," he says. "The surveillance team is in place in a house nearby, and we're moving Subject Seven tonight."

I steeple my hands over the book open on my lap. "Good. I'll expect an update when the pieces are in place. And remember, Subject Seven gets nothing but water. No food. She's stronger than she looks. We want her weak. Fragile."

Gareth nods. "Will do, sir. She's in bad shape already, and the scans this morning came back looking just the way you wanted. Significant deterioration in the frontal lobe. Her long-term memory is going to be Swiss cheese by the time she's found. She won't remember enough to make any trouble."

"*If* she's found," I say, voice hard. "If she isn't...."

The threat doesn't need to be spoken. Gareth knows what happens if he's lost our subjects. If he's lost them, we'll have to turn to Atlas for help finding them, and Atlas's help always comes at too high a price.

The pack of wolves who murdered my daughter and her children was slaughtered by his hands. In payment, he took his pound of flesh.

Several pounds, in fact, in the form of my wife's legs from the knees down.

We didn't know that's what the monster would ask for when we begged him to help us take vengeance, but Bea doesn't regret it. She would have given her life to punish Natalie's killers.

In her mind, her legs are a small sacrifice.

In mine, they loom so large that sometimes I can't bear to look at her, can't stomach the sight of her amputated limbs beneath the covers. The guilt is crushing, a half ton weight on my chest, squeezing the life out of me.

I wish he'd taken his fee from me. But that's why he carved away pieces of my wife, making me watch from behind the glass as he slashed a fiery arm through each leg, severing and cauterizing in one fell swoop, while Bea screamed until she passed out from the pain.

Atlas didn't want the limbs. He wanted the pain, the emotional agony, the absolutely helpless terror.

Sometimes I think he feeds on it. Sometimes I think he's just bored and taking his entertainment where he finds it.

"I've already got three search teams in the area." Gareth clears his throat. "But I can add more. If you really think..."

Bea makes a panicked sound low in her throat, but I reassure her with another smile. "It's fine. It's going to be fine. I promise you."

"I'm sorry, sir," Gareth says. "I wouldn't have bothered you at home, but you told me to come to you the moment I had news."

I reach a hand out to Bea, threading my fingers through hers and squeezing. "It's fine, Gareth. You did well. You can go now. We'll talk more in the morning."

"Yes, sir." Gareth leaves the room, shutting the door softly behind him, leaving Bea and I alone in our too-warm cocoon.

Alone, but not alone.

The dead are always here with us, hovering overhead, reminding us of how much we've lost.

"He'll find them. I know it." Bea's voice trembles but her eyes are steady and full of faith. Faith in me. Still, after all the ways I've failed her, she believes I can move mountains.

"He will," I promise, refusing to let her down again. I will get eyes and ears inside the girl's innermost circle. I will report back to the creature who pulls my strings, and someday soon this will all be over.

The threat will pass, and the work will once again take center stage. And when all the shifters are dead but one, and he, safely tucked away on his throne, certain he will always be king of his castle, my family will be safe. Wendy will be able to grow up in a world where there are no monsters hiding among us, no claws and teeth bared and waiting in the dark.

"I'm ready to sleep now," Bea whispers. "Help me into my chair?"

"Of course, love." I lift my wife into her chair and

wheel her toward the elevator by the fireplace, hoping sleep will come easy for both of us tonight, though I already know it won't.

Nothing is easy, and nothing will be easy until Atlas has the girl's head mounted on his wall.

CHAPTER 7
CARRIE ANN

Once upon a time, there was a girl with blond curls, blue eyes, and a laugh so loud her parents were embarrassed to take her out in public. The *aw-shucks-I-know-but-she's-cute-right?* kind of embarrassed—her mother all giggles and apologies for her obnoxiously happy kid and her father beaming at the both of them.

His girls.

That's what he called us.

His girls, with such pride I knew it was something special to be a girl, especially one who belonged to my tall, handsome, guitar-playing daddy, a man who fronted a band and smoked classy cigarettes he rolled by hand and had a singing voice so deep and lonely it made strangers cry.

I thought it was beautiful back then—all those tears pouring out of people who, until my father stepped up to the mic, had been laughing, guzzling beer, and about as in touch with their emotions as the average earthworm.

Daddy worked hard at bringing the emotional gut-punch, laboring over every note, every key change, and turn of phrase. He was never happier than when he had a room full of barflies mopping up tears with their shirtsleeves and sniffling into their bandanas.

He was happy. And we were happy—his girls, the most loyal fan club any minor rock star could have asked for.

Even when gigs got fewer and farther between, and Jerry, the drummer, quit because "the Reminders were a bunch of doped-up has-beens," we were happy. We had each other and the music, the tears in the audience and the laughter in our beat-up RV, and magic waiting around every turn in the road.

And then, in the blink of an eye, we had nothing at all.

Every member of the band and most of their families were on the chartered plane bound for Singapore, embarking on the first leg of an Asian tour that was going to turn it all around for the Reminders, when the engine exploded two minutes after leaving the runway.

I don't remember anything about the crash, nothing between the excitement of takeoff and waking up in a hospital room days later, hurting all over and somehow knowing that my mother was dead.

I thought Daddy was gone, too.

I assumed I was headed to an orphanage—even though I was twelve and had been cooking meals and doing RV-cleanup for my bohemian parents for years—unless I could run away from the hospital first.

I was plotting my escape from whatever evil Miss-Hannigan type the state was sending to fetch me, when Daddy swaggered into my room sporting two black eyes and a sling. He ran teasing fingers over the toes poking out of my cast and announced we were going home.

It was the last time he ever touched me, skin to skin.

In the years that followed, as his grief over losing Mom and the band and an audience eager to give away their pain ate at him, Dad touched me in other ways. He'd whip a belt against my thighs, slam a door on my fingers, press the tip of his classy cigarette into my skin, burning constellations into my flesh between the freckles. But there was never a hug or a hand on my shoulder when I was crying in my room, missing Mom so much it felt like my heart was gobbling a hole in my chest.

I took off twice; Dad sold my dead grandparents' farm so I'd have nowhere to run. I asked a counselor at school for help; Dad convinced her I was a liar and then he fucked her in the bathroom of the teacher's lounge while I waited in the car.

I gave up and came to heel. I learned to read his moods and keep my mouth shut. But no matter how hard I tried, I was never small enough or quiet enough to avoid the belt, the door, the cigarette.

By the time I was fourteen, I couldn't remember what it was like to be part of a family. By sixteen, I was out on the streets most nights, preferring the violence of strangers to that of a blood relative.

Easier not to take it so personally that way.

That's when I met Dr. Highborn, the man with the silver-streaked black hair, steady brown eyes, and hands that touched his patients with such gentleness and respect. We were homeless and filthy, every one of us who shuffled into the free clinic, but Dr. Highborn—call me Martin, he told his favorites—treated our wounds and listened to our problems. He gave us sack lunches to take with our medicine, just in case we didn't feel well enough to stand in line at the soup kitchen across the street.

He even had free pads and tampons in big jars by the clinic's front door, winning him the affection of every homeless chick between the ages of thirteen and fifty. A dude who realized it sucked even harder to be a girl on the street and took steps to make our lives easier?

Be still our beating hearts...

Looking back, I know Martin took advantage of us. Of me. I might as well have had "Daddy Issues" tattooed on my forehead, and he was way too smart not to leverage that to his advantage.

But at the time, I needed so badly for someone to listen, to care—even a little bit. It was a matter of life or death, and Martin was the one who reached out, took my hand, and pulled me back into the land of the living.

And then he made me a shifter.

He gave me superpowers. And a job. And money when I needed it and special attention that made me feel superior to all the other lab rats who worked as his spies. I thought I was special. I believed it so fiercely that I betrayed my best friend, maybe the only person in the world who truly loved me with no strings attached.

I hate myself for it, even though I can't remember exactly what I did...

The past few years get hazier with every passing minute. Whatever Martin gave me in that IV drip along with the Devour Virus, it isn't just eating away at my flesh and bones. It's wolfing down my memories, nibbling holes in my history, turning my brain into a cartoon landscape filled with so many black holes it would be easy to tumble into one and get lost. Forever.

But as I lay curled in the corner of this dusty bedroom, alone in the dark, waiting for something I can't recall, yet dread all the same, he's still there.

Daddy and his belt.

And his cigarettes.

And his voice assuring me I'm never going to amount to jack shit.

"You were right, Dad," I croak as tears stream down my hollow cheeks. "Look. You were right."

Deep in my mind, neurons fire, electricity dances, and my imagination wastes valuable energy showing me Daddy on the stage, mic cupped in his hands, eyes closed as he sings his favorite song. The one about the girl who spends her entire life mourning the boy who got away, only to die the day before his love letter arrives in the mail.

I bite down on my bottom lip until I taste blood. The sharp, iron-and-sugar taste comforts me, making me stronger, though I can't remember why it feels so good to bite.

To bite and claw…

I lift one trembling hand, but no matter how I ache for the escape of my animal form, my fingers remain pale and slender. Weak and frail. Human.

Martin took that away, too. I can't shift without a trigger from his goons.

From…those men…

I used to know their names. Now they're just silhouettes retreating into impenetrable darkness.

The world narrows, fades, evaporates.

I lose so many names and faces that I'm not surprised when the two men who wake me in the middle of the night seem to know who I am but I can't recall a thing about either of them.

Nothing at all, though they seem kind. Good guys, not bad ones.

One of them—the slimmer one with the shaggy brown hair and the smell of wood smoke lingering on his skin—has tears in his eyes as he asks who did this to me.

"I don't know," I answer honestly. I can't remember anything. I am a cracked vase, all the water I once held spilled out onto the floor. But I do know one thing, and I confess it to the man in a whisper as I beg, "Please don't cry. I can't stand to see people cry."

It makes me feel sick, but I don't know why.

I don't know much of anything.

Not even my own name, a fact I confess, as well.

"Carrie Ann," the golden-haired man says, his eyes nearly as sad as his friend's. "Your name is Carrie Ann. You're Wren's friend, which means you're our friend.

We're going to take care of you, okay? No one's going to hurt you again. I promise."

It's a lovely promise, one I want to believe so much it hurts.

But I don't. Something deep inside knows instinctively that promises are made to be broken and that I'll never be safe, no matter how far I run or how well I hide.

"Leave me here," I say, panic I can't name churning in my chest. "Leave. You can't help me. No one can."

"There are ways," Brown Eyes—Dust—says. "My people have had success turning the Devour virus around. We'll take you with us, and I'll do everything I can to get you the help you need." He smiles. "As long as you don't mind a ridiculously long plane flight. The doctors who take care of my family haven't left England in a hundred years, and they aren't about to start now. Not even for a friend."

"We don't know that she's a friend," the other man mumbles beneath his breath, earning a hard look from Dust. "No offense," Golden Hair says, dividing his attention between me, and something over his shoulder. "It's nothing personal. I'm programmed to be suspicious of everyone these days."

"Friend or traitor, it doesn't matter now," Dust says, not unkindly. "She's in no condition to do anyone any damage."

For some reason, his words send a chill skittering up my spine on tiny spider feet.

"Speaking of damage, this place is a fucking wreck," Golden Hair says. "Clearly the assholes got here before we did. If there's anything here worth bringing back, I'll eat my own fist."

"I'm inclined to agree with you, but let's do a sweep anyway." Dust reaches out, patting my hand gently. "Hang tight, and we'll get out of here as soon as possible."

"I'm afraid," I whisper.

"It's all right," Dust says, compassion knitting his features. "We'll be right back. I promise."

That's what I'm afraid of, I think, but I don't know why.

So I don't say a word. I simply nod and continue to lie in an aching, suffering puddle on the floor, waiting for my heroes to rescue me, though I'm certain I don't deserve it.

Not even a little bit.

CHAPTER 8

WREN

I lie awake until the wee hours of the morning—long after Kite and Luke's breathing has grown slow and even—listening for the touchdown of a magical creature in the woods. But the night remains still, without even the comforting patter of the rain to break the silence between the cries of night birds and the softer yips and squeaks of the raccoons raiding the dumpster outside.

I can't fight the feeling that something is wrong.

Or that something *will* go wrong if I drop my guard long enough to get some rest.

I can feel Atlas closer in these moments, when I'm a whisper away from dreamland. He can't kill me in my dreams, the way he could if I risked another visit to the shifter spirit world we share, but he can make me suffer. My nightmares are filled with the tortured cries of the people I love, littered with bodies and bloodshed and violence so depraved I can't bear to talk about it in the morning.

I know why Dust kept his secret.

Sometimes the bad things are so bad you can't bring yourself to share them, even when you know you should.

Finally, close to four a.m., I drift into a fitful sleep, but this time it isn't Atlas who waits for me on the other side of consciousness.

My eyes blink open to daylight—bright and dazzling. I'm standing barefoot on cool spring grass in a field of cherry trees. Their limbs wave back and forth in the breeze, tossing blossoms that drift like fluffy white snowflakes in the air all around me. The sky is a soul-shattering shade of blue, and the air is perfumed with flowers and the occasional waft of fresh-baked pastry drifting from the cottage at the top of the rise, the one with the view of the orchard, the stream, and the forest beyond.

And all of it's ours.

Was ours...

"And it will be again." A deep, familiar voice speaks behind me, and I turn to see a dragon with shimmering green scales curled in the back of my dad's old red truck. It's so big, it barely fits, but dragons like cozy spaces to curl up in.

Just like cats.

The memories of the house and the truck and everything my father taught me about dragons in between rides to the pasture on his always-toasty back come rushing into my heart, as familiar as a favorite song.

"Daddy," I whisper, my voice breaking in the middle of the word.

The dragon smiles, its green eyes, the same color as Scarlett's, like the purest, palest Jade, wrinkle at the edges, the way they did when he was in his human form. Daddy wasn't around as much as my mother—he had a big job somewhere that took up a lot of his time—but we were close. Close enough that I don't hesitate to rush across the orchard and throw my arms around his neck as he leans down to greet me over the side of the truck bed.

"I love you, sweetheart. I'm so proud of you," he says, his voice a rumble that vibrates through my chest, my bones, making every breath feel like home. "But I can't stay long. I don't have the gift for it your mother does."

I pull back, fighting tears as I look up into his fiercely gentle face. "I love you, too. I'm sorry I forgot you for so long."

"The Church makes the children forget," he says, his scales shining brighter in the sun. "There are things Dust won't remember, either. You need to go deeper than memory, open all the doors to the past, no holding back. You'll need to life fast."

"Life fast," I repeat, fighting to commit the words to memory.

"All the beasts of antiquity can guide a life fast," my father says, the light reflecting off his scales so fierce that I lift a hand to shield my eyes. "Tell him not to be afraid."

I blink faster, fighting to keep my eyes open as I'm blinded by the glare.

I don't want to shut out the sight of my father, but finally, I can't help but cringe against the unbearable brightness, my lids squeezing shut.

. . .

W hen I blink them open again, I'm back in my bed at the hotel.

I sit, squinting against the light filtering through the curtains someone must have drawn this morning. At four a.m., they'd still been open, granting me a view of the stars spiraling lazily across the sky as the world turned oh-so-slowly.

Slow, slow, every minute that Creedence and Dust are in danger making me feel knife-edge anxious.

That's what "on edge" means, I've decided. It's not about tumbling off the edge of the world the way I once thought. It's a blade pressed tight to something soft and vulnerable, threatening to transform anxiety into suffering with the flick of a wrist.

The thought brings it rushing back, that feeling that I've misplaced something important. That I've left the stove on, the water running, the baby in the bathwater with no one to stand watch to ensure she doesn't drown.

Running a hand through my hair, I turn to survey the quiet room.

Beside me, the bed is empty, nothing but rumpled sheets and a faint whiff of evergreen needles to hint that Kite spent the night here, too. The other bed is equally vacant, and Luke's pallet is rolled up and tucked into the corner behind the floor lamp, making me wonder how long I've been asleep.

Leaning forward, I catch a glimpse of the clock, pulse leaping when I see the numbers read ten fifteen. Luke and I agreed to meet in the glen at ten-thirty.

But it isn't being late that has my heart knocking against my ribs as I vault out of bed, each rapid beat a plea, a prayer that I'll stumble outside to find all four of the men in my life hunched over coffees at the picnic tables or arguing about how best to fix the tear in our Mustang's ancient drop-top.

I scrub my face and teeth, run a quick comb through my hair and pull it into a knot on top of my head before lacing up my tennis shoes and sprinting for the door in my pajamas. This is why I sleep in leggings and a hoodie, so I can be ready to go at a moment's notice.

And because I only have three changes of clothes to my name.

The old me, with her closet full of work, leisure, and special occasion clothes would have found that unthinkable.

It's amazing what you can get used to. And how quickly.

I don't miss my closet, but I would kill for a pair of waterproof shoes. My sneakers, still damp from yesterday's walk, squish as I pound down the stairs, letting off faint whiffs of funk that warn I'd better get them in a dryer soon.

Outside, the morning air is still cool, but the sun is up, busily burning away yesterday's rain, promising today will be Rocky Mountain summer hot. I scan the parking lot and the picnic area, with its crooked grills and swing set so rusty it could give a kid tetanus from looking at it too hard. But aside from a pair of squirrels arguing over an apple core, I'm alone.

The Mustang is no longer in its parking spot by the dumpster, an absence that sends a whisper of unease shivering across my skin.

It's not unusual for someone to make a morning run into town for food, but Luke and I are meeting in a few minutes, and Kite wouldn't normally leave without jotting a note.

It makes me wonder if I missed something upstairs, but there isn't time to run back to the room and check or I'll be late to meet Luke.

Luke, who will hopefully know where Kite is, and whether Creedence and Dust made it back last night.

Fingering the gold coin around my neck and hoping Dust won't need an enchanted talisman to track me down, I start toward the trailhead. There's no sign of my trainer, but I'm not surprised Luke started the run without me. He's insanely fast. Getting off the suppression meds has done wonders for my speed and stamina, but naturally superior shifter genetics will only take a girl so far. I'm going to need hardcore training to get into fighting shape by the end of the summer.

Too bad that doesn't make me one iota more excited to start boot camp...

I'm a lover, not a fighter. Yes, my instincts for self-preservation kick in if I'm threatened, but I'm never going to be the type of person who's spoiling to get in the ring and throw punches. I'd rather spend the morning getting a root canal.

Enduring pain, I'm good at. Causing pain in others isn't my forte.

I'm deep in thought, questioning for the hundredth

time whether Fate made a big mistake when she made me a Fata Morgana, when thick arms band around me from behind, drawing me against a solid wall of flesh. The breath rushes from my chest, and my heart stutters once before pumping into high gear, but to my surprise, I don't hesitate to act.

Remembering the self-defense moves Kite taught me yesterday, I jerk both arms high into the air, palms facing the attacker behind me. Curling my fingers, I draw them down hard and fast, hooking the man's arm and dragging it far enough away from my throat for me to slither from his grip.

I fall to the ground and roll away before popping up to run back to the hotel. A cry for Kite is on my lips when I get a look at my attacker and my jaw drops.

"Pretty good," Luke says, grudging respect in his eyes. "Looks like you might have some instincts after all."

"You scared the hell out of me," I huff, crossing my arms at my chest.

"Good." He nods. "Get scared and stay scared. Maybe then you'll show up to train on time."

"I was two minutes late! Not even two minutes. And I—"

"I don't want to hear excuses." He jabs a finger toward the trail. "I want to hear you breathing hard. Two miles. Go. I'll tell you when you can stop."

My lips part, but before I can insist that he promise never to attack me like that again, he barks, "Now, Princess. Waste another minute of my time, and we'll make it five."

"Fine," I grit out as I spin on my heel and jog into the woods. Thanks to the infuriating man trotting beside me, I'm faster than usual, but by the time we reach the glen Luke's chosen for our sparring session, my anger has cooled and I'm back to wondering what the hell I'm doing here.

Proving my successful foray into self-defense was most likely a fluke, for the next hour and a half, I proceed to suck ass at all the things. My reflexes are slow, my dodging instincts are non-existent, and after hundreds of practice jabs at the couch cushion we're using as a makeshift punching bag, Luke calmly pronounces that I "hit like a princess, too" and tosses the cushion on the grass.

"What's that mean?" I prop my hands low on my hips, breathing hard.

"It means you hit like you've never had to fight for anything in your entire life," Luke says, wiping the sweat from his forehead with the back of one lightly-furred arm. The temperature has jumped dramatically since we started. I'm down to my tank top, and Luke shed his shirt a few minutes ago, making it even harder to focus on keeping my knees bent while following through with my right hook.

My gaze keeps drifting to the scars on his chest—shiny streaks of hairless flesh that I'm guessing are knife wounds—and the star-shaped birthmark on his back, the reason he's here, the mark that pegged him as a potential Fata Morgana mate.

And then there are his sculpted abs and chiseled chest...

I don't *want* to look at them. I don't *want* to be affected by them. But what I want hasn't meant much lately, and this morning is no different.

I want to tell Luke to go to hell, yes. But I also want to lick him. All over. Repeatedly.

"That's not true." I lift my chin, working to keep my gaze fixed on his stupid face. "I fought every day. Since I was a kid."

"No, you didn't," Luke says. "You endured. You kept going, even when it was hard, and that's good. That'll make you a better fighter in the long run, but it isn't going to help if you refuse to show up in the ring."

I start to insist that I have shown up—I'm standing right here—but shut my mouth. Because he's right. I'm here in body, but not in spirit. My heart isn't in this. At least, not today.

"I'm worried about Dust and Creedence," I confess. "And Kite. He didn't leave a note before he left this morning. I'll have better focus next time. I promise."

Luke nods. "I talked to Kite before he headed out. Said he had an errand to run, but that he'd meet us at the room a little before one." He glances down at his watch. "Which gives us just enough time to do some strength training. Drop and give me twenty push-ups and then we'll get you up a tree or two before we head back."

I arch a brow. "Up a tree?"

"Climbing trees is a good workout. Don't worry, I won't let you fall." Luke smiles, sending a tingling sensation across my skin before he adds, "I need you alive to get across the border, right?" and the tingles go cold.

"Right." I hold his gaze for a beat before I sink down on my knees.

I'm just a meal ticket to Luke, a means to an end, and I would be stupid to forget it.

So I don't. Every time he touches me—his fingers at my waist when he lifts me up to reach the first tree branch, his hand on my hip or shoulder as he points out a path upward—I remind myself that this is all business.

Soon, the tingling sensation fades to a faint fizz that I can almost ignore.

Almost...

But when we're finally done, and Luke helps me down from the last tree, plucking a leaf from my hair with a sigh and murmuring, "We've got a lot to do, Princess. A whole lot," I have to fight the urge to lean into his chest and apologize for being the worst student ever.

Luke doesn't want my apologies or my friendship or anything else, a point he drives home by nodding toward the trail and adding a gruff, "Now we run back. Keep pace, or we'll be late to meet your people."

My people, not his or ours. *Mine.*

Feeling more alone than I have in days, I grab my sweatshirt from the ground, tie it around my waist, and start back toward civilization, Luke jogging effortlessly beside me while I huff and puff, every dragging breath a reminder that I'm in over my head with no way out in sight.

CHAPTER 9
WREN

I burst from the woods not far behind Luke, proving I've got more stamina than I would have given myself credit for.

But there's no time to celebrate baby milestones.

Not if I'm going to keep Luke from killing my mate.

The moment I see the woman sitting on the hood of the Mustang beside Kite, I know the shit is going to hit the fan, and Luke, the poster boy for Trust Issues doesn't disappoint.

"What the fuck did you do?" Luke growls as he comes to a stop beneath the trees shading the car from the midday sun. "You stupid, fucking kid."

Kite stands, shoulders back and his brow furrowed. "Before you fly off the handle, let me explain."

"And don't talk to my brother like that." Leda stands beside Kite, her hands propped menacingly on her hips. She's a foot shorter than her younger brother, but what she lacks in size she makes up for in presence. I'm sure that's helpful in her role as chief of the tribal police, but it won't hold much weight with an ex-con.

"You don't tell me what to do," Luke snaps back, unpleasantly predictable. "And your brother is an idiot." He jabs a finger at Kite's chest, transferring his rage. "What the hell were you thinking? We just had the fucking 'we can't trust anyone but each other' talk and you think that's a good time to go crying to Big Sissy for help?"

"She has important news, asshole," Kite says, his grip on his own temper beginning to slip. "Shit that changes everything."

"And *I* found him, not the other way around," Leda snaps, dropping her voice as she adds. "And I kept a low profile while I was doing it. If you'd like to continue to *not* attract attention, I suggest we sit the fuck down and talk like rational people."

Luke's hands ball into fists and his jaw clenches so tight a muscle begins to dance near his temple, but I sense the worst of the storm has passed.

"Let's head up to the room." I motion across the pine-needle strewn picnic grounds. "The maid should be finished by now, so we'll have privacy."

"No, we won't," Kite says, his gaze fixed on Luke as he adds, "There's someone in there."

Luke curses. "Great. Why not throw a party and invite this Atlas guy as the guest of honor while you're at it?"

"Atlas is why I'm here. And why the woman in the bedroom is here." Leda crosses to the picnic table. "Now sit down and shut up. The faster I bring you up to date, the sooner I can get out of here. I need to be home before nightfall. We're still running double guard patrols."

Maybe it's the reminder of how much the bear kin lost, or maybe Luke simply has the sense to realize when he's encountered an unstoppable force, but after a beat he exhales sharply, crosses the glen in four long strides, and hops up to sit on the table. "Talk," he snaps.

Leda mutters something under her breath about wolves, as I sit beside Luke and cast a worried gaze Kite's way. But for once he doesn't smile or let down his walls to let me know what he's feeling.

Quite the contrary. He's shielding so hard I can't tell what's going on, leaving me every bit as blindsided as Luke when he says, "The night that I took Wren from her house, the night we went into the river... When we thought Sierra died..." He exhales sharply. "She didn't. Atlas fished her out of the water."

"Oh God," I murmur, my hand coming to cover my mouth. I've never met Atlas in person, but what I've seen of him in Dust's vision-sharing and in my dreams is more than enough to send dread twisting through my insides.

Kite's throat works. "He tortured her. We're not sure for how long. She says it was at least a few days, but it could have been longer. The pain made her lose track of time."

"And lose most of a limb while she was at it," Leda adds, her eyes glittering. "The sick fuck started with her fingers, one every few hours. He cut off all five, then her hand, and then her arm up to her elbow before she gave in and agreed to help him find Wren."

Acid laps at the back of my throat. "I can't blame her. I *don't* blame her."

"But that's how they found us, right?" Luke says, his voice low. "At the reservation. Those monsters and whoever was shooting from the vehicles on the road."

Leda nods soberly. "Sierra said she smuggled Atlas into resistance headquarters. He got the information about your mission he needed and then slaughtered everyone."

"But not her. Not Sierra." The lilt in Luke's tone makes his suspicions clear.

For once, I can't fault him for it. Her survival, when so many other highly trained people were no match for Atlas, is suspect. "He's right. Like I said, I don't blame her. I'm sure I wouldn't last long in the face of torture, but we can't trust her. She shouldn't be here."

"Atlas left her alive because she bears the mark," Leda says. "Of a potential Fata mate. He was going to add her to his harem, but she managed to get away. The second she was free, she came straight to the reservation to warn us."

"She was too late," Kite adds. "But she tried. Tore through the skin on her paws, she was running so fast."

"Give her a medal, then," Luke says. "But you shouldn't have told your sister where we were. You've fucked every one of us, Kite. None of us are safe now."

"Like I said, he didn't tell me jack," Leda shoots back. "I'm Kite's cub-mother. I could track him down anywhere in the world, no matter how hard he tried to hide."

"It's like a godmother," Kite explains. "But with a built-in blood-tie GPS."

"Which is why, as soon as I find a capable replacement to take over for me on the force, I'm going into hiding." Leda's delivery is as no-nonsense as ever, but I can feel the regret beneath her resolve. She doesn't want to leave her people, but she wants to risk being tortured into revealing her brother's location even less. "But I had to bring Sierra to you first. Yes, it's a risk, and she's been through hell, but she can help you."

"She's been to Atlas's stronghold," Kite says. "Several times. And she's sure, once she's back in the area, she'll recognize the secret path to get in."

"Or she could follow along at home," Luke says. "Hook her up to us via an untraceable signal while she's locked away somewhere safe. She can tell us if we're getting close. *We* don't have a traitor along for the road trip. Everybody wins."

"Only shifters who have already passed through the portal to Atlas's realm can pass through again without him. Then she can open the gate from the inside," Kite explains. "Without her, we're not getting in. Maybe we'll be able to find another way in before go-time, but until we do, Sierra is our best bet."

I chew my bottom lip, not liking this any more than Luke does. "It still feels wrong. I understand the logic in what you're saying, but it's too dangerous. She's betrayed us once before. Who's to say she won't do it again?"

"I do." Leda crosses to stand in front of Luke and me, shifting her steady gaze between his face and mine. "That's my kin gift. I can see a person's truest, inner-most self. Their core being. Sierra's soul is clear. All she wants to do is make things right. To put our planet back on course and Wren on the Fata throne where she belongs. I'd bet my life on it."

"But you're not betting your life. You're betting ours," Luke says.

Leda nods. "You're right. Ultimately, it has to be your choice. But I've talked this through with my mother a hundred times since she told me what was really going on with you five last week. We dug through every scrap of information we could find on Atlas and his whereabouts. No one has ever found the portal on the other side of his killing fields, let alone gotten inside his castle. Sierra's been through hell, but she's willing to go back for you. For all of us. I think that's something you should consider before you dismiss how valuable she could be."

Luke holds her gaze before turning to Kite. "You know more about the fairy tale shit than I do. Does what she's saying check out? Is Sierra really our best shot?"

"Probably our only shot." Kite props his hands low on his hips, his lightly-whiskered jaw working back and forth. "But we should assume there's a chance Leda was followed, no matter how careful she tried to be. Which means we've got to make tracks. Now. Get new wheels, swap out the license plate, and get off the radar. So, we have to make this call fast. We can't debate for hours, and we can't wait for Dust and Creedence."

His words send anxiety flaring to life in my chest. I don't want to leave without Dust and Creedence—splitting up is dangerous for all of us—but Kite's right.

"All right." I sit up straighter, my hands curling into fists on my thighs. "I want to see her. Get my own read on where she is emotionally. Then we'll vote."

"Sounds good." Kite arches a brow Luke's way. "Agreed?"

Luke grunts. "I get a vote? Even though I'm not part of the in-crowd? I'm not going to be there when you cross the killing fields to kill the goblin king or whatever mystical quest shit you two are up to after we part ways. I'm here to get Wren battle ready and then I'm gone."

"Well, then, you might be with us for a long time," I snap, losing my patience with his "Can't Be Bothered to Care About Anyone but Myself" bullshit. "Because you know how much I suck at fighting. And dodging. And climbing things. And everything else I'm supposed to be able to do in order to defend myself. So, cut the passive aggressive crap and tell us if you're on board with the plan to talk to Sierra and vote after. M'kay?"

Leda snorts in what sounds like muffled laughter.

I expect Luke to lose it. Instead, he smiles, and his head bobs slowly. "Nice. Now if we can get you in touch with that anger in training, we'll have you ready to kick ass in two, three...maybe five years, tops."

I start to demand an answer, not a backhanded compliment, when Luke adds, "I'll talk to her and vote after, but I'm not going to pull any punches. We have enough tender-hearted people spraying empathy all over the place around here. Someone has to ask the hard questions."

"Don't be cruel," I warn. "She's been through enough. I'm not sure I trust her, either, but there's no reason to be cruel. Ever."

Luke's eyes narrow. "That is where you and I will always disagree, Princess. But I'm not going to kick this girl when she's down. I'm a realist, not an asshole."

My lips pucker and shift to the side, and Luke chuckles, a silky rumble that makes my already aching muscles feel squishier. "Point taken, Princess. But in my defense, you can be a fucking handful."

I am *not* a handful. I am as far from a handful—let alone a *fucking* handful—as it's possible to get. But before I can defend myself, there's a shift in the wind. The cool, early summer breeze goes hot and smoky, coming in sharp gusts from the north instead of easy wisps from the west.

Instantly, my heart lifts, and my shoulders relax away from my ears.

They're here. Dust is back. Creedence, too. I can feel the hum of his energy beneath the wind from Dust's wings.

I vault off the picnic table, hurrying down the trail toward the clearing with Luke, Leda, and Kite close behind. It feels like they've been gone so much longer than a day. There's so much to tell them, and I'll feel so much better making decisions as five instead of three.

I may be the only irreplaceable member of our crew, but I want all of us to have a voice.

But when I reach the clearing, I draw up short, stumbling to a stop several feet from the center of the glen, where Dust and Creedence are pulling on their clothes.

They aren't alone. There's someone with them. Someone who, judging by the feel of her energy, is sick. Very sick.

And very familiar.

"Carrie Ann." Her name rips from my throat as I break into a run, rushing to where she's lying, fevered and delirious, on a bed of pine needles.

CHAPTER 10

DUST

After the others fill us in on the latest crisis, Luke, the unlikeliest of heroes, offers to carry Carrie Ann up to the room. While he's at it, he suggests leaving both her and Sierra here while we hit the road, but he helps.

Carefully.

Gently.

It gives me a spark of hope that things with the wolf might turn out in the end. Even with a secret weapon with knowledge of the monster's lair in our corner, if we can't win him over to our side before we face Atlas, the odds won't be in our favor.

Back in the day, Sierra and I were constantly butting heads, both of us too stubborn to give an inch when we were certain our way was the only way, but having a friend come back from the dead changes a person.

It has changed me, that's for damned sure.

The moment we step into the room and I see Sierra

—smaller, frailer, missing part of her arm, but still with that crazy spiked black hair and that passion for the cause in her eyes—I cross to the bed and pull her into my arms. She resists for a moment, but only a moment, before sagging against my shoulder with a weary sigh. "I'm sorry, Dust. I'm so sorry. I tried to down the tablet, but he took it. He's so fucking strong. And everywhere. All at once."

"You did the best you could. There's no doubt in my mind about that." I insist, rubbing a hand in circles on her back.

If Sierra had taken her emergency tablet, the one all resistance operatives carry to make certain we won't be tortured into revealing our secrets, she would be dead right now. And I can't wish her dead, not even to wish the bears we lost alive again.

Especially since her sacrifice might not have made a difference.

Now that Atlas knows he's been hunting the wrong girl for two decades, he won't stop until Wren is dead and the rest of us along with her.

"Celeste is dead," she whispers, her voice breaking.

I wince and hug her closer. Celeste, my mentor and boss, was Sierra's lover. They'd been planning a wedding for the spring.

"I tried to warn her," Sierra continues tightly, "to warn them all. But that thing was in my fucking head. I couldn't say no to him when he got like that, no matter how hard I tried."

"How did you get away?" Luke asks as he draws the covers over an unconscious Carrie Ann, who he's settled into the other bed. I suppose it's just as well we're going back on the run—this room is getting more crowded by the minute.

Sierra pulls away from me, crossing her arm and bandaged stump at her chest as she hunches over her crossed legs. "He left me alone at that park, the one by the water, where you stopped on your way to the reservation."

Wren sits down on the mattress on Sierra's other side. "You were there?"

Sierra nods. "Hiding under the fucking trashcan not five feet from you guys, but I couldn't make a sound until Atlas let me out of that mind-grip he gets on people. But the second he flew off, I went after you. I tried like hell to catch up, but he'd infected me with something, and I had to keep stopping every few minutes to get sick."

"She was dangerously dehydrated by the time she reached us," Leda confirms. "For the first twenty-four hours, I wasn't sure she was going to make it."

"He uses biological warfare?" Wren shakes her head, looking horrified. She keeps telling me she understands what we're up against, but I'm not so sure.

If she did, she wouldn't be surprised by that.

By anything.

"He becomes the bacteria, mama," Sierra says, the shadows beneath her eyes darkening as she tips her chin closer to her chest. "He can become anything he wants. And not even just one thing at a time. He splits himself into pieces. Say, maybe eighty percent of him is back at his castle with his creepy soldiers, and the rest is flying around the world as a cockroach or whatever, stirring shit up." Her lip curls. "But he fucked up with me. I've always had one hell of an immune system. By the morning after he flew off, I'd already shit him out and was on the mend."

I clear my throat, and Sierra turns my way, sadness flooding her eyes. "I missed that. It's crazy what you miss, like your judgmental sniffing and throat-clearing when you think I'm being crass."

"I'm just glad you're okay," Wren says. "Leda told us about the secret path and the spelled entry. You sure you feel up to helping us get in?"

Sierra's eyes narrow. "Yes. But we can't go in unprotected. We're going to need boosted immune systems, charms against bodily invasion, and every trick up your fancy shifter sleeve, girl. Combat training, weapons, and business, as usual, ain't gonna cut it."

"Does that mean I can skip sparring with Luke?" Wren smiles, clearly trying to lighten the mood.

Sierra's brows lift. "When I say we're going to need all the help we can get, I mean all the fucking help we can get. You never know what's going to save your life. Could be that right hook you pick up in training. Could be your body's talent for explosive diarrhea."

Wren nods. "I'll get to work on both, then."

Sierra makes a rusty, coughing sound that it takes me a moment to realize is a laugh. A moment later she buries her face in her hands, her shoulders shaking as she says in a thick voice, "Sorry. I lose it over the stupidest shit lately."

I rest a hand on her shoulder. "It's all right." She

leans into me, and I draw her close. But this time I don't stop at physical comfort. I drop my walls, letting my kin gift free, wrapping us both in a veil of illusion.

A sharp intake of breath from Wren and a "Where did they go?" from Creedence, who's leaning silently against the far wall, assure me the test was a success.

"I had to check," I tell Sierra as I withdraw the cloaking shield. "Just in case." I meet Wren's wide eyes across the bed. "If someone were tracking her with a kin gift, I wouldn't have been able to cloak her with mine. She's clean. Magically, anyway."

"And I swept her with my wand the day she showed up and before we left home this morning," Leda adds. "No technological tracking devices, either."

Wren touches gentle fingers to Sierra's knee. "It's not personal. I hope you understand that. We just can't afford to take any chances right now."

Sierra nods, her gaze resigned. "I get it. If I were you, I wouldn't trust me, either. I betrayed you. It doesn't matter if I lost most of an arm first. I was tested, and I failed."

"You didn't fail," Wren says. "You were human."

"But I'm *not* human," Sierra says, her eyes blazing. "I'm forest kin. We're faithful, trustworthy, loyal to the bitter end. It's who we are. And I betrayed all of that to save my own stupid life." She swallows hard, her throat working as she adds, "I wouldn't have had the guts to show my face to any of you if I weren't the only one with a chance of getting you through the portal. You don't have to like me or trust me, just use me. That's why I'm here. And on the off chance you find someone else capable of taking my place, I'm happy to step aside, get out of your lives for good."

"No one wants that," Kite rumbles from across the room, his voice thick with emotion. He was running the mission when Sierra was lost, and I imagine he's feeling his share of guilt for what happened to his friend and partner. "We're glad you're here and grateful for your help."

"But we should get on the road." Luke motions toward the bed, where Carrie Ann is muttering softly to herself in her sleep. "You could cloak her, too, right?"

I nod in response.

Luke shifts his attention to Leda. "Can you give her a sweep with your wand? Make sure she's clean before we step outside to vote on who's coming and who's staying?"

Leda starts toward the door. "Yeah. Let me grab it from the trunk."

I stand, ready to make the case for taking both women along with us—Carrie Ann until I can arrange for transport to England, and Sierra for the foreseeable future—when Sierra's fingers close around my wrist.

"Chain me up," she says softly, for my ears only. "Lock me in a cage if you have to, if that's what it takes to get the others on board. I have to come with you, Dust. I have to do something to make this better, or I'll never forgive myself. I was there the morning after you left the reservation." Her dark eyes glitter. "I saw them. The bodies. The kids. I can't... I know nothing can bring them back, but I have to tip the scales. I have to make that monster pay. I don't care if I die in the process."

I shift my arm, taking her hand in mine, but I don't say a word. Danger is part of the job description for a Fata Morgana and her allies in Atlas's world.

But it's a chance we're ready to take, whatever we have to do to rip that sick bastard off his throne.

CHAPTER 11
WREN

"I would say the shit couldn't get any deeper, but I don't want to jinx us more than we're jinxed already." Creedence leans back against the filthy beige camper he somehow managed to talk the owner of the motel into signing over to us in exchange for our Mustang.

It's a clunker, but Dust assured us the engine was sound before we made the trade.

The Beige—or Da Beige, as Creedence has christened the monstrosity—will get us to the border and anywhere we need to stop in between.

Where to next, of course, is the current subject of debate among the four men in my life. Dust says we should head east—better to hide out somewhere closer to our eventual crossing point until we're ready to make the journey. Luke says south—our enemies won't expect that—and Kite says west because they *really* won't expect that.

Creedence is the only one keeping his opinion to himself.

"What about you?" I ask, hoping he'll break the tie. "East, west, or south?"

"I'm a north guy myself."

I glare at him, but he only laughs in response.

"It's your call, Slim. You've got as good a gut as the rest of us."

I twist a lock of damp hair around my finger—we're all grabbing lightning fast showers before we head out in a rig with nothing but a spigot on the wall above the camper's toilet. "I don't know. I'm so worried about Carrie Ann I can't think straight. We need to get her on a plane. Yesterday." I'm glad we voted unanimously to take both Carrie Ann and Sierra with us, but Carrie isn't in any condition for a road trip. She needs to be in a hospital under twenty-four-hour observation, with access to cutting-edge immune therapies to put the virus into remission before it's too late.

But of course, that's a risk we can't take.

Infecting my best friend with the virus I was told I had for years and dumping her near-lifeless body in our alleged "safe house" was clearly intended as a message for me. A message and a threat—we know where you are, we know where you're going, and we won't hesitate to hurt the people you love on our way through them to you.

"I know it looks bad, but she's holding up okay," Creedence says. "She's got time, even without serious meds. She's a tough kid, that one. A fighter."

"She is. I just wish she didn't have to be so tough.

And I wish I knew my parents were all right," I say, forcing the words out through my tight throat. "If whoever did this to Carrie Ann gets to them..."

Creedence rests a hand at the small of my back. "I'll see what I can find out about your parents."

I tilt my head, peering at him from the corners of my eyes. "How? Dust says we can't risk contacting anyone in Seattle."

"I have my ways," he says with a wink. "Trust me?"

"Of course."

"Good," he says, his expression sobering as he adds. "But be careful with your fight coach, okay? Hit the pause button on that trusting nature of yours until we're sure his story checks out."

I narrow my eyes, wishing I could read Creedence as well as he reads me. "What's going on? What aren't you telling me?"

"Those ways I was telling you about," he says softly. "I've got a few feelers out with people in the San Diego area. So far no one's been able to pinpoint Luke's family's pack of origin."

"And?" I ask, wishing I'd had the time to take a Shifter Culture 101 class before being thrust into the middle of it.

"Pack of origin is sacred to wolves. They live and die by their allegiance to their birth alpha and the greater good of the wolf nation. They can marry into a new pack or be recruited as foot soldiers by their allies, but unlike my people, who live to fight and tell each other to fuck off, they don't just go wandering off on their own." He holds my gaze with an intensity that makes it clear how deep his suspicions run where Luke is concerned. "The pack is life. The only way you end up a lone wolf family is if you've been banished. Kicked out for crimes against your kin."

"I'm guessing crimes more serious than shoplifting?"

Creedence's brows bob. "Yep. Could have been his mom or pop who got the family in trouble. But it could have been Luke or one of his siblings, too. He's got a few more than he's been claiming in that backstory of his about his poor dead brother."

"Losing his brother was painful for him. I believe that part is real, but…" I trail off with a sigh, lids sliding closed as I rub the backs of my aching eyes "But the lies are troubling. Are his parents and siblings still alive?"

"The parents, no. But he's got an older half-brother who lives in Mexico, and an older half-sister somewhere in SoCal. That's where my sources are focusing, seeing if they can get Sister Dearest to give up the goods. I'll let you know what they dig up."

"Sounds good." I glance up at the door to the hotel room to find it closed and Dust, Luke, and the two women still inside. Kite went with Leda to get supplies in town—medicine for Carrie Ann, food for the trip, and clean sheets to put on the mattresses in the camper. Even with clean sheets, I'm not looking forward to sleeping in the cramped hidey-hole at the back of Da Beige, but no one said being on the run was going to be a five-star affair.

And I'm so damned tired.

So tired it takes my brain a few beats to connect Creedence's concern to its likely source. "Did you see something when you were casting forward yesterday? Something in the future that has you doubting Luke?"

After a hint of hesitation, Creedence shakes his head. "No. Not really."

"Not really. What does that mean?" I press.

He laughs beneath his breath. "It means I learned a long time ago not to share everything I see, doll face. Worrying about a dozen things that are never going to happen is a good way to make people crazy, and I prefer to keep the crazy to myself."

"You're not crazy."

Pushing away from the camper, he spins in a swift half circle, bracing his hands on the dusty metal on either side of my face as he leans in close. "Maybe I'm just the kind of crazy you like. Admit it, Slim, you're still thinking about that kiss last night. I know I am."

Pulse picking up, I meet his gaze. "Maybe."

His full lips curve into a wicked grin that sends heat racing across my skin. "Maybe? That's all I get? A maybe?"

"Maybe I want more than chemistry. Maybe I want to know you, Cree. The real you. Not just the charming parts."

"You shouldn't look down your nose on chemistry and charm, sweetheart. I promise you, fireworks like this don't happen every day." And then he kisses me, his tongue sweeping into my mouth, stroking against mine as his right hand slides down to cup my bottom through my leggings, drawing me against him.

I gasp into his mouth as I feel the hard length of him nudging between my legs, making it clear what he wants from me. Instinctively, I wrap a leg around his waist, keeping that long, thick part of him close as our kiss grows hotter, deeper.

Sex is still so new to me, and when I'm alone with Kite, a voice in my head insists he should be the only man in my bed. But when Creedence touches me like this, I forget all about that voice. I forget that, according to the Church, only "bad girls" sleep with more than one man before they're married. And only a truly depraved hussy would consider sleeping with more than one man on a regular basis.

Let alone more than one man at the same time…

But I would be a liar if I said the idea doesn't excite me, that it doesn't make me wet to imagine Kite behind me, stripping my leggings down my thighs as Creedence slips his hand up my shirt for the first time.

Creedence tugs my bra down, finding my nipple and rolling it with an easy confidence that takes my breath away. His skin is warm against mine and his erection is hard between my thighs and his kiss is like too much wine—something I'll probably regret later, but that feels too good going down to care.

"I want you on top of me, Slim," he growls against my lips as his grip tightens on my ass, urging me to rock against him through our clothes. "I want to suck these pretty tits while you come for me. We can keep it casual. No need to rush into a mate bond or any of that crazy."

The words penetrate the haze of lust swirling through my head. "What?" I pull back, heart jerking as I meet his gaze and see the hunger obvious in his eyes. "I thought… Kite said once we slept together there was no going back. We'd be bonded for life."

Creedence gives an indulgent roll of his eyes. "Yeah, that's bears for you, baby. They'll fuck any feline or canine shifter that moves and say it's all just for fun. But the second they get naked with another bear, it's for life. Guess Kite considers you bear enough for him."

He pinches my nipple again, sending another shudder of desire working through me, making my voice tremble as I say, "But I didn't know. He didn't tell me we could wait to make that decision."

"You probably couldn't. You love him, and he loves you. Love plus sex equals mate bond, no going back on that. Though, you do get to choose when you get knocked up." Creedence stops teasing my nipple, making it easier to think as he asks in a tighter voice, "Kite did tell you about that right? Made sure you knew not to think about babies while he's getting you off? I mean, kids are great and all, but the last thing we need right now is baby makes six."

I nod, cheeks heating. "He told me that. But I… I feel so stupid. About the mate bond. I feel like I never know what the hell is going on until after it's already happened. Like I'll never find my footing. I'm always going to be ten steps behind playing catch up."

"Nah, don't do that. Don't feel bad, I want you to feel good." His mouth finds mine again, kissing me lazy, sexy sweet until my muscles relax and my blood thickens. "And I'll teach you all about cats, beautiful," he murmurs. "Everything you need to know, starting with what amazing fuck buddies we can be."

I huff in soft laughter, a sound that becomes a moan as Cree hitches my legs around his waist and pins me against the side of the camper, bringing all that delicious hardness into even more intimate contact with where I'm aching for every inch.

"I can make you come without making you mine," he says, grinding against me through our clothes while I cling to his shoulders. "It's all about intention, sweetheart. Until love enters the picture, sex is just sex. Just a good time, a release, a way for us both to let off steam." He leans in, nipping my neck with his teeth as he adds softly in my ear, "I'm dying to be inside you, Slim, and I know you want this, too. I can smell you, baby, how wet you are for me. I can't fucking wait to get my tongue between your legs and show you what a grown man can do to your body."

I'm so turned on I'm about to tell him "yes," to beg him to take me—here against the side of the camper with nothing but the dumpsters to conceal us from the rest of the parking lot and half the rooms on the second floor—when someone clears his throat.

Loudly.

And I'm guessing not for the first time.

I emerge from the lust fog to see Dust standing by the concrete block wall surrounding the industrial trash containers. Unlocking my legs from around Creedence's waist, I slide to the ground, hastily pulling at my clothes, wondering what the hell is wrong with me.

When did I become a sex fiend, and how long until I'm back in my right mind?

Never, the no-bullshit voice in my head pipes up. *Not*

with men like this around. Say goodbye to your right mind and dry panties while you're at it.

I frown at the thought even as I hurry to apologize for wasting time making out when I should be helping get the camper cleaned and loaded, "Sorry, we were—"

"No, I'm sorry to interrupt," Dust cuts in, a faint pink to his cheeks. "But there's a problem. With Carrie Ann. You've got to see this. Now." He turns, hurrying back toward the hotel.

With one last glance at Creedence who assures me, "Right behind you," I jog after Dust, praying this latest crisis isn't the straw that breaks our collective backs.

CHAPTER 12

CARRIE ANN

I *don't know much, but I know I love you...*
Scraps of a nearly forgotten song drift through my head, warming my heart.

Tiny heart, beating so fast, but so strong.

Take that, Doc, you piece of fucking shit. I'm not supposed to be able to shift without a cue from a handler, but I did. I did and right now I'm feeling six inches tall and bulletproof.

It's the claws. And the tail. I've got a magnificent tail, perfect for tucking under my head as I catch my breath, sinking into a puddle of reddish-brown fluff on the faded flower comforter.

Another thing about claws and tails—they suck at placing phone calls. And even if I managed to punch out the numbers, Dr. Highborn doesn't speak squirrel.

I smile and the man with the dark eyes and silky black hair past his shoulders smiles back at me from the end of the bed. I can't remember his name, but he's familiar now. The longer I can stay in my kin form, the faster I'll be able to fight off the virus, and the sooner my memories will return.

And I need them back. Desperately.

I feel that truth in my bones, even though I can't yet remember why.

The door opens, and the man with the accent, Dust, returns, nodding toward me. "There. On the bed."

"Oh my God." A young woman with big blue eyes and brown hair wild around her flushed face comes to a stop behind him, sending a thrill through me. She's a friend. I know it instantly, though I don't recall how we met or who she is to me. She blinks, shock blanking her features for a moment before she lifts a wary brow. "Carrie?"

Yes, that much I remember. My name. I lift a claw—the universal sign for "Here, teacher,"—before letting it fall again, still so weak that even small movements make my head spin.

"Did you know she was a shifter?" Dust asks.

"No idea." The woman shakes her head, her gaze still fixed on me. "Not even after I got off the meds. She doesn't smell like kin, does she? Is that because her animal form's so small or—"

"It's because she was made in a lab. Not too long ago, I'm guessing, after the mad scientists learned how to adjust for scent to help their shifters go unnoticed by the rest of us." The golden-haired man from last night studies me with kind but wary eyes as he crouches beside the bed. "Someone did this to her. She wasn't born this way."

"Highborn," the woman says, sending my arm shooting into the air again. *Ding, ding,* now they're on the right track.

She kneels, bringing her gaze level with mine. "How long? How long have you been able to shift?"

I shake my head, rolling it back and forth across the pillow of my own tail.

"You can't remember?" she asks.

I shake my head again, even slower this time. I'm so tired, so heavy, even in this body, with its enhanced capacity to heal.

The woman's breath rushes out. "It's okay, Carrie. We're going to help you. I promise. But we might have to take certain...precautions until we know exactly what's going on."

I bring my front paws together, crossed at the wrists, summoning a sad smile to the young woman's lips as she says, "Yeah. We need some kind of restraints. But we'll do our best to make you comfortable."

"Looks like you're headed back to town, Kite," Golden Boy says as he stands. "They had rabbit cages and drink dispensers at the hardware store. Right near the backyard chicken supplies."

The man with the long black hair nods but doesn't rise to his feet or shift his focus away from me. "I'll head back now, but the rest of you need to talk to Leda. She's on the phone by her car. A call came in from the team assisting with the investigation. Sounds like they found something we should know about before we decide to take one of Highborn's creations on a road trip." His mouth softens. "Sorry, Carrie Ann. It isn't personal. Not even a little bit."

I sigh. Maybe it would be for the best for me to stay here, though I have no idea if my species is indigenous to the area.

Before I can think of how to communicate my willingness to stay behind, the woman shakes her head. "No. We can't leave her. She's like family to me, and you don't leave family behind. Even when things get complicated. We'll find a way to make it work, Carrie Ann. Get some rest. We'll be back."

Rising to her feet with a strength and ease I instinctively know isn't the norm for this woman, she starts for the door. "Let's talk to Leda."

After a beat, the three men follow her out into the sunny day, one by one, with the Englishman bringing up the rear.

He pauses in the doorway, turning back to me with a sober expression. He holds my gaze for a moment, before he slowly, deliberately releases the handle, leaving the door cracked a few inches as he trails after his friends.

The invitation is clear, and for a moment I can see myself rising to my feet, bounding off the bed and slipping out into the warm summer day.

But my head is so heavy and my eyes even heavier, and before I know it, they're sliding closed.

It's okay to sleep, I decide.

These people aren't stupid. Whether they decide to take me or leave me, they've got a shot. A chance. A good chance, I think, especially if I can stay small and furry until I remember why my human form is so dangerous.

Though, what human form isn't?

We are incredible and terrible creatures, we humans —a beautiful disaster I can't help but think the world might have been better off without.

CHAPTER 13

LUKE

Never let them see you sweat.

Better yet, don't sweat. Don't even *think* about sweating.

Sweat is weakness, and weakness is death, and even after all the shit I've been through in my life, I don't want to die. Not yet. Not until I've had a taste of that freedom everyone is always talking about.

Slave to my crazy fucking family, slave to my body turned traitor, slave to the street gang that promised to make me a king only to take everything good in my life and flush it down the toilet, slave to the cell block and the rules of the iron jungle and all those hundreds of days waiting to be crossed out in red...

It's *my turn* to be free. It's time to lift two middle fingers to the rest of the world and leave the fucking building.

Instead, I'm still here, standing in a circle in the

shade with people who have no idea who I am, what I've done, or how dangerous I could be if…

I clench my jaw, shutting down the thought.

There is no if.

There is no when.

I haven't shifted in nearly seven years, and I'm not going to start now. No fur, no fury—that's my creed and I'm fucking sticking to it.

Especially now…

"The guy wasn't just genetically modified to shift into whatever that monster thing was, he had also had tech implants. A camera in both eyes and a mod in his ear canal that we're guessing provided audio," Leda continues, her almond-shaped eyes scanning the circle of faces surrounding her. "But the wildest thing is the chip the team found in his brain."

She's short, forcing her to look up to all of us—even the princess—but she demands attention, respect. She reminds me of my favorite guard at the prison, a tiny Italian mama who commanded obedience from every man in her block with nothing but a hard look and the respectful way she said an inmate's last name.

It's about respect—you have to give it to get it.

That's what the rest of these people don't understand. You can't kidnap a man, jab a finger at the mark on his shoulder, and expect him to jump at the chance to risk his life to save a world that's been trying to chew him up and spit him out since the day he was born.

You can't demand loyalty, not the real stuff. That has to be earned.

So I keep my mouth shut, not offering contribution or commentary as Leda adds, "It was equipped to receive radio signals, and our doctors are ninety percent sure it was used to force the kid to shift. They don't know how yet, but apparently this is something the Frankenstein doctors have been working on for a while now."

"And one of them succeeded," Dust mutters darkly.

"Looks like it. And since this guy came from High-born's lab, we can assume the U.S. Government is either on board with this shit or turning a blind eye while they wait to see what Highborn will be able to deliver down the line. I don't know about you guys, but remote-control shifter soldiers sound like the kind of thing the people in charge of this great nation would get hot under the collar about," Leda says, wrapping up her report on the body at the reservation.

The body of the man I killed.

The man who, if Leda is right, was as innocent as Wren has been insisting since the second my bullet punched a hole through his skull.

I suppose I should feel guilty about how things went down, but I don't.

That kid's life was over. He was a Gen Mod monster. There's no going back to being anything close to human, or shifter, after your DNA has been scrambled like that. The kindest thing for him was to put him out of his misery.

But somehow I doubt the princess is going to see things that way.

I cut my glance her direction, but her sharp blue

gaze is fixed on Leda's face. "That would check out with what he said to me before he died."

Died, not *killed*. Not murdered.

It's a telling choice of words.

I'm damned sure it's a deliberate one, too. Wren is careful in her thoughts and deeds. She's a thinker and a feeler, always weighing the pros and cons and evaluating the emotional impact of her choices. She would be a great politician—truly great in a way our country hasn't been lucky enough to experience in decades—but all that thinking and heart-bleeding isn't going to keep her alive.

She needs to trust her gut, that slimy shit deep down in her core, the primordial ooze that wants to stay alive at any cost.

"He said he couldn't control it," she continues, "that *they* couldn't control it, and begged me to help him make it stop."

"Unfortunately, according to the doctors, we have no way to do that yet," Leda says. "It's going to take time to reverse engineer biotech this sophisticated. And until we figure out how it works, there's no way to make it un-work."

"And even then, we wouldn't have been able to put him back the way he was. Not after a genetic modification that severe," Kite offers, saying what I'm sure most of us are thinking.

All of us except Princess, who's been kept so ignorant of our world she might as well be an infant. A baby, toddling around, headed for the nearest cliff the second we handlers turn our backs.

She's dangerous. Foolishly unpredictable.

Flat-out fucking terrifying, because as much as she pisses me off, I don't want to watch her tumble over the edge. It would be a waste of a decent person's life, and that's not okay. Not even my ice-cold heart can look into Wren's kind, innocent, I-want-to-save-the-world eyes and say she's better off dead.

She's better off back where she came from, sheltered and protected, loved and coddled. Sure, she was slowly dying, but aren't we all?

Some of us not so slowly. The chances of getting over the border and getting my walking papers before one of the many people out to kill this girl catch up with us are slim to fucking none.

I know that, even before Leda pipes up with another piece of encouraging news, "And in unrelated bullshit, the Kin Born Forces have deployed packs to the woods along the border. Cascadia and Cheyenne packs for sure —our spies saw them heading out a few days ago."

"Fucking wolves," Creedence grumbles, shooting a narrow look my way. "Why do your people have to be such narrow-minded fuck-heads, Luke?"

I hold his gaze, my face expressionless until he finally looks away.

Those wolves aren't my people. I don't *have* people, but I'm not about to share that with a suspicious, know-it-all cat who thinks he's got my number.

"Don't," Dust warns. "Luke isn't responsible for this, and not all wolves agree with the Kin Born. They're not all out to destroy lab-made shifters."

"Just ninety percent of them." Creedence grins, and

Dust rolls his eyes, but my features are made of stone. He's going to have to work a hell of a lot harder to get a rise out of me. I don't give my power away that easily.

Not to him, not to anyone.

"This is why it's going to be so hard to find another canine kin who bears the mark, isn't it?" Wren asks. "Because most of them consider me the enemy?"

"They consider *us* the enemy," Kite says. "Dust and I have been working with the resistance for years, standing up for lab-made shifters they want dead. You're guilty of associating with us, that's it. They couldn't care less that you're the Fata Morgana or what that means for the planet or the future."

"Most of them don't believe it means anything," Dust seconds. "Like other fundamentalists, they have a great gift for ignoring facts that don't support their insanity." He glances my way. "Which is one of the reasons you're so valuable to us, Luke. It's not just that you bear the mark. It's that you've got a level head on your shoulders."

"Yeah, the rest of us had to have special skills, Wolf Boy," Creedence says. "All you had to do was have a pulse and not be bat-shit crazy."

I smile, hoping he can read the unspoken "fuck you" in my eyes.

I don't know where he got the idea that I'm not crazy, but he's going to regret making assumptions. One day he's going to push me too far, wake up with his pretty nose smashed through to the other side of his face, and realize just how crazy I am.

"Cut the shit, kitty," Leda says with a sigh. "You need

the wolf. He's going to be able to sense the packs' movements better than any tech or spy network. If I were you, I'd stay on his good side. At least until you get across the border."

Jaw clenching, I pretend to be engrossed in study of the grass and dirt beneath our feet. I will my mind to remain empty, refusing entry to the dangerous confessions lurking at the back of my thoughts.

Never let them see you sweat.

Never let them smell your lies.

Never let them know you aren't what they think you are.

If they get wind of the truth, they'll dump me by the road so fast my head will swim. They're my only shot at a fresh start. They owe me that much for having me kidnapped and delivered in chains to their basement, breaking my parole in the process. You can't order a person like a fucking pizza and expect his unfailing loyalty in return.

As much as I want to kick his teeth in, the cat is the only one of these fools with sense, a fact he proves by being the lone "nay" vote on whether to take Carrie Ann along for whatever comes next. Even Kite comes around, agreeing that keeping her caged should ensure our safety until we can find someone to take her to Dust's people.

The rest of them take an unreasonable amount of comfort in the fact that Leda's wand sweep proved Carrie Ann hasn't been equipped with audio or video surveillance implants. As if that would prevent her from picking up a phone, calling the fucking doctor, and telling him exactly where we are.

Even when they're being cautious, they're fools.

I decline the opportunity to vote, not wanting any part in making it easier for the lot of them to have their heads removed from their bodies.

"You should have your say. You're part of this for the next few months, at least." Wren's gaze is piercing, but not accusing. Apparently, she isn't going to get up on her "I told you so" soapbox with me. Not here in front of the rest of them, anyway. I don't know whether to be grateful or to resent her careful handling.

I'm not a fucking child. I can admit when I'm wrong.

But I wasn't wrong. The kid is better off dead, and we might be, too.

Before I can say something I'll regret, a thunderous clatter-smash fills the air. Dust flinches, Leda does a swift one-eighty to face the problem, and Wren...disappears.

One second, she's standing between Kite and Creedence, calling me out. The next, she's nothing but a pile of soft cotton clothes.

A wiggling pile of clothes...

"Sorry," a young male voice calls out from near the soda machines behind the office. "Just taking out the recycling. Didn't mean to scare you guys. So many bottles upstairs today. Someone must have had a party last night, eh?"

I glance up to see the towheaded twenty-something grinning in our direction, a large blue bin propped on his narrow hip. He doesn't seem to have noticed Wren's transformation, but I step in front of her, just in case. Keep what you are a secret—it's pretty much the only law all the shifter factions can agree on, and one I've been happy to embrace from day one.

Secrets get a bad rap. I like secrets. They're the most solid defense I've found against all the forces out there that like nothing better than destroying the circles that don't fit into their square holes.

As the kid heads back up the stairs to the second floor, I crouch down, freeing Wren from her T-shirt. But instead of the fox shape I'm expecting, I uncover a flop-eared rabbit with white paws and a black patch over one startled blue eye.

I shake my head as I grab her gently by the scruff of the neck, lifting her into my arms while Kite gathers her clothes. "You're heading in the wrong direction, Princess. You're supposed to be getting scarier, not fluffier."

Wren wiggles her pink nose, clearly irritated, but she's too cute to be taken seriously.

"At least the shift was fast." Kite runs a gentle finger over the fur between her ears. "And you made Luke smile. That's an accomplishment all on its own."

"I'm not smiling," I say. "Got a cramp in my jaw."

"Was that a joke, Wolf Boy?" Creedence huffs. "Not great, but I'll take it. You could stand to lighten the fuck up once in a while."

I grunt in response as I lift Wren to eye level. "Straight to the camper or do you want to go upstairs first? You've already packed, right?"

She nods grudgingly before pointing a tiny arm toward the camper.

For a beat, I'm possessed by the urge to press my lips to the pink of her paw, to feel the silk of her fur against my cheek, to pull the Wren smell of her into my lungs.

She always smells the same, no matter what skin she's wearing, like a sea breeze kissed with citrus, flowers, and a whiff of homemade bread. She smells like… home, though not any home I've ever lived in.

She's the kind of home I longed for as a tiny kid, back when I thought sitcoms were real and that someday, if I tried hard enough, I would live in a place like that—where there was always enough food, everything was polished and clean, and any problem could be cured with a hug and a laugh track.

But I figured out a long time ago, I'm never going to have a happy home or a family or a pretty little wife waiting for me with a kiss and a beer when I get off work. Survival as a lone wolf is the best I can hope for.

So I don't kiss her paw.

Of course I don't. That was never an option.

I tuck her against my chest and start toward the camper, trying not to enjoy the feel of her warm and close. It feels so damned good to touch her, but that feeling is a lie, too, just like everything else.

I am a lie.

And I always will be.

CHAPTER 14

WREN

I wake up groggy, disorientated, and naked, and it all comes rushing back.

A bunny. I terror-shifted into a flop-eared rabbit over the sound of bottles being dropped into a bin.

Worst. World saver. Ever.

I sit up on the gently rocking bed, dragging a weary hand through my tangled hair as I draw the sheet up around my chest. Blinking into the semi-darkness, I see the interior of the camper, bathed in the faint red glow of an ancient nightlight plugged in near the bathroom. Carrie Ann's cage is strapped into a bucket seat near the lavatory and it looks like she's still asleep, curled up in the cedar shavings.

Faint snoring from the top bunk of the built-in bed across from the kitchen area makes me think Kite must be sacked out there—my big bear is the only one of us who snores, a fact I find oddly charming when it isn't loud enough to wake me from my few stolen hours of sleep—and the curled fingers dangling off the lower mattress give Luke's location.

Even in sleep, he keeps his hand in a fist. Just in case.

He's a violent man. A convicted murderer, who has made it clear he has no qualms about killing again. I should be afraid of him. But I'm not.

In fact, I'm pretty sure I enjoyed being cradled against his strong chest in fluffy-bunny form way too much.

"What is wrong with you," I grumble softly, my voice scratchy with thirst.

"Tough question, but your clothes are by your pillow if you'd like to get dressed." The lightly accented words come from outside the entrance to my lofted full-size mattress. "I think we should talk."

Scooting forward, I poke my head out to find Dust leaning against the closest part of the kitchen counter. The clock on the microwave mounted behind his head reads two ten a.m., making it clear whatever he wants to talk about is serious.

But isn't it always?

We're serious together these days, Dust and me, and I have things I'd like to talk to him about, too.

"Give me a minute, then come on up," I whisper. "And bring some water with you, please? Shifting makes me so thirsty."

He smiles and gives a two-fingered salute in agreement.

Drawing the homemade privacy curtains—tent-patterned fabric that's stiff with dust and age—I crawl back to the top of the mattress, flick on the small reading light set into the roof, and dress in the cramped space, doing my best to be quiet.

Creedence volunteered to take the first driving shift, which means Sierra must be in the bed beneath me. I don't want to wake her, or any of the others. They need their rest and Dust and I need privacy, or as close as we can get to it considering we're all literally sleeping on top of each other.

Once I've pulled on a fresh pair of navy leggings, socks to ward off the chill, and a long-sleeved gray T-shirt, I scoot to sit cross-legged on one side of the mattress. A few moments later, Dust appears with two water bottles and a plate, which he sets between us as he settles in across from me.

I squint at the selection of snacks and lift narrowed eyes to his face. "Carrots?"

He grins, instantly taking five years off his face. "I couldn't resist. I'm sorry."

"You're not sorry, not even a little bit." I grab a carrot stick, biting into it and chewing with a mock glare.

"No, I'm not," he says, his eyes dancing. "It felt like an appropriate celebration. And I brought cheese slices and raisins, too."

"A celebration? Of what? The fact that I excel at shifting into tiny furry things no one in their right mind would be scared of?"

Dust's lips settle into a soft line. "Yes. You've found three forms in less than two weeks. That's incredible, Wren. You should be proud."

I shake my head. "But I didn't choose to shift. Or what I was going to shift into."

He shrugs. "So you've got good instincts. A rabbit was as good a choice as any for running from sudden danger."

I arch a dubious brow. "Like I said, it wasn't a choice. And I think the fact that Kite had just gotten back from buying a rabbit cage deserves as much credit as any instincts on my part. It was just fresh in my mind." I take a cheese slice from the plate, breaking it in half and holding the pieces up between us. "So, if I eat this cheese and think of mice, maybe that will be next?"

"Mice can sneak under an alarming number of doors. You never know when that might prove useful." Dust smiles as I pop the cheese into my mouth and chew soberly, refusing to dignify that remark with a response. "But I understand this is frustrating for you. Once we're settled, I'll have more time to help with that part. I'm obviously not dealing with the range of options you are, but I had to relearn how to shift later in life. I remember how unpredictable it was at first, and some of the tricks that helped me gain control. We can work on those together in the afternoons, once Luke has worn you out in the sparring ring. I found that at first, the more tired I was, the easier it was to slip my skin. The less the brain's involved, the better."

I brush my fingers off over the plate and unscrew the top on my water. "That reminds me of what I wanted to talk to you about. I had another dream while you were gone."

I fill Dust in on the message from my father and the

part of my mother's message I initially left out, then lean back against the side of the compartment, sipping water and waiting for his thoughtful expression to become something he's willing to share.

I can tell he isn't upset that I withheld information—enhanced empathy is a comforting thing at times—so I'm happy to wait, watching the glow of passing street-lights flash on his face as we near a town big enough to light the road beside the highway.

We ended up heading east, though I'm not sure how far we're going. Cree assured us that he'll "know our place" when he sees it, and for once, no one wanted to argue.

We're all tired. None of us have been sleeping well. We need to find safety and establish some sense of routine before we're too exhausted to be of use to anyone.

Finally, Dust tucks his increasingly long hair behind an ear and offers softly, "Your father was right. I've never life-fasted before, but I'm willing to try. But I'd like to talk with my parents first. I've got to reach out to them about arranging transport for Carrie Ann, anyway. I can ask for advice on how to manage it then. I do know there's a certain amount of risk involved."

"What kind of risk?" I ask, draining the last of the water from my bottle.

Dust exhales. "Um...madness? General brain damage?" He laughs, his eyes twinkling into mine. "If one partner is mentally stronger than the other, they can accidentally push things too far. It can have some messy results."

I bare my teeth. "Yeah, so maybe we shouldn't do that."

"Don't discount it yet. Let me talk to people I trust. It might be fine. And it would have benefits aside from figuring out what might be locked away in my head from those years with the Parsons. What better way to teach you how to shift than for you to experience those memories with me, as if you were in my body?"

I lengthen my legs out along the mattress, toes wiggling. "Sounds intimate."

He dips his chin closer to his chest. "Well, yes. I'm sure it would be. Is that a problem? Getting that close?"

"No. Not a problem." I shake my head, lips tingling as memories of yesterday's kiss—our first kiss—flit through my thoughts.

I've never been alone in a bed with Dust, and though I'm way too tired for anything more than sleep, I would like to lay down beside him, to hold him, our arms and legs tangled together as we drift off. I want to feel his heart beating steadily beneath my palm and relish the comfort of knowing at least one person from my past is going to be a part of my future.

Because Carrie Ann has to go. Soon.

It isn't safe for her, or us, to have her along for the ride.

"Why do you think Highborn left Carrie Ann at the safe house?" I drop my voice to a whisper. "Even after he knew we'd found the tracking device and ditched the Hummer? I mean, there was a good chance we weren't going to show up there at all. I understand 'he was delivering a message' is the prevailing theory, but the more I think about it, the less I buy that."

Dust leans closer, his elbows propped on his knees. "That's been bothering me, too. As well as something else..." He reaches into the back pocket of his suit pants —only Dust would choose suit pants and a button-down shirt rolled at the sleeves as road trip attire—and pulls out his wallet. "I found these at the house, tucked under a board by the fireplace. It was one of the places Celeste liked to hide things when she was designing a safe space, so I knew where to look. I didn't show them to Creedence. I wanted to talk to you first."

He hands over a small stack of passports, most of them U.S. blue, though one is burgundy red. United Kingdom, I realize, as I flip the oddball open to reveal Dust, looking even more serious than usual. "Archibald Knowlton? Good Lord."

Dust smiles. "Not the best alias I've had, I'll admit. But wait until you get to yours."

I flip through two more—Kite alias Curtis Freemason and Creedence aka Flynn Baxter—until I find myself. I press a fist to my lips, stifling a laugh.

"I told you." Dust gives my knee a teasing squeeze. "Dearest Mildred, I hope you will allow this humble Archibald the honor of taking you for tea and scones at your earliest convenience."

"I love tea and scones, but..." I huff. "Mildred Munchin? Seriously? I sound like I'm a hundred years old."

"Two hundred. Mildred hasn't been a common name for over a century," Dust says, his tone sobering as he points toward the last passport. "But that's where the real trouble is, I'm afraid."

I hold his gaze. "What is it? Is Luke's out of date or something? You know he's only sticking around to get across the border."

"Open it," he says. "You'll see."

With a bracing breath, I open the final folder to reveal...a stranger.

"Who is this?" I hiss, eyes wide as I search Dust's face.

"Diego Garcia, alias Lucas Rivera," Dust murmurs. "The real question is who is that?" He points deeper into the camper, where our wolf sleeps with his fingers curled into a fist.

Only he might not be *our* wolf at all.

And the shifting sand beneath our feet just got even more unsteady.

CHAPTER 15
WREN

Somehow, I fall back asleep, tucked against Dust in the small spoon position as the gentle rocking of the camper lulls us into unconsciousness. But once again, I wake up alone.

For a woman with four potential mates, I do an awful lot of that.

When all of this is over, I would like to wake up with someone I love still in bed beside me, I decide, as I spread up the covers as best I can in the cramped quarters. It's a simple wish, but it's something to fight for, to look forward to in the event I live to see my twenty-fifth birthday.

Crawling to the bottom of the mattress, I draw back the curtains to reveal sunlight and stillness. We're parked somewhere very quiet. Even when I strain my ears, clicking into that wide range of hearing now available to my shifter side, all I can hear is the breeze, birdsong, and a faint rushing in the distance.

A river or a creek, I'm guessing, the thought making my heart feel lighter. I showered before we left the hotel, but shifting always makes my skin feel too tight. A swim sounds luxurious, and I can't help hoping we've reached our final destination, not just a pitstop along the way.

I maneuver the three rungs down the ladder to the floor and bend to pull on the tennis shoes someone has placed there for me. The movement brings my face low enough to peek into the bottom bunk, where Sierra is still asleep, her thin arm flung over her face. A glance at the microwave clock reveals it's barely six. Still early, but everyone else is already out and about.

Including Luke.

Or whoever he is.

Dust and I agreed not to say anything to the others—or to Luke—for now, at least until Dust gets in touch with the members of the L.A. pack who delivered Luke to make sure there hasn't been some sort of innocent mix up. But it's not going to be easy to keep my new knowledge from affecting the way I look at the wolf.

I was starting to admire him, damn it, if not necessarily trust him or agree with all his choices. Yes, he shot an innocent man, but he did it to protect me, the bears, and the rest of our people.

Or so I'd assumed.

But now...

Now, I don't know what to think, except that I'm glad to see Carrie Ann bright eyed and bushy tailed—literally, her tail looks incredible this morning—as I walk by her cage on the way to the door. "Hey? How are you feeling?" I whisper, reaching for the door to her cage. "You want to come outside with me?"

She shakes her head and backs to the corner of the enclosure, wrapping her small paws tightly around the bars before shaking her head again, more vehemently this time. "All right, that's fine." I lift my hands, signaling that I respect her decision to stay wherever she feels safe. "I'll bring you something to eat soon."

Her shoulders relaxing, she nods and curls up again, her tail looped around her small body.

I have to shove my shoulder into it a couple of times, but the door to the outside world finally pops open, spilling me out into a picture-perfect postcard of a day, with crisp, cool air that smells of sweet grass and honeysuckle, and a view that takes my breath away. We're parked in a copse of trees at the edge of a wide field atop a mountain at the edge of the world.

Or at least that's what it feels like.

Turning in a slow circle, I can't find a sign of life anywhere on the surrounding hilltops or valleys. Nothing to hint at human habitation except Da Beige and what looks like an old cabin leaning drunkenly against a large tree a bit deeper into the forest.

I'm studying the cabin, wondering if it was built crooked or gradually got that way over time, when Kite circles around the side of the building. The moment he sees me, his face lights up, and I know right then.

We've found it. Our home away from home.

"How's the well?" Creedence asks from behind me.

I glance over my shoulder to see him approaching through the grass wearing nothing but a smile, and I blush. The parts of him I have yet to see up close are covered by the corpse of the large turkey he's holding in front of his hips, but there's enough of him on display to make me hot all over, from my cheeks to my toes and everything in between.

"Good," Kite replies, coming to stand beside me, looping an easy arm around my shoulders. "Spring fed and clean. It will be a pain in the ass lugging buckets to the kitchen, but it could be worse."

"And the cabin?" Creedence shifts his attention to the tilting structure as Dust appears in the doorway.

"The back porch is rotten, and there's something clogging the chimney." Dust thumps the heel of his hand on the doorframe. "But it's in better shape than I thought. Nothing a good scrubbing and a few fresh boards and nails can't fix."

"What is this place?" I lean into Kite, relishing the feel of him so close after a night apart. "It's so beautiful here."

Creedence grins. "An old trapping cabin. They're all over this part of Montana and up into Canada. My folks used to shack up in them when they needed to lay low for a while. We stayed here once when I was six or seven."

"I can't believe you remembered how to get here," Kite says.

"Yeah, well, it was a fun summer." Creedence shrugs. "Lots of fishing and swimming and running wild through the woods with my sister. We didn't have a lot of summers like that when we were kids. Makes you remember the good times."

Kite hugs me closer. "I hear you."

The good times...

I'm not sure any of those are in our near future, but hopefully, we've found a safe place to hide while we get ready for the fight of our lives. The thought is barely through my head when Luke appears from around the rear of the camper. "We're clear visibility wise. No sign of civilization on any of the hills around here."

"Good to know," Dust says, but all I can think about is all the things we *don't* know about the man ambling over to lean against the shady side of the camper.

Who the hell are you, Luke? I wonder silently, but my hard look yields nothing but a lazy smile that makes my stomach flip in spite of myself.

Trouble. Luke is a trouble enchilada smothered in trouble sauce with a side of frustration salsa. But for now, he's part of our crew and we're all safe.

If I've learned anything in my life, it's to be grateful for little miracles.

"Welcome home pancakes, anyone?" I ask, with a smile. "I'm making."

I make twenty pancakes and we eat them all, smothered in syrup and crushed walnuts, while watching the sun light up the hills, the view so pretty it would be easy to start believing in happy endings.

Or at the very least, happy beginnings.

CHAPTER 16
WREN

The first day on the Compound, as we eventually come to call it, I'm so busy trying to pretend I don't know that Luke isn't who he says he is—and to keep from coughing up a lung during our five-mile sprint down the mountain, or our sparring practice and weight training, during which Luke proves he does not intend to take it easy on me until I build up my stamina—I don't notice much else.

I know Carrie Ann sleeps most of the day in her cage and that Sierra isn't doing so well—she gets panicked in open spaces and takes a plate back to Da Beige to eat alone rather than join us for the evening meal at the outdoor table Kite rigged up from an old barn door—but neither is much of a surprise. Carrie Ann is sick, and Sierra has been through hell and lost the love of her life in the process.

I can't imagine I would be in the mood for company if I were in either of their shoes.

So I make a mental note to check on Carrie Ann more often and to ask Sierra if she'd like the paperback copy of Lonesome Dove I found under the sink in the camper when I'm done reading it, devour three peanut butter sandwiches, drink a half gallon of water, and pass out from exhaustion by nine o'clock.

The next day is a repeat of the first, except that I'm so sore it hurts to move and throwing a punch is probably the most painful thing I've ever experienced, second only to *taking* one. Luke isn't hitting me with anything close to his full strength, but getting kneed in the stomach or elbowed in the face isn't a pleasant experience any way you cut it.

By the time Kite helps me into a bath he's heated for me, kettle by tedious kettle on the wood stove, I practically weep with gratitude as I slide into the steaming water. I'm too battered and bruised to even pay much attention to his concerns about Carrie Ann.

Yes, she's still refusing to come out of her cage, but every time I checked on her, she was bouncing away with an encouraging amount of energy.

Surely that's a good thing. Certainly, better than Carrie Ann in her human form, curled up on a bed, pale, sweating, and close to death.

Day three introduces me to levels of muscle soreness I didn't know exist.

Day four it rains, and Luke, or whoever the hell he is —Dust still hasn't been able to get in touch with the L.A. pack, his parents, or anyone with information about our fake passports—beats me up in the mud.

Just to add variety to the torture, I suppose.

I'm face down in the muck for the fifth time, in fact, being told to, "Get up. Let's go again. You're still leaving your left side undefended," when Kite comes rushing down the hill, rain streaming down his worried face.

"What is it?" Luke's ever-ready fists curl at his sides.

"Carrie Ann," Kite pants, his breath coming fast. "She's having seizures."

I struggle to my feet, slogging my way through the ankle-deep mud as fast as I can. "Where's Dust? We have to get her to a hospital."

Kite shakes his head. "No, we've got to get her out of the cage. But she jimmied the door. I can't get her out without breaking the fucking thing and I'm afraid I'll hurt her in the process."

Luke starts up the hill. "So, you hurt her, man. Better hurt than kin bound for the rest of her life."

I hurry after him, Kite beside me. "What's that?" I ask, swiping the rain from my eyes. "What's he talking about?"

"It's what I was telling you the other day." Kite jogs easily over the rocky ground, making me feel clumsier every time I nearly trip and fall. "If we stay in kin form too long, we get stuck that way. That's one of the ways humans got rid of us in the past. Lock a shifter in animal form in a cage and don't let him out for long enough, and pretty soon you have nothing left but the animal. We can't shift behind bars."

"Why not?" I ask, yipping in surprise as the toe of my tennis shoe catches on a root hidden beneath the leaves and I pitch forward.

"Woah. Got you." Kite grabs me by the elbow,

holding me up until I'm able to find my feet. "We just can't. Like how some animals can't live in captivity. We can't shift inside it."

I wince as he releases my arm and the blood comes flowing back into the bruised flesh. He notices, and a shadow falls over his features. "You don't have to do this, you know. Train this hard. We have time. Luke promised to stay with us until you're ready, no matter how long it takes."

"I know. But I have so much to learn, and who knows how long we'll be safe here. Danger has a way of catching up with us. Any word on the howling we heard last night?"

"Not yet." Kite takes my hand, threading his fingers through mine as we move out of the woods and into the thinner trees surrounding the homestead. "Creedence should be back soon, though. He left before Dust, and Dust got back ten minutes ago. That's the only reason I felt safe leaving Carrie Ann. He's watching her, ready to smash the hell out of the cage if we have no other choice."

I bite my bottom lip and immediately wish I hadn't as I get a mouthful of earthworm-flavored mud. "Yuck. Gross." I turn my head, spitting onto the wet ground.

Unexpectedly, this earns a chuckle from Kite.

I glance up at him, eyebrows raised. "My unladylike behavior amuses you?"

He shakes his head. "Nah. You're just cute when you spit."

"You're crazy." I sniff, brow furrowing. "And I'm too

worried to be cute. What if Carrie Ann gets stuck? Is there any way to bring her back?"

Kite's expression sobers. "Not that I know of. But... that's the thing, Wren. That's what I was trying to prepare you for the other day. It isn't always something that's done against someone's will. Sometimes shifters *decide* to go kin bound. They choose to give up their human life. And if that's what Carrie Ann wants..."

Pain flashes through my chest and the backs of my eyes begin to sting. "No. You can't believe that. You said you're going to break the cage if there's no other way to get her out. There's no way you're on board with letting her die."

"She won't die," Kite says gently. "She'll go wild, become an animal and lose all memory of who and what she used to be. She'll have a simpler life. Different, shorter, but no less worth living."

I shake my head. "No. That's not what she wants. I know it. She has so many dreams for her future. She wants to start a band and learn to speak French and kiss a boy on every continent. She can't do any of that if she's a squirrel. She's sick. Out of her right mind. She doesn't understand the risk she's taking."

"Maybe not," Kite says. "That's why we have to break the cage. Before we honor her decision, we have to be sure she understands the full implications of her choice."

Fighting to swallow past the lump bobbing in my throat, I nod. "Yes. We'll do that." As we near the entrance to the cabin, I swipe my muddy hands on the front of my muddier shirt, but the overall effect is just more smearing and more dirt crusted under my fingernails.

I pause by the back steps, shaking like a dog to the get the worst of the mess off before I remember who I am.

And what I can do.

What I can do...

I look up at Kite, heart racing. "I have an idea."

CHAPTER 17
WREN

I don't get it right on my first try.

I'm not sure what I change into, but it feels unnatural—twisted in my guts and too tight in the spine—and the sight of me makes Kite go so pale I'd laugh if I still had human lungs.

If I weren't trying to focus…

And if a part of me wasn't terrified that I'm going to end up stuck in a monster body and not be able to get out. I've never tried to control my kin form. I've always let the shift take me wherever it wanted to go.

Now, this reaching, molding, searching blindly through the dark with nothing but instinct to guide me, is maddening. If I could enter my spirit realm, it wouldn't be like this, Kite's mother assured me, I'd have more control. But my spirit world is occupied by an evil dictator. I can't risk popping in there for even a moment. It might tip Atlas off to our location, and another monster under our beds is the last thing we need right now.

So I stretch and roll, clawing my way out of the creepy-feeling skin and into something that feels closer to squirrel. When I'm done, I'm trembling and sweating, but when I lift my chin up, up, up to catch a glimpse of Kite's face, his expression is soft with relief.

"Good work," he says, his words loud and garbled. Squirrel hearing is different than fox or rabbit, and when Kite reaches down to pick me up off the porch, I realize I can see his hands moving closer and the door opening behind me at the same time.

Squirrels apparently really do have eyes in the back of their heads. Or so far to the side they have a close to a three-hundred-and-sixty-degree view, maybe?

I'm not sure, but the fisheye lens on the world makes me queasy and it becomes even harder to focus on drawing meaning from the rumbling sounds Luke makes as he gestures toward the far side of the room.

I hunch lower in Kite's cupped hands, willing my stomach to stop pitching and my eyes to focus forward. After a moment, I home in on the cage on the table by the fireplace and Dust crouched beside it, a worried look on his face. Carrie Ann is still inside, her front claws wrapped tight around the thin bars and her sides heaving as she fights for breath.

In this form, I can hear her heart pounding and the rattle of air in her lungs. I can hear the scratch of mice in a nest on the far side of the fireplace and the flap of tiny moth wings near the candles flickering on the mantle, and other faint scritch-scratch melodies of indeterminate origin.

There's music in the natural world if you listen hard enough.

It's the first thing I say to her in the new language that rises inside me with an ease so much more organic than the initial shift into this body. But that's something I'm learning about shifting and life in general—if the infrastructure is sound, everything else will follow. But if something's rotten at the core, nothing is ever going to be right.

Carrie lifts her head, her eyes wide. *Is that you, Wren?* she asks with a weak chitter and a flick of her tail.

It's me, I assure her, circling to the side of the cage closest to her and curling my claws around the bars. *I'm here to talk you out of that cage, babe. You need to make a visit to your human form.*

Her chin trembles. *I can't. The virus is active in my human form. It will take my memories again, and you won't be safe. None of you.*

Blood going cold, I lean my face between the bars. *What are you talking about, Carrie? What have you remembered?*

I put the tracker on your truck at the gas station, she says, wincing as another shudder works through her small body. *Your parents didn't know. They thought I was telling the truth about being on your side. I'm sorry. I didn't think I had a choice, but I did. I should have taken Highborn's plans to the grave and kept you safe.* Her hind legs curl closer to her stomach. *I'll do the right thing this time.*

No, I bark loud enough to cause some uncomfortable

shifting from the three men standing in a semi-circle around the cage. They can't understand squirrel, obviously, but I guess fear translates into any language. *You're not going to die. You're going to tell me what's going on and let me help you.*

You can't help, Wren. Her lips curve on one side in something almost like a smile. *He's in my DNA. As soon as I go human, he'll run the Trojan Horse protocol.*

My tail ripples in response. *What is that? What does it do?*

It doesn't do anything. It's me, Wren. I'm the Trojan Horse. He made me sick so you would take me in, and stole my memories so I couldn't warn you about the danger until it was too late. But there's a glitch somewhere. I shouldn't have been able to shift without a trigger, but I did. She clings more tightly to the bars as another seizure grips her full-force, arching her spine and making her voice almost unintelligible as she adds, *But he's pulling. Calling. I can feel it tearing away inside me. If I leave this body, he'll be in control, and I can't let that happen. I won't tell him where you are. I won't help him destroy my best friend.*

But if you don't shift back, you'll be stuck, Carrie. Panic makes my heart pound faster, though not nearly as fast as hers. I wouldn't be surprised to see it punch right through her heaving chest and spill out the other side.

She doesn't have much time.

I have to make my case and make it fast.

You'll get stuck in this form forever. I crouch low, bringing my face closer to hers. *You'll become a squirrel for real. You won't be human, you won't remember me or Kite or any of your dreams. Paris is waiting for you, honey, and sweet French boys who love to sing as much as you do, and a whole world waiting to be explored.*

I want to do this. Her stomach draws in sharply and her eyes squeeze shut. *To do the right thing. Don't try to stop me. Let me be proud of something before I go.*

No, Carrie, please, I beg, reaching an arm inside. But I'm still too far away to take her hand, and she's shivering so hard I don't know if I would be able to hold on to her even if our paws could touch. *Please, Carrie! You'll have the lifespan of a squirrel, too. Even if you can avoid predators, you'll only have a few more years. Don't let Highborn steal your life away. We can fight him. We'll tie you up, keep you from betraying us until we can figure out how to help you. There aren't any phones here, no way to get a signal out. Or we can send you to Dust's people and—*

Atlas! She pants for air, her heart galloping behind her ribs as something irreversible draws so close I can feel its breath hot on my neck. *He owns Highborn. He calls the shots. They both want you gone, all of you. All of us. He'll kill his own creations before he's finished. Every last one. Oh God, Wren, it hurts. I'm sorry, I'm so sorry.*

Get her out! I back away from the cage, jabbing a frantic arm at the enclosure. *Get her out now! Now!*

Kite launches into motion, lifting the cage and swinging it into the stone fireplace, sending cedar shavings flying and the water bottle sailing across the room. Carrie clings to the bars for the first few hits, but then she lets go, going limp. I watch her too-still, too-heavy body knock back and forth with a sick knot in my stomach.

After only a minute, maybe less, the top of the cage

breaks away from the solid metal base, but it's too late. I know it the moment Dust reaches in and gently lifts Carrie Ann's body from the wreckage.

She's not there anymore. Not the way she was before.

I look into her glassy eyes and see...curiosity. Fear. A wondering in the flick of her tail that makes it clear she isn't sure what she's doing in this place. But no pain. No suffering, no regret, no sense of humor.

No humanity.

After a beat, she skitters out of Dust's hands, zig-zag-dashing across the room as she retreats to the currently unoccupied corner of the cabin. She hops onto a chair by the open window and then onto the sill itself.

And then she leaps out into the rain and bounds across the wet leaves toward the trees without looking back. Not even once.

My brain goes hot and my chest tight, but no tears rise in my eyes.

Squirrels can't cry, I guess, not even with a human soul inside of them.

Carrie Ann will never cry again.

I try to take some comfort in that as I shift back into my girl body, heart bruised and sobs squeezing miserable sounds from my throat.

CHAPTER 18
DR. MARTIN HIGHBORN

As she leaves the cabin, the movements of the camera embedded in Subject 7's corneas—the ones my tech crew are so proud to have made undetectable by even the most sensitive scanning equipment—grow increasingly jerky and unpredictable. There's no rhyme or reason to her direction, and repeated signals to her shifter trigger produce no response.

Because she's not a shifter anymore.

She's a squirrel.

"Fuck. We've lost her. Fuck!" Gareth shoves his headset off onto the table between us. There are four other members of the team in the control room, but it's quiet enough to hear the leaves crisping from his headphones as the thing that was once Carrie Ann crashes along the forest floor before leaping onto a tree and clawing her way to higher ground.

She was once human.

She was once one of us.

It's a bigger loss than one of our pretty monsters. Subject 7's shifter DNA could have been deactivated. She could have returned to her mortal life, *would* have been granted another shot at humanity and salvation if she'd done as she was told.

Instead, she gave it all away—gave her life—to protect her friend.

It's beautiful. And stupid. And any moment, I expect a message from Atlas that it's time to move in on their location. There will be no more waiting, watching, or observing Wren and her people without Carrie Ann's camera in the same room with them. We'll be blind and deaf. They could pack up and head out tonight, and we'd be none the wiser.

I'm not sure what he's watching or waiting for, anyway. The girl is a threat that should be neutralized as swiftly as possible.

At least, that's what I would be thinking if I were the man she was training so hard to kill. She's getting stronger faster than any of us believed possible. She has at least four kin forms that we know of, but there could be more, and with each passing day she moves more like the predator she is. She glides, graceful and powerful and sure of herself, no longer the awkward girl with the sloped shoulders and the halting stride.

If I were Atlas, I'd want her dead.

But as the sun sets and the night vision on Carrie's camera clicks on, there's still no sign from the man himself. No note delivered by cockroach, no message eaten by a swarm of flies into the cheese of the pizza we have delivered a little after nine.

I call Bea to say goodnight and ask Gloria, her nurse, to stay late, still certain I'll be needed to call a mission before sunrise. But by eleven thirty, we all realize the hammer isn't going to fall.

Not tonight.

I'm about to send the team home, leaving our second string to keep watch, when the feed suddenly leaps sharply in my peripheral vision. I turn to see the world jerking back and forth.

"Shit," Gareth murmurs, leaning closer to the screen. "Are you seeing this, sir?"

"I am," I confirm, my skin crawling.

"Something must have her in its mouth," one of the others offers as a final, sharp jolt rocks the feed. A hot, squelching sound fills the room, and then the camera is still again.

A moment later, Subject 7's head rolls away from her body.

Someone behind me makes a gagging sound, and Gareth curses again. I sit down hard in my chair.

Carrie Ann is dead.

Subject 7, I remind myself. She isn't that kid who looked at me like I hung the moon for handing out free antibiotics. She hasn't been for a long time, not since the day she decided to sell her humanity for a used car and a few thousand dollars cash.

She was tested, and she failed.

But so have I.

Hours later, after more radio silence from Atlas and

a shift change that takes Gareth home to sleep off his failure to control his Trojan Horse, I fall asleep at the surveillance desk, the sounds of the faraway forest wild in my ears, weakly wishing I could go back to the day that skinny girl arrived on my clinic's front steps and keep the door locked against her.

Keep her outside, where the mean streets and her abusive father were the biggest things she had to fear.

She was safer then. So was I. Back before I made so many ethical compromises that it's getting hard to see the difference between the monsters and this man.

Harder with every passing day.

⚜

I wake with a stiff neck hours later, with still no word from Atlas. The next day passes and then the next. Soon, an entire week has rolled away, eaten up by classes and surgeries, by physical therapy for Bea and counseling for Wendy and trips to the gym that leave me feeling on edge, no matter how hard or long I run.

⚜

One week becomes two and then three, and still there's no word from Atlas, no directive, no orders to storm into the mountains and slaughter every living soul. If I were a more optimistic man, I might dare to believe the nightmare is finally over, that my life is, once again, my own, the way it was before I heard the name Atlas or realized there were scarier things in the world than garden variety shifters.

But I know better.

The axe will fall. It's already swinging.

Sometimes, when I wake up in the middle of the night in the tomblike silence of our bedroom, I swear I can hear it singing as it arcs through the air.

The only question is, who the target will be.

The girl? Her men? Or someone closer to home?

If Atlas thinks I've failed him…

If he decides I'm no longer as useful as I once was…

I pause at my assistant Delilah's desk early one morning, tapping my fingers gently near her nameplate. "Can you get me an appointment with Bruce? This afternoon, if possible. Tell him I want to review my estate plans, make sure everything is in order for Bea and Wendy."

"Of course, sir," she says. "Right away." The look in her pale green eyes is somber, maybe even concerned, but she doesn't ask if everything is okay. She's ranked high enough in the organization to know that all is not well.

And that it might never be again.

CHAPTER 19
DUST

We fold Carrie Ann's clothes and tuck them into an empty shopping bag from my last flight into town for supplies. Wren writes a letter, telling the story of the girl who gave her human life to protect the people she loved, and tucks it inside.

We bury it at dawn the next day, standing in a circle around the grave with our heads bowed. Even Sierra, who has barely set foot outside for more than a few minutes since we arrived.

When it's over, and we're walking back to camp, she says, "I've been thinking... The day Atlas was spying on you in the park... Afterward, he had me place a call to a man he called the doctor. I don't know why I didn't make the connection before, but it must have been Dr. Highborn, which would line up with Carrie Ann's story."

"I thought you were sick," Luke says in a soft but

dangerous voice. "Stuck in your kin form with a nasty bug?"

Sierra holds up a hand, fingers spread wide. "I can dial a phone in my kin form. Raccoons don't have opposable thumbs, but we're pretty close. A keypad isn't a problem."

"So, Highborn speaks raccoon?" Luke shoots back, making me want to pop him in the nose. For a man who's been lying to all of us since the moment we met, he's awfully quick to get up on his high horse.

But Sierra just shakes her head. "I didn't have to say anything. It wasn't even a person who picked up. It was some sort of answering service. I had to punch in a code and that was it."

"Carrie Ann had no reason to lie. I trust that she was telling the truth about the Atlas-Highborn connection," Wren says, her voice rough with lack of sleep. She was up all night writing Carrie Ann's story and a carefully worded letter to her own parents, warning them not to trust anyone connected with her old friend, without giving too much away in case the message is intercepted.

I've promised to mail it the next time I fly to town, but who knows when that will be. There's no sick girl to arrange transport for now, we're well stocked with supplies, and I've gotten as much information as I'm going to get on Luke. There's only one high-ranking member of the resistance still alive. I finally contacted Bill yesterday, and he had nothing on Lucas, aka Luke, and the L.A. pack hasn't been forthcoming, either.

I have to get Wren alone and tell her we've hit a

brick wall with him, preferably before she heads back into the woods alone with a man we still know so little about aside from the fact that he's a liar.

"But why?" Kite squints into the sun peeking out from behind the mountains to the east. "I get why Highborn wants to drive shifters to extinction, but what does Atlas have to gain from it? He's still taking marked mates, right? Those will be hard to come by if there aren't any shifters left in the world."

Sierra crosses her arms, cupping her hand around the stump at the end of her elbow in a self-conscious way that makes me ache for what she's lost—not just part of her body, but the confidence that made her a force to be reckoned with. "I don't know. He's got a dungeon full of women at his stronghold, but you're right—sooner or later, he'll run out. We've got longer lifespans than humans, but we don't live forever."

Especially when you have a habit of eating the people you marry, I add silently. But I keep that to myself.

No need for this conversation to take a turn for the truly gruesome.

"That's another thing I don't understand. About the mate-bond process..." Wren stops in front of the camper, turning to face us with her hands propped low on her hips, drawing my attention to her newly broadened shoulders. She's getting stronger with a speed that's mind-blowing. Luke is good at what he does, which is the only reason I'm even *considering* letting him stay.

That and the fact that I'm hoping the dirt I have on him will give me the leverage I need to force him to take his commitment to the next level. He's a canine shifter with the mark. Like it or not, we need him.

It makes me sick to my stomach that I've been forced into the position of coercing a man I don't trust into forming a mate bond with the girl I love. But I'll do whatever it takes to protect Wren, even nudge her into the arms of another man.

"Creedence told me the other day that you have to consciously choose to form a bond. Either that or be so in love with the person that your heart makes the choice for you." Her cheeks go pink, but she keeps her head up, making eye contact with each of us as she continues, "So how does Atlas force these women into the bond? Is it like Sierra said? Some kind of mind control? And if so, does that count as a conscious choice?"

"It must," I say. "He's thousands of years old and gets stronger with every passing decade. Whatever he's doing, it's getting the job done. But that doesn't explain why he's helping Highborn."

"He's not helping Highborn." Wren paces, one finger tapping her lips. "Atlas is a megalomaniac. He considers himself a god. He doesn't *help* humans. Humans *serve* him. Whatever the cause, it's his cause."

"She's right." Sierra lifts anxious eyes to the sky. "But right now, my cause is getting inside. Daylight makes me nervous. I'll start water for oatmeal."

"Thanks, Sierra." Wren stops beside me, plucking a small white feather from the sleeve of my shirt. She lifts it to her face, studying the architecture of the fluff and bone through narrowed eyes. "I need a flight form. And it needs to be bigger than a breadbox. You can carry two people. If I can lock down a form big enough to carry two, then we've got an emergency exit strategy off the mountain. Just in case."

"I may have something that will help with that," I say, seeing the perfect excuse to get her away from the others. I motion to the coin around her neck. "I spoke with Jasper yesterday, my parents' advisor. He walked me through the life-fast process. It's allegedly easier with a charm to help keep both parties grounded in the real world. If you're up for it, we can give it a try later. If all goes well, you'll be able to experience what's it's like to shift into a larger form. It should give you guidance at the very least. But if we're lucky..."

Wren's gaze sharpens. "I might have a griffin shape by the end of the day." She nods. "Let's do it. The sooner we have a backup plan, the better I'll feel. Obviously, Carrie Ann didn't place any calls to Highborn from her cage, but he got too close."

"And we were too clueless," Luke adds.

"Speaking of close and clueless." Creedence scrubs a hand across his unshaven jaw. "I tracked the howling we heard to the source. It's just a normal pack of wolves. But they've been a few miles away all this time, and it took days for us to realize we were in wolf territory." He shifts his gaze to Luke. "Care to explain how you missed that, Bucko? I thought you were supposed to be our canine-sensing secret weapon."

"I was in prison for almost a decade," Luke shoots back without missing a beat. "If I hadn't found a way to dull my instincts, I would have lost my mind in close quarters with that many humans. And I've only been out a few months. I'll work on getting my senses back in shape, but I can't make any promises. If you're that worried about pack movement, you and Kite should start swapping out surveillance shifts."

"Aren't you worried about it?" Creedence asks. "And are your legs broken? Why are Kite and I the ones in charge of taking up your slack?"

"Because Dust is the only one who can fly to get supplies and I have to save my energy to get my girl in shape," Luke says, lips curving in a deliberate taunt.

As expected, Cree's eyes flash and his jaw clenches tight. "She's not your girl. She's not your anything. You're on your way out of this happy family, remember?"

"It's never more than a second from my thoughts," Luke says.

"Enough." Wren steps between them. "Luke, see if you can help Kite and Creedence figure out where and how far they need to patrol. Your instincts may be dulled, but you still know more about pack movement and habits than the rest of us. I need the day off from training. Dust and I have other work to do."

"Whatever it takes to get you airborne, Princess." Luke glances up at the pale blue sky. "Having another route off this mountain would help me sleep better at night." He jerks his head toward the camper. "I'll help Sierra with breakfast. I want you to double up on protein, even if you are taking the day off. Nuts on your oatmeal, and a protein shake."

"All right. Thanks." She smiles tightly as Luke heads

inside, waiting to roll her eyes until he's out of sight. "I thought I was going to get a day off from the chalk dust. I swear, they must *try* to make that protein powder taste awful. There's no other explanation for how bad it is."

"I'll grab another brand next time I'm in town," I say, casting a pointed glance toward her increasingly chiseled arms. "But Luke's regimen is definitely working. I wouldn't want to meet you in an alley after dark."

Wren smiles—a real one this time—and nudges my booted foot with hers. "Right? I might turn into a bunny rabbit and jump out of a hat. Scare you half to death."

"Or a griffin," I remind her. "If the life fast works."

"I want to stay with you two today," Kite says, his brow furrowed. "Life-fasting can be dangerous. I want to be there to help if I can. Offer backup."

"I think it's best done in private," I say. "Every secret we've ever had will be laid bare. We're both going to feel vulnerable enough without an audience." I know Kite is concerned for his mate, but Wren will most likely be *my* mate someday, too. I can be trusted to do everything in my power to keep her safe.

At least, I hope she'll still consider me mate material after she's seen every dark, shadowy corner of my soul.

"Dust's right." Wren takes Kite's hand. "But we'll be fine. I promise."

"You can't make promises like that," Kite says before adding in a softer voice, "and I'm sorry if you felt deceived about the mate-bond process. There *wasn't* a choice for me. I was already in love with you. And I knew you were in the same place. I could feel it. It wasn't going to be a one-sided thing, so I didn't even think to talk about that."

"No, it's fine. I don't feel deceived," Wren says, clearly uncomfortable.

Kite's brows arch, and Wren's jaw tenses in response as energy Creedence and I can't sense flows back and forth between them.

Sometimes I envy their empathic connection.

Other times, I do not.

There are occasions when it's nice to be able to soften the truth for the one you love, and when feelings are best kept close to the chest.

"I'm not angry or resentful," Wren insists. "Truly, I'm not. I love you so much. I just would have liked to be in possession of all the facts from the beginning. Like what you just said..." Wren lifts a hand, motioning to Kite's chest. "Is it possible to form a one-sided bond? Could it happen for one person, and not the other?"

"That's an attachment—one person hooked for life, but not vice versa," Creedence offers, casting a longing look toward the door to the camper, where breakfast and coffee are waiting. "A bond requires two invested parties."

"My people don't see it that way." Kite's eyes narrow on the other man's face. "Neither do the wolves or other forest kin. There are cultural differences between people who have lived in close-knit communities for millennia and lone cats who would sell their own children for the right price."

Creedence laughs. "Don't pick a fight with me, Pooh-bie. It's not my fault you're in the doghouse with your old lady. I'm an innocent bystander." He lifts his hands in surrender. "And I don't fight this early in the morning. Or before breakfast. Or after funerals."

He turns, climbing into the camper as a pall settles over the three of us who remain.

"I know she's still alive," Wren whispers, hugging her arms around her chest. "Out there in the woods somewhere. But..."

"But her human spirit is gone," Kite says, sliding an arm around her shoulders. "And it hurts."

"Yes. That." Wren leans into him, resting her forehead on his chest, their brief squabble apparently forgotten.

"I'll make tea for anyone who wants some. See you inside." I back away, for once not the slightest bit jealous of Wren and Kite's closeness.

If things go well today, Wren and I will be as close as two souls can get.

And if they go badly...

Well, if that happens, I won't be lucid enough to fret about it. I'm physically bigger and stronger than Wren, but her will is a force to be reckoned with. Her mind might very well crush mine like a bug.

It's a chance I'm willing to take.

I will do anything for her. Absolutely anything.

Dust and I sit cross-legged across from each other on the floor in the center of the cabin, the gold coin on the boards between us and potential energy thick in the air.

By the end of this, we could have the answers we've been looking for. Or, if it goes badly, one of our minds will be broken, maybe beyond repair.

Maybe forever.

"You're sure?" I ask, meeting his gaze in the hazy light filtering through the curtains Kite hung yesterday, giving our compound a homey feel.

"I'm sure." He holds out his palms, face up. "But if I don't come out all right on the other side, I want you to know something."

"What's that?"

"I don't regret any of it," he says, his gray eyes steady and true. "Not a single sad, ugly, difficult step. Because every one brought me back to you."

Emotion tightens my throat. "You're going to make it out. We both are." I slip my hands into his, shivering as electricity dances across my skin and that increasingly familiar ache curls low in my body. I'm crazy attracted to Dust, a fact he's going to know when he has a front row seat to every detail of my entire life.

But I'm not nervous about that part of the life fast.

Even now, with our breath coming faster simply from holding hands and looking deep into each other's eyes, I think it's clear that we're not just childhood friends anymore. We're grown-up friends on the verge of becoming something greater.

"We'll start by focusing on the coin, breathing deep and keeping our hands pressed lightly together," Dust says. "When the connection is secure, I'll start counting backward, and at a certain point, the fast will take over."

"How will you know the connection is secure?"

"I'll just know." A lopsided grin lilts across his face, reminding me of all the times we got in trouble together as kids and how often that grin got us out of it. "Some things you just...know."

"True," I whisper. Like the way I know I'm not going to regret letting Dust this close. He's already a part of me. I'm ready for this, for whatever comes next in the adventures of Dust and Wren. "I'm glad you're back in my life," I say, curling my fingers lightly into his palms.

"Me too, Snow."

I smile. "You have a Snow White fetish."

"I have a *you*, fetish," he says, making my cheeks go hot and my grin stretch wider. "Now close your eyes. I'm going to start at one hundred. Just in case."

As my eyes slide closed, I immediately become more aware of the texture of his hands—warm and dry, with callouses on his right hand from target practice—and his scent—like smoke and forest, like summer nights and the kitchen after a lovely meal prepared and eaten with people you love. Like care. Like love.

He's on seventy-eight, and I'm thinking about love, about family and what ours might look like if we live to make a real life together, when the birds chirping outside go silent. My skin warms, and my mind softens as I sink into something deeper and wider than any dream.

Within a few moments, the memories start to come like waves, rocking me gently as they soak into my soul, undulating in kaleidoscope colors behind my closed eyes.

At first there doesn't seem to be any order to what I'm experiencing—I am Dust at six hunting with his father, Dust at seventeen kissing a beautiful girl beneath the mistletoe at Winter Solstice, Dust at two running naked through the castle halls with griffin wings sprouting from his shoulders and laughter bubbling from his chest, Dust at ten, whispering with me in his fort as we planned a water balloon attack on the kids next door with the giant slingshots he'd made.

I shudder, shaken by the sensation of being in two bodies at once as my side of the same memory ripples through me, swelling my heart with happiness.

Suddenly, I understand.

Joy. These are the bliss-filled memories, coming fast

and messy and out of order, but connected by a thread of beauty, play, and love.

I relax into the flow, laughing aloud as I slide down a snow-covered hill on a silver platter Dust snuck out of the kitchen and take to the sky with my mother, my kin form unfurling from deep inside me like a puzzle I've always known how to solve.

Dimly, as if from a great distance, I hear Dust laugh, too, but instinctively I know he isn't seeing what I'm seeing.

If I'm in his life, then he must be in mine.

And he's finding joy there, too. Even amid all the pain, there was love and happiness, a fact I'm grateful for as the waves grow colder and the memories deeper.

Now I'm Dust as a small boy, screaming as someone snatches him from the woods, carrying him far away from home. I'm Dust in the hospital, fighting for his life, wondering why he can't remember how he got here or how he came to live with his adopted parents.

I'm Dust with tears streaming down his cheeks because he can't keep up with the other kids on the playground, can't make it across the neighborhood on his bike without calling for help, can't pick Wren up off the ground and carry her back to their parents after she collapses by the snow cone truck. She's cut her head, and it's bleeding so badly it's scary, but when I touch the red, smearing it away from her eyes, there's an unexpected shivering sensation, like electricity coursing up my arm.

Strangely, it makes me feel strong, maybe strong enough to help.

My chest tightens, fear and love throbbing against my ribs as I bend my knees and lift Wren—lift *myself*, a tiny, sickly girl, pale and limp on the ground.

And for a few amazing steps, I'm doing it! Carrying her on that miraculous wave of strength. But all too soon it fades. I fight to hold on, but barely make it two more steps across the grass before I collapse.

We're both so weak, so vulnerable it's terrifying.

Terrifying….

Now I'm in a car, racing down a narrow country road with Wren unconscious and suffering from a gunshot wound beside me, and I know I will never forgive myself if she dies. She *can't* die. Not when I've finally found my way back to her after so many miserable fucking years apart.

Years of shame and brutality and never being allowed to forget that I failed my family, my people. I allowed myself to be taken, and I failed them all.

The waves are coming faster now.

Deeper.

Colder.

I'm back at court after my rescue from the cult, but the castle isn't the vibrant, life- and love-filled place it was before. My mother never fully recovered from the kidnapping. The pain devastated her, so much so that she still holds me at a distance, as if she can't bear to love me for fear I'll be stolen away again, taking what's left of her heart with her. And Father is too busy holding on to the throne by the skin of his teeth to notice the way I'm treated after my return.

Or maybe he thinks I deserve the hazing from my

peers, the beatings from my cousins, the way my uncle twists my skin in his fingers and hisses that I should have stayed away, that I should have stayed in the human world where the taint of my weakness couldn't make Meadwood vulnerable to attack from our enemies. A crown prince who spent five years drugged in captivity, who didn't shift for so long he had to relearn the skill like a child, who is so far behind in his studies and spell work he will never be considered fully Griffin, is a liability.

They're all relieved when I enlist in the resistance, when I volunteer for a mission that requires me to forfeit my place in the line of succession. Now Cousin Phillip will be king when my father dies, and the court returns to a state of relative peace.

And I am happy for a while. Working hard and playing hard.

I even fall in love.

Visions of a beautiful woman with golden hair and a sunshine smile flit through my mind. Her name was Josephine and she was five years older, already an up and coming resistance operative when I was a clueless new recruit.

She teaches me everything I know about pleasure, and then she leaves me to marry a much older man, making me feel like a fool, a toy she'd grown tired of and tossed aside. I sleep with half the class of new recruits, fucking myself into a state of even deeper despair before I swear off women to concentrate on my duties.

Two weeks later, I'm asked to lead the mission to

extract the Fata Morgana from her human family, as one of her potential mates. I see her face in the pictures Celeste shows me, and suddenly everything makes sense again.

It's Wren, *my* Wren.

From that day on, through two years of grueling training to prepare for the biggest mission of my life, I sleep alone. I don't want to be with anyone else. I want to wait for her, the girl I loved, the girl who's become a woman so beautiful and strong I can't wait to meet her again.

To love her again.

To make love to her, to show her with every kiss, every touch, how much she means to me. God, every cell in my body aches when she's close. I'm in a constant state of semi-arousal, my cock refusing to get the message that she doesn't want me that way. She desires Kite and Creedence, but I'm just her friend.

"Not just my friend," I murmur, as the magic of the life fast fades away and Dust and I slowly retreat to the separate oceans of our own subconscious minds.

Dust sighs, and I open my eyes to find him watching me with an intensity that makes my skin hum all over.

"What's that, beautiful?" he asks, fingers curling tight around mine.

"I don't think of you as just a friend," I repeat, pulse picking up as love and hunger mix in his stormy eyes.

"I know that now," he says, adding in a husky whisper. "I liked being in your skin. Even the hard parts."

"Me, too."

"I'm sorry I left you alone for so long, Snow. If I'd

known how much you missed me, I would have found a way back to you. Somehow. Even if I was just a kid."

"You're here now. That's all that matters," I say, my heart beating swift wings in my chest as I lean closer. "Though, I would like you to kiss me, please."

I don't have to ask twice. One moment we're facing each other across the lightly melted remains of our lucky coin, the next we're devouring each other from the mouth down. He tears my shirt over my head, and I return the favor, and soon there is nothing between us but skin and heat and a love so real nothing will ever come between us again.

CHAPTER 21
DUST

I'm lost in her. Found in her. I'm drowning, sucked into the depths of her beautiful heart, and I don't ever want to be free.

I don't need air.

I don't need food or water or anything but the shelter of her arms.

"Yes. Oh please," she murmurs against my lips as I cup her breast in my hand, rolling her nipple as she rocks on top of me. She's still wearing panties—somehow I missed those in the initial clothes-tearing frenzy—but it doesn't matter. The feel of her grinding against my cock is still the most electric, euphoria-inducing thing that has ever happened to me.

I don't feel the hard floor beneath my back or the ache of the pain I so-recently relived in Wren's body. All I feel is her heat and softness and the increasingly damp fabric between us that leaves no doubt that she wants me.

She's seen every ugly, sad, pathetic moment of my life and she still wants me.

"I love you," I confess against her lips as I slide a hand between us, reaching down the front of her panties to slide fingers through her wetness. I groan as I feel how ready she is, how drenched with heat because of me.

Because of *us*.

"I love you, too." She gasps, trembling as I glide two fingers inside her.

"Then we can't do more than this," I say, forcing the words out even as a primal voice deep inside shouts for me to shut my fucking mouth. "If we take things any further, we'll be bonded for life."

"Good. I want you for life," she says, making my chest ache. "And I don't want to wait. I want to be yours. I want you to be mine. God, I want you, Dust. I need you."

I suck in a breath, fighting to keep what remains of my wits about me. But it's so insanely hard with her riding my hand and the smell of her desire making me wild, ravenous. "We're too close, Snow. We should wait, give the spell-rush time to wear off."

"I don't want it to wear off." She sits up, hands braced on my chest, her face flushed with desire and her lips softly parted. "I want to be this close. Even closer."

Looking up at her, with her nipples tight and her breasts flushed, she is the most beautiful thing I've ever seen. She is magical, ethereal, a goddess, impossible to resist. I'm going to worship her all the days of my life. I'm already falling, ripping, tearing down the center, making room for the woman I love to be stitched into the heart of me.

There's no use in fighting this. Resistance is futile.

And stupid. Why on earth should I resist something that feels so damned right?

So when she rises onto her knees and reaches for the top of her panties, I pull my fingers away and watch her dispose of the last thin barrier to what we both want. I reach down, gripping my aching cock at the base, heart in my throat as Wren straddles me again and guides my swollen tip to her center.

My hands come to her hips, squeezing tight as she lowers herself down, oh-so-slowly, her eyes locked on mine as she takes me in, every inch, until I'm buried in her heat, her sweetness. Until there is nothing but love and hunger and her breath coming faster as we begin to move.

A part of me is desperate to pull her closer, to get her nipples in my mouth and her lips hot against mine, but I'm too lost in her eyes. I can't look away. I don't dare. I don't want to miss a moment of the feeling dancing across her delicate features. She's here with me now the way she was in every dark and beautiful moment in my past. And as we get closer to the edge, bodies straining and breath tight in our chests, I can see the future stretching out ahead of me.

And it is her—beautiful and perfect and filled with hope, the wild kind that spreads like blackberry vines in spring.

"Yes, oh yes," she says, as if she sees it, too. And then she comes, staring fearlessly into my eyes as her body locks tight around my cock, and I follow her the way I always have. The way I always will.

The release that twists through me is so powerful it's almost painful.

Almost. But it's not.

This isn't pain. This is...everything. The bond knits away the last of the separation between us, and I find the place that I've missed so desperately. My home, the one Wren made for me in her heart and kept warm with love and memory, no matter how the years stretched out between us.

She is mine. I am hers. And it is the rightest thing I've ever done.

I only pray it's the same for her.

"No regrets?" I ask after, as she's lying limp and heavy on top of me, with my softened cock still tucked inside her and the evidence of how much we enjoy each other sticky between us.

She hums softly. "Never. You?"

"Never." I run a hand over her head, smoothing her wild hair. "You're all I've ever wanted, Snow."

Wren lifts her head, gazing down at me with shining eyes. "Thank you. For coming here. Coming back to me..."

I cup her face in my hand, running my thumb lightly over her swollen lips. "No thanks necessary. You're where I belong."

"Ditto." Her lips curve up on one side and an unspoken question flickers across her face. "You aren't... You couldn't possibly..."

I smile. "You know how long it's been since I've been

with a woman. What do you think?" I slide my hands around to cup her bare bottom, squeezing as I lift my hips, pushing my increasingly thick cock deeper into her welcoming body.

She bites her lip. "I want you on top this time."

"The floor is hard," I warn her.

"I'm not scared of the floor. I'm tougher than I look."

"Don't I know it," I agree as she rolls to the side, dragging me with her.

I take her again, give myself to her again. I am lost and found in her again, and it is as beautiful as it was the first time.

But like all good things lately, our stolen moment comes to an end far too soon.

The only thing that makes it bearable is knowing that she's mine. Forever. As long as we're both living and breathing, and maybe even longer.

"So, we're no closer to finding Scarlett. No secrets of that sort locked inside you. Though, there was one strange thing." Wren cocks her head. "When you touched me while I was bleeding, when I was a little girl... It made you stronger."

I nod. "My blood would do the same for you. We're both from ancient bloodlines, the beasts of antiquity. These days, my people use blood therapies to help each other heal from sickness. In the old days, it was an... uglier practice."

Wren arches a brow. "Do I want to know?"

I shake my head. "No. That's a dark story for another day."

"I believe you," she says, shivering. "So what about

Luke?" She slowly pulls on her T-shirt, seeming as reluctant to get back to the real world as I am. "What do you think we should do about that situation?"

I fill her in on what I learned—or didn't learn—from Bill and lean back against the cabin wall by the door. "But his name is Luke, and the other man's name was Lucas. There's a chance it's just a case of mistaken identity, not foul play on the part of the L.A. pack or Luke himself."

Wren's eyebrows form a WTF squiggle across her forehead, making me smile.

"Yeah," I agree. "Not my gut-take either. The L.A. pack knew Luke. He wasn't part of their crew, but he was friendly with several people who are. They knew he wasn't Lucas Rivera, but they kidnapped him and brought him to us, anyway, instead of the man who volunteered for the mission. And now they're refusing to take my phone calls. It doesn't look good."

Wren's eyes narrow. "Maybe this Lucas guy can help. Can you get in touch with him? See if he knows where things went sideways?"

I clear my throat. "My contact tried. Lucas has been missing for weeks, since the night Luke was taken."

"So...he's dead." Wren's expression tightens. "Or being held prisoner somewhere to keep us from finding out we have the wrong wolf."

"Either is possible."

Wren paces toward the window, giving me no choice but to admire how fetching she looks wearing nothing but a pair of tiny black panties and a thin cotton tee.

When she turns back, I quickly lift my gaze to her face, but I'm too late.

She grins. "So I guess you don't miss all the court finery and fancy lingerie?"

"You don't need fancy lingerie," I say, already regretting putting my pants on. I know we have more important things to do than make love all day, but I'm suddenly having some intense fantasies about Wren naked on the dining table. "But you'd be stunning in court dress. As soon as this is all over, I'm going to have something made for you. In artic blue to match your eyes."

"I don't need a dress. You've already given me something way better." Her eyes dance as she reaches for the bottom of her T-shirt.

I'm feeling optimistic about my table fantasies becoming reality, when she adds in a breathy voice, "Open the door."

I catch on, heart beating faster as I open the door and quickly shed my pants, determined to join her. A first flight isn't something she should do alone, or something I want to miss.

I don't want to miss another moment of her.

"Stay close to the trees." I shove my boxers down as she strips off her panties. "I'll cloak us both, so you won't have to think about anything but enjoying the ride."

"I can do this..." She pauses in front of me, her toes wiggling in the patch of afternoon sunlight painting the floor a rich gold. "Right?'

"You can do anything you set your mind to, Snow," I say, believing it with all my heart.

Wren turns to me, smiling so big and bright it banishes all the darkness, and nods. "Then let's fly."

She jogs out the door, taking the first step on her human legs before leaping off the porch. She shifts in midair, skin rippling into feathers and claws and wings so wide there's barely room for her to rise between the trees.

With a whoop of victory, I follow her, wings unfurling to push hard toward the wide-open sky.

CHAPTER 22
WREN

They say time flies when you're having fun, but no one ever mentioned how fast it goes when you're actually flying.

The next few weeks swoop past in a rush of learning to fight even harder, honing my shifting skills, and fine-tuning my control of the kin gifts I gained when Dust and I formed our mate bond. But it's the evenings spent soaring above the clouds that seem to last forever and no time at all.

It's all I want to do.

Well, not *all* I want to do...

I cast a glance across the fire at Dust, who's busy whittling something with his curved knife, before shifting my gaze to Kite, who's rereading Lonesome Dove for the fourth time. Before I was bound to two men, I worried I might have trouble managing a sex life with more than one partner, if only because I have a lot of other things on my plate right now.

But, as so often happens, reality is completely different than what I anticipated.

I'm having zero trouble keeping both of my loves busy in the bedroom. In fact, the more I'm with them, the more I want them. I want them so much there are times when it's painful to have Dust on top of me, making me feel a thousand beautiful things, and know that Kite is only a few hundred feet away, all alone.

I want them both with me, their skin hot on mine, their hands everywhere, and no heart left out in the cold.

But how to start a conversation like that? With two men who clearly have zero interest in each other sexually? Would they be at all open to something like that? Or would they think I'm a freak who's gone from virgin to deviant so fast I've probably set some kind of sex-pervert world record?

Freak. You're definitely a freak. I pop my lightly toasted marshmallow between my lips and let the caramelized sweetness dissolve on my tongue. But sadly, it does nothing to banish my bitter thoughts.

It's not just my increasingly voracious appetite for carnal pleasure that's bothering me. Life-fasting with Dust was one of the most incredible things I've ever experienced, and I don't regret it for a second, but it didn't get us any closer to finding my sister. And I still have no clue which of my remaining three has the secret to discovering her location locked inside him.

At this rate, if or when I finally figure it out, it could be too late.

We've been here nearly a month, and Sierra's stories

about Atlas's gift for being everywhere, all at once, are the opposite of comforting.

"How about a walk, Slim?" Creedence tosses his marshmallow roasting stick into the fire, where it begins to sizzle, letting off sugar-scented smoke. "See if we can get your lynx going tonight?"

Dragging my eyes away from the flames, I nod. "Sounds good."

It doesn't sound good. I'm exhausted from training for three hours with Luke this morning, a run with Kite this afternoon, and an hour of cloaking work before flight training this evening, but I'm not doing anyone any good sitting here brooding.

"Let me grab a flashlight," I say, starting toward the camper, where Sierra has already gone to bed.

"You don't need it. I'll be your secret weapon." Creedence holds out a hand, his eyes going brighter gold around the edges as his pupils narrow.

I scrunch my nose. "I can't decide if that's really cool or really creepy."

"Creepy," Kite offers without taking his eyes off the book in his hands. "Keep that up, and they'll get stuck that way."

Chuckling softly, Creedence nods toward the darkness. I thread my fingers through his, and we start off through the trees, around the back of the silent cabin where Luke turned in early, not long after sunset. My ears strain as we pass the screen door Kite installed last week to let the warm, summer breeze through at night, but I don't hear a thing. Not the whisper of a dream of a snore. Not the slightest shuffle of covers.

Luke must sleep like the dead.

"Wolf Boy is one of the reasons I wanted to have a chat," Creedence says, apparently able to read my mind nearly as well as Kite. "Watch your step. Big rock."

I step over the obstacle, glancing over my shoulder at the crooked silhouette of the cabin against the campfire flickering on the other side. "What's on your mind?"

"Dust showed me the passport photo a couple days ago. Let me in on the fact that we've got the wrong guy."

I knew Dust was ready to tell Creedence. I agreed it was time to tell Kite, as well—we'll have to decide what to do about Luke before we cross the border, a milestone that grows closer with every passing day—but I hadn't realized Dust had already spilled the beans.

I haven't noticed any increased animosity on Cree's part. In fact, he's been a little nicer to Luke lately, easing up on the verbal jabs and general sneering.

"What are your thoughts?" I sway closer to him, curling my arm into the crook of his elbow as we move into the deeper shadows of the forest proper.

"No clear thoughts yet, just suspicions. Theories. I flew into town with Dust yesterday, checked my voicemail. I finally had something from my source in San Diego, the one looking into Luke's family."

"And?" I ask, peering up at him in the scraps of moonlight. We've reached a clearing, the same one where I lost the battle against the mud a few weeks ago.

The place where I first learned that Carrie Ann was dying. Leaving.

I shiver. Some places have bad energy, and I have a feeling this one's is about to get even worse.

Creedence lets out a long, slow breath. "His sister isn't a wolf."

I blink. "What kind of shifter is she?" I know shifter species can intermarry—my own father was a dragon and my mother a fox—but I've learned most of them don't. Wolves are especially sensitive about pack members mating with anyone but another wolf kin. Even other canine shifters—jackals, hyenas, etc.—are frowned upon.

In some circles, it can be grounds for banishment from the pack.

"Is that why their family went lone wolf?" I ask. "Because one of their parents broke pack mating traditions?"

"That would have been grounds for expulsion by the L.A. pack. The San Bernardino pack, too. But that's not what we're dealing with. His sister isn't a shifter at all, Slim. She's human."

I stand up straighter, thoughts racing. "You said she's his half-sister?"

"She is," Creedence confirms. "But even fifty percent shifter is enough. They have the same father, different mothers. So there's a chance Luke's mother was part shifter, the father was part shifter, and that was enough to make him go wolf, while his sister, born to a purely human mother, didn't get the supernatural mojo. But I'm thinking there's a simpler explanation."

"I'm listening." I cross my arms at my chest, wishing I could see Cree's face better. But the moon has checked out, disappearing behind the low-lying clouds crouched on the mountaintops, biding their time.

It's going to rain before morning, but not for another few hours. I've learned to read the weather, too, Kite teaching me how to decipher Mother Nature's secrets in the scents lingering in the air. But I can't read Cree. He's learned to shield so completely against my empathic gift that I all I get from him is static, a steady buzz that insists there's nothing for me to hear.

I reach out, placing a hand on his chest, feeling the steady beat of his heart beneath my palm. "Tell me," I whisper. "I can handle it."

"I know you can, but..." He sighs. "I'm at odds with myself on this one. A part of me wants to suspect the worse. But the more I think about the evidence, the more I think I've misjudged Wolfie. I still don't like him, but..."

"Really? I never would have guessed."

Creedence chuckles. "Yeah, well... I'm not used to being in close quarters with other people for this long. Makes me cranky. Aside from shacking up with my sister once in a while between gigs, I've been on my own since I was sixteen."

"What kind of gigs?" I ask, intrigued by this glimpse into Creedence's life. Aside from Luke—our resident brick wall—Creedence is the most secretive of the crew. I know he grew up in a con-artist family, had a rough childhood, and has a grown sister with two kids. That's about it.

"Photography," he says after a beat. "Wildlife mostly, but fashion every now and then, if a buddy needed a second shooter."

"That's amazing," I say, ridiculously pleased by this tiny morsel. "How did you get into it?"

"I started out doing some kinky modeling for rent money and eventually picked up enough on set to get behind the camera."

I smile. "Of course you did."

"What's that supposed to mean?" He pinches my waist playfully, making me laugh and dance back a step, tennis shoes shushing in the leaves.

"You're so pretty. It makes sense that you used it to your advantage. And it makes sense that you leveraged that into a career where you get to call the shots. You like control."

He makes a soft growling sound, but without seeing his face, I can't tell if it's his amused growl or his irritated one. In the end, I decide I don't really care. Let him be irritated. I'm tired of begging for scraps of trust from this man who's supposed to be one of my ride-or-die allies.

"You do," I push on. "You can be easy going, but sometimes it's all an act. A shield you throw up to distract people from the plots and plans behind the scenes."

He rumbles again, the sound vibrating across my skin as he moves closer. "Is that right? And what am I so busy plotting and planning, Slim?"

Ignoring the voice in my head that insists I shut my mouth and be nice, I say, "How to manipulate people and situations to your advantage. How to get the dirt on others while revealing almost nothing about yourself.

How to stay safe when people let you down. Because they've always let you down. Haven't they?"

I lift my chin, searching the darkness for his face. I catch a flash of yellow as his eyes reflect some tiny spark of light, but that's it. Then, nothing but black and silence and my breath rushing out as his hands settle on my hips.

A moment later his lips are at my temple, moving against my skin as he whispers, "And what about you, sweetheart? What about the people you've trusted? Looks to me like we're in the same boat."

I flatten my hands on his chest, fighting to think clearly as hunger prickles across my skin. "My parents were brainwashed by a cult. They couldn't help it."

"They still lied to your face every day of your life."

I swallow hard. "You're right. They did. But they've changed. So had Carrie Ann. She gave her life to keep from betraying me."

"Again," Creedence says, not pulling any punches, either. "From betraying you *again*. After years of spying on you, pretending to be something she wasn't, and planting a tracking device on our vehicle that would have gotten us all killed if Luke hadn't found it in time." His fingers curl into my hips. "Which leads us back to Wolf Boy. He's either the real deal, someone we can trust to have our backs, at least until he gets what he wants. Or…"

"Or what?"

"Or he's another layer in the conspiracy onion. As far as I know, he hasn't shifted a single time since we met him. And if he has, it hasn't been in front of any of us. Right?"

"Right," I say, brow furrowing. "So, what does that mean? What are the implications?"

"Either he's got such a mangy kin form he's ashamed to show his muzzle in public," Creedence says, clearly not buying that theory any more than I do, "or he's hiding something. Maybe something like the fact that he gets into his kin form in fits and starts, jerky and slow, like all the lab-made shifters made before the mad scientists perfected their crazy."

My lips part, but the more I think about it, the more sense it makes. "He's lab-made. That's why his sister isn't a shifter."

"And why his pack instincts are for shit. He's never been part of a pack, so how the hell would he know how they work?"

I nod. "That would explain why he's so cagey, too. We've already been betrayed by a lab-made shifter. He's probably worried he'll lose what trust he's gained if he tells us the truth now."

"I'm guessing he's more concerned about losing his free ride across the border into his shiny fresh start when we realize he's not the right wolf," Creedence says. "But here's the really weird thing. Luke bears the mark. It's on his right shoulder. The wolves who brought him to the safe house showed it to me before they dumped him and drove off."

"Right. I've seen it." I've spent enough time fighting with a shirtless Luke to memorize every muscle and mark on his body, no matter how hard I try not to drool over his stupidly gorgeous chest. "Why is that weird? It wouldn't make sense to bring an unmarked man. The mark is the whole point."

"It is," Creedence agrees. "But to my knowledge, only Kin Born shifters have ever borne the mark. It's something you inherit, not something you whip up in a petri dish."

"But inherited traits come from DNA," I say, wishing I'd paid better attention in experimental biology my sophomore year of college. "That's how they're making these shifters. With DNA therapies. It follows that the genetic code for the mark might have gotten mixed in with the rest of it."

Creedence grunts. "Not ten years ago, when they were still targeting one or two base sequences with enzymes and a prayer. They weren't doing the bulk infusions and code overwriting they do now. It was more specific, a snip here and a replacement there, just enough to get the shift going in both directions. And according to the timeline I've been able to piece together, Luke's been wolf for at least fifteen years."

The skin at the back of my neck prickles. "Then how does he have the mark? It's real. I've seen it up close. It's a birthmark, not a tattoo or makeup or anything else."

"Up close, huh?" His arm bands around my waist, drawing me against his lean, hard, oh-so-delicious body. "Anything you want to share with the class, Slim? Cause if you're feeling this guy, it might be worth locking down the mate bond and worrying about how he came by that mark later. If he's lab-made, he won't have a kin gift to share with you, but he'll still make you stronger." His free hand skims up my side, molding around the ribs below my breast. "The chances of us finding another marked wolf before we head off to face the Big Bad are slim to fucking none. They don't want any part of this."

"Luke and I aren't anywhere close to that," I say, though I can't deny there's a part of me that looks forward to his hands on me, even if he spends most of our time together kicking my ass. "Which makes sense, considering he's not who he's pretending to be. But what about you, Cree?"

"What about me, Slim?"

"Why are you so far away?"

He draws me closer, until his erection pulses between his belly and mine, making my blood run hotter. "I'm not far away. I'm right here."

I cup his face in my hands. "Are you really? This is the first time we've been this close since we got here. I was starting to think you'd lost interest."

He hums. "Oh, I'm interested. But you've been busy."

"Not that busy."

He cups my breast, making my pulse spike. "You've got two men in your bed, baby girl. I'd call that pretty fucking busy. Literally." He laughs, teasing my nipple through my shirt as he adds in a softer voice, "I have to confess, I was thrown by you and the captain. I thought I was going to be your number two."

My breath rushes out against his lips; the electric bliss tingling from my nipple downward makes clear thinking difficult. "But I... I didn't think you were ready to commit to a mate bond."

"I'm not. But I still thought I'd be the second man in your bed. Guess I overestimated the chemistry, huh?" He pinches my nipple tighter, making me gasp and my heart begin to beat between my legs.

I want him, want him so much the last of my shyness evaporates, burned away by the heat sizzling across my skin.

"My panties would tell a different story," I say, digging my fingers into his shoulders and holding on tight.

"Oh yeah? And what kind of story is that?"

"Why don't you find out for yourself?" I whisper.

"You want me to touch you, sweetheart?" he asks, voice going husky as his hands smooth down my ribs. "You want my fingers inside you?"

I shiver. "Yes. So bad."

"No, it won't be bad," he says, thumbing open the button at the top of my shorts. "It's going to be good, Slim. I'm going to make you come so hard you're going to forget everything that ever made you cry."

I moan my endorsement of this plan, and a beat later, Cree's hand slides into my panties, his fingers teasing through where I'm already almost embarrassingly slick. But the growl vibrating against my neck as he guides us both to the leaf-covered ground leaves no doubt that Cree likes me this way.

Wet and ready for him, dying for his touch, his kiss...

"In a rush?" I tease, breath catching as he rips my shorts and panties down my legs with one swift motion.

"Yes." He fists the hem of my shirt in his hand. "Now,

take this off, and play with your tits for me, Slim. I need to drown myself in your pussy. Your safe word is Flea Collar."

My lips twitch. "What will I need a safe word for?" I strip off my shirt, pulse racing as Creedence spreads my legs, baring me to him as he shifts lower, positioning his face only inches from where I'm dying for him to touch me. The moon peeks out from behind the clouds, granting me a heart-stopping glimpse of the heat in his eyes as he drinks in the sight of me, swollen and desperate for his attention.

"In case you decide you don't like biting," he says, making my breath come faster. "But I think you will, gorgeous." He shakes his head, the muscle in his jaw ticking. "Fuck, I think you will."

And then his mouth is on me, kissing my sex the same way he's always kissed my lips, with devoted abandon that drives me wild. His tongue dips into my entrance, swirling and teasing, building the ache inside of me until I'm writhing in the leaves, the musky scent of the forest floor making me even wilder, hungrier.

And then he starts to bite.

To bite me *there*…

At first just little nips at the top of my thighs, then capturing the swollen folds of my sex between his teeth, and then…

Oh, *God*, and then…

I cry out his name, driving my fingers into his thick hair and holding on as his teeth pulse around my clit— tighter, harder, until it hurts so good. So insanely good. He drives two fingers inside me, hooking them as he drags them out again, electrifying every tingling, dancing nerve, and I come so hard a sky full of stars is born behind my closed eyes.

Waves of bliss pulse across my skin as I buck into his mouth, knowing I'm never going to get enough of his kiss. His teeth. His hands cradling my hips, drawing me close as he moans against my slick skin, as if he's never tasted anything as delicious as my body wet and aching for him.

"You..." I moan, my back arching off the ground as the biting becomes suckling and his fingers continue to work inside me. "I want you, Cree. Please."

"Not tonight, baby." His breath shudders out against my thigh. "My pants stay on tonight. This is all about you."

"I don't want it to be all about me." I tangle my fingers in his hair and tug lightly, wanting him up here with me. Wanting to taste myself on his lips and feel his cock hot and hard between my legs. "I want to make you feel good."

"You already make me..." Cursing softly, he sits back on his heels, pressing the heel of his hand to his temple. "Shit. My head...it's fucking exploding."

"What's wrong? Are you okay?" I sit up fast, reaching for him.

"No, don't, I—" His words end in a choked sound as my palms brush his chest and suddenly the night rips down the center.

It's like half the world just...peels away, revealing an entirely new one on the other side of the clearing.

My jaw drops, terror and wonder mixing in my

chest as I watch time twist and curl back on itself, granting me glimpses of what might come to pass.

Cree's kin gift...

This is what it's like, I realize. It's intense, so much more real and present-feeling than I imagined.

I see myself years from now, my hair in a long braid and a baby in my arms as three beautiful children roll down a grassy hill in front of me. I'm laughing at Creedence, who's not far behind them, still a kid at heart though there's gray threading his golden beard and wrinkles around his smiling eyes. I see a cabin in an orchard, a kitchen big enough to feed a small army, and the men I loved gathered around the holiday tree as we hand out presents to friends and family, pretending not to notice the kids sneaking cookies from the plate we're going to leave out for Santa.

I see happiness and love and a family that struggles to find its feet sometimes, but always comes through in the end, no matter what hardships we face.

But I also see...

Pain. And death.

So much death...

I suck in a breath that gets trapped in my lungs as Kite takes a fatal arrow to the heart, Dust falls from the sky into a churning ocean, and I walk through the rain dressed in black, on my way to yet another funeral, my heart aching and my arms empty.

There is no family in this future, no joy, no children because it would be cruel to bring a baby into this world, where there is only misery and suffering.

So much suffering...

The vision writhes forward again, rolling across time with a speed that makes my stomach pitch and Creedence cry out in agony.

Creedence.

God, what have I done to him?

I flinch, pulling my hands away from his chest. The moment the connection is severed, the other world cuts off like a door's been slammed, locking me firmly on the other side.

But Creedence isn't so lucky.

He collapses onto the leaves, clawed hands gripping his head as he fights for breath, his lids fluttering so fast I can only imagine what he's seeing behind his closed eyes. "Get help. Help. Please."

"I'll be right back," I swear, fighting the urge to reach for him again, knowing my touch isn't going to make anything better. Instead, I scramble to my feet, backing toward camp as I shout, "Hold on, Cree. Hold on for me!"

And then I turn and run like I'm being chased by a monster.

The monster responsible for setting fire to our beautiful future and burning it all to the ground.

CHAPTER 23

WREN

I race through the woods naked for one heart-hammering, panic-stricken minute before I remember what I am and turn to my animal friends.

That's what they feel like—my various shapes are me, but *not me* at the same time. I'm still Wren inside a furry skin, but I'm also channeling primal energy unique to each kin form I welcome in.

Tonight, I call on my mama bear, my newest and most powerful land bound shape. She'll keep me safe as I run through the woods in the dark. She'll charge fast and furious into camp and have Kite and the others on their feet in seconds, ready to rush back to Creedence.

I reach down inside me with invisible hands, digging psychic fingers into the thick fur of my bear and drawing her close, swirling her around me like a cloak as I send out a silent thank you for coming to me, for helping me be something more than a girl alone.

The increasingly familiar twist-pull-pop starts in my stomach and ripples outward, transforming human skin into tooth and claw. My feet leave the ground bare and vulnerable and touch down the next heartbeat thickly padded and ready to rumble.

With a roar of warning that one of our own is in trouble, I gallop through the woods toward the smell of burning wood. By the time I reach the cabin, Luke is bursting through the door, shrugging on a sweatshirt as he moves, and the others are crashing through the woods toward me. Kite is already a big, burly, take-no-prisoners bear. Dust and Sierra are not far behind, both carrying flashlights and moving fast in human form.

I jerk my head and do a one-eighty, hurrying back the way I came.

I've only been gone five, maybe six minutes, but by the time I get back to the clearing, Creedence is so pale he practically glows in the darkness, and his heart beats so slowly a panicked moan rips from my chest, echoing through the night.

"Give me room." Dust falls to his knees beside Creedence, bringing his fingers to the other man's throat. "What happened?"

I tense, every muscle in my massive head straining as I try to reach out to Dust telepathically, the way he's been teaching me to do, but I can't find the link to my human voice. I'm too scared for Creedence, too panicked that I've done something terrible I can't take back.

If I'm the death of him, I will never forgive myself.

After another beat, I give up and reach for the

strings tying me to my bear. I pull hard—too hard, sending myself into the shift so fast I land in my human skin with a scream and a wave of nausea so intense I fall to my hands and knees in the dirt, fighting to keep my dinner in my belly as I gasp, "We were together and—"

"Together how?" Dust demands. "Having sex?"

I shake my head. "No. Not yet. He was kissing me, and then he said it felt like his head was exploding. I reached out to him. When my hands touched his chest, I could see it. What he sees. The futures."

"His kin gift." Dust exhales sharply. "You must have enhanced it. The way you did Kite's, even before you were bonded."

"That's the problem. It's not just her power anymore." Luke strips off his sweatshirt, using it to cover Cree's bare upper body. "She's channeling you and Kite now, too. I can feel the difference when we're sparring. It might have been too much for Creedence. All three of you pumping into his kin gift at once."

Creedence moans, and his lids flutter, but his eyes stay closed.

I desperately want him to wake up and tell Luke to go fuck himself, to insist that he can handle anything the rest of them can and then some, but he doesn't. He stays flat on his back, unmoving except for the twitching behind his lids and the occasional jerk of a hand or foot.

"We have to do something." I snatch my shirt and panties from the ground, pulling them on. "We have to get him out."

Kite, still in bear form, groans softly and bobs his

head, clearly knowing better than to try to reach me with telepathy right now.

"If our bond triggered this in some way, then there's a chance the three of us together can turn it off. Kite?" Dust reaches for Kite, who crosses quickly to him, dipping his head low enough for Dust to thread his fingers into the fur on his neck. "You too, Wren."

I kneel on Kite's other side, gripping his coarse, sweet-smelling fur like a lifeline as I meet Dust's gaze. "What do we do now?"

"We try to reach him." Carefully, Dust places a hand on Creedence's forehead, his jaw going tight. "Jesus…"

"What is it?" The backs of my eyes sting, but I refuse to cry. Crying isn't going to help undo this mess. "What's happening?"

"Give him a second, Princess," Luke says, in what I assume is intended to be a calming voice.

But I'm not in the mood to be fucking calm.

Or to take orders from a liar.

"You don't tell me what to do," I snap, low and cold.

Luke's brows shoot up, and Kite rumbles low in his throat, but I don't back off. I double down, my eyes glued to Luke's. "Unless we're in the ring, keep your opinions to yourself."

Luke's lips part, but he wisely shuts his mouth before anything stupid comes out.

A beat later, Dust whispers in a shattered voice, "Touch Creedence, Wren. Complete the circuit."

I turn back to Dust. His eyes are closed, but the grief tightening his features makes it clear whatever he's seeing isn't good. But good or bad, it doesn't matter. All that matters is that we bring Creedence back to the present before the future breaks him.

Fingers trembling, I reach out, settling my hand on Cree's forehead next to Dust's.

Instantly, the world tears again, shredding into a dozen different pieces, two dozen, more…ribbons of time fluttering in the air all around us. But this future isn't just about us.

It's…everything.

Everyone.

And they're all in pain. In hell, right here on Earth.

Kite groans miserably, and I tighten my grip in his fur. I feel what he feels through his kin gift, the agony and despair choking the people on most of these time-lines, the utter hopelessness and rage, the final violent death rattle of humanity as it succumbs to an apoca-lypse of its own making.

It's all darkness. All wasted.

I'm too late. Already too late. Even if I destroy Atlas and fight like hell to turn it all around, there will be no avoiding impact. The best we can hope for is a course adjustment, a shift away from utter and complete ruination.

"Focus on the dirt, the leaves," Dust says, his tight voice breaking through the waves of despair. "Send your energy into the earth. We have to ground ourselves in the present, help him shut out the future."

Shivering, I fight to block out the chaos, but it's so hard. We're huddled on a tiny island in the middle of a storm made of nightmares. Everywhere I turn, there are horrifying new things to see, but it's impossible to look away. Especially when I realize what most of these futures have in common.

They're what happens if we fail.

And we almost always fail.

Almost.

Always.

I squeeze my eyes shut, tears streaming down my cheeks as I focus on the ground beneath my shins. I focus on the feel of Creedence's forehead hot against my fingers, on the soothing drone of Dust's voice as he urges us to deepen our breath, on the comforting bulk of Kite's fur so rough-soft in my hand.

All three of them are so precious to me.

And all three will likely be dead before the year is out. And I will be, too. And the only bright side is that we won't live to see the world and everyone we love go up in flames.

My ribs lock tight, but it isn't misery that squeezes the air from my lungs this time.

It's rage, white-hot to the touch.

How dare they? Atlas and all the greedy, human monsters that are like him? How dare they doom us all? How dare they defile the sacred gifts we've been given? The gifts of love and hope and this planet teeming with life so wild and miraculous every piece of it hums with magic?

How *dare* they?

My head falls back, and a howl of fury explodes from my chest. I scream for everything that's lost, for all the suffering no one can stop, for all the senseless greed and violence that's led to this. To the end. The miserable, wretched, not at all fitting end. We were terrible, humanity, but we were also so beautiful.

We could have turned out differently. We could have been so...good.

I feel like I'm dying, like my life is pouring out of me along with this soul-deep wail, when suddenly there's a hand on my ribs and a voice begging me to breathe.

The moment the hand touches me, the ribbons of time are slashed and fall away. I'm back on the forest floor, the darkness soft around me, and Luke's arm wrapped tight around my waist.

Cree's eyes are open now. So are mine. All our eyes are open. Horribly, miserably open.

"Thank you, Luke," Dust says, his voice rough, worn. "Though, I wish I'd known you were vision blind five minutes ago. You could have pulled Creedence out on your own and..."

And we wouldn't have had to see all that, goes unspoken, but we all hear it.

I shake my head. "No," I murmur, sounding as hollow as I feel. "It's better to know. It's reality. It is... what it is."

"You guys are going to have to fill me in." Sierra steps into the glow of Luke's flashlight, worry knitting her features. "But I have a feeling I'm not going to like what you saw any more than you do."

None of us respond.

I don't know about Kite and Dust, but I don't have it in me right now to talk about what just happened.

Seeing it was hard enough, so hard that it takes every bit of strength left in me to help Creedence to his feet, gather the rest of my clothes, and limp back to camp, defeat weighing heavy on my shoulders before we've even started to fight.

CHAPTER 24
WREN

The sun creeps slowly over the sleeping peaks, lighting up the world with a kiss. Sunrise around here is always beautiful, but this morning it's so dazzling, so precious that it breaks my heart. Soft, silent tears cut paths down my dirty cheeks to drip off my chin, but I don't move to swipe them away.

I sit cross-legged in the damp grass at the top of our mountain. And stare. And wish I could gather the world into my arms and hold it close.

Protect it. Preserve it.

Or shake it until humanity comes to its senses and changes its ways.

But it's already too late. Even the best scenario isn't a best scenario. Or even a decent one. We've pushed too far, taken too much, remained willfully ignorant for too long to turn back now. Now, there is no happy ending, only a lesser of all the available evil.

Visions of the hundreds of possible futures twist and flutter behind my eyes, like playing cards tossed into the air, making my synapses groan under the burden of this impossible puzzle, this mess I can't clean up, no matter how hard I try.

It's a miracle Creedence isn't stark raving mad. I can't fathom how he's borne this gift for so long without losing his mind, let alone his sense of humor.

But there he is, walking across the field with two steaming mugs in hand, his golden hair and prickly beard shining like a sun god come down to save the world from the darkness. And he's smiling. Exhausted, sad, but still smiling.

"Hey there, Slim. Thought you could use some coffee."

"Thanks. How are you feeling?" I take the mug and scoot over, making room for him on my blanket. "Get any sleep?"

He settles beside me with a soft groan, cupping his coffee close to his blue-flannel covered chest. "Some. Enough to take the edge off. What about you?"

I shake my head, gaze fixed on the view as the morning light creeps into the nooks and crannies between the mountains and bird song begins to drift from the valley. "I couldn't sleep. I couldn't quit thinking. Trying to find a way…" I trail off as my ribs lock down, as if by holding my next breath hostage they can freeze time, keep this moment from becoming the next and the next until God only knows what nightmare is waiting for us down the line.

"Understandable." Cree reaches into the back pocket

of his jeans, pulling something out and pressing it into my hand.

I glance down to see an old-fashioned handkerchief, white with tiny bluebells embroidered on one corner. "Thank you." I mop up my face, but the tears keep coming. Slower now, but insistent, a steady drip inspired by the miracle of morning and the smell of the sweet grass and the revelation of the sunlight warm on my face.

"You don't know what you've got until it's gone, I guess," I murmur.

"It's not gone. Not today. And today's all we ever have, Slim. We can't do a damn thing about tomorrow."

"That's not true," I say, sniffing. "If it were, then we wouldn't be here, busting our asses to take the reins of the world away from a monster." I swallow hard. "But the monster's already won. And it isn't even all the monster's fault. A lot of it was us, Cree. Just...people. Scared, stupid, blind, selfish people. We're like children, hurling our toys against the wall and then wondering why all the beautiful things are broken. Why we can't ever put them back together again."

He puts an arm around my shoulders, the gentleness in his touch making it even harder to breathe. All the love in this world. All the wild, fierce, devoted, tender, miraculous love, but what is it good for?

If it can't save the innocent?

If it can't turn back time, undo the damage, wipe the slate clean?

I squeeze my eyes shut, shaking my head. "I don't know where to go from here," I confess, voice as strained and broken as I feel. "I don't know how to keep hoping."

Creedence makes soft shushing sounds, rubbing a hand up and down my back. "I'm sorry, kid. This is why I kept my distance. I saw how the mate bond made Kite feelier and Dust hidier, and I got to thinking…"

My lips twitch in spite of myself. "Feelier and hidier…" I lean into him, resting my head on his shoulder. "And now you're seeier. I'm the one who should apologize, Cree. I'm sorry. So sorry."

"Hush." He hugs me closer. "There's nothing to apologize for. It's nothing I didn't know deep down. I might not have been able to see that far or that much before, but in my gut, I'd already clocked on to what was coming." He sighs. "The clouds were churning and spitting fire on the horizon, Slim. I knew the chances the sky was going to clear up and we'd all go on a picnic weren't great."

"But at least there was a chance. A sliver of hope."

He pulls away, setting his coffee down in the grass and turning to face me. "And there still might be. We don't know what comes after the shit storm. But we saw that far and wide with just a touch connection and some extra juice from Kite and Dust. Think about what we could do with a mate bond?"

I shiver. "It's kind of a scary thought."

Creedence's eyes crinkle at the edges. "It is. But now that we've confirmed Luke's superpower is being the ultimate magical wet blanket, we know there's a way out if things get too intense." He glances over his shoulder. "About Luke, by the way. Do you remember…"

"I do," I whisper. "If we make it, Luke is there with us. Part of our family."

"I'm not saying I'm ready to trust him completely, but that's definitely changed since the last time I looked forward." He nudges my shoulder gently with his. "You're getting through to him, Slim. You've got this. Just keep doing what you're doing. Keep fighting the good fight, and we'll get where we need to be. We'll hand Atlas his walking papers, get your pretty ass on the throne where it belongs, and make all those happy possibilities a reality."

He doesn't mention the children by name, and I'm grateful. It already feels like they've died. I can't bear to think about those four beautiful possibilities too much or my heart might never get up off the floor.

It's going to be a battle as it is.

I search Cree's face. "But we have to face facts, Cree. Even if we win, we're in for hard times like nothing humanity's ever seen. The best we can do is minimize the suffering, but there's still going to be more than enough to go around."

His expression softens, his eyes filling with a vulnerability that strums every string in my heart as he says, "But that doesn't mean we stop fighting, baby. We're all born to die. That doesn't make one second of this life any less precious. And this is what faith is all about, believing that love is the biggest truth out there, no matter how hard the evil shit tries to convince you otherwise."

Tears streaming faster down my face, I nod. He's

right. I know he is, but… "It still hurts. I'm so sad. And so angry."

"That's fine. Be sad and angry. Grieve until you're done grieving. And then we'll get up and keep going. This isn't about the end, it never was. It's about every step we take down the right path, every shaft of light we shine into the darkness." He pauses, his throat working. "And you shine brighter than anyone I've ever met. Even after everything you've been through—the lies and the pain and facing down death every morning over your cornflakes when you were just a kid—you've still got this big, beautiful heart. You can still love and be loved and risk your life for people you don't even know, and that's brave as hell."

"But that's hard, too," I confess in a whisper. "Sometimes I want to give up. I want to run away and build a wall and hide behind it so I won't have to hurt like that ever again."

His lips curve. "Understandable. But you keep ripping those walls down and getting back in the ring. And that's why you're the shit, girl."

For some reason that makes me cry even harder, even as I start to laugh—a snotty laugh that's as messy as my life right now.

"Come here, Slim. You need a hug." Cree reaches out, gathering me into his arms and lifting me into his lap.

"No, I'll get snot on you," I say, swiping at my nose with the now soggy handkerchief.

"Good, I like snot," he says, making me laugh-sob again. "And I like you." He brushes the tears from my chin before trapping it gently between his fingers and thumb, "I more than like you."

I sniff, the tears finally beginning to slow. "I more than like you, too."

He holds my gaze as he adds in a soft voice, "That's why I kept my pants on last night. I'm afraid I'm already there. If we fuck, it won't be fucking. I'm not going to fuck you, Slim. I'm going to make love to you, baby. And since I'd rather not get into a one-sided situation with the mate bond…"

I run my fingers along the whiskers on his jaw. "Next time you should take your pants off."

He arches a brow. "Yeah? You're sure?"

"I'm sure. I already loved a lot of things about you, but this morning…" I smile, even though it hurts. "I adore this man. He's my hero."

Creedence's eyes begin to shine. "No. Like it or not, you're the hero. You're the one who's got to steer this ship. But I'll be there with you, every fucking step of the way."

"I know." I wrap my arms around his neck, hugging him tight.

"Did you just Han Solo me?" he asks.

"What?" I pull back, smile-frowning into his handsome face.

"Did you just Han Solo me?" He shakes his head like I'm the one who's talking nonsense. "You know, the part where he's about to be imprisoned in carbonite for all eternity and Princess Leia says she loves him. And he's like 'I know' and that's it?"

I grin. "Is this a book? Or—"

"A book? No! It's a movie, a fucking classic of twentieth-century cannon. Maybe the most famous old movie ever."

I shrug. "I wasn't allowed to watch many movies. But I'll watch this one with you if we can find a copy. Though, this guy sounds like a jerk."

"I know," Creedence says, eyes narrowing. "He does, doesn't he? What kind of person responds to a confession of undying love like that?"

"I didn't!"

His glare sharpens, making me laugh harder.

"I didn't," I insist. "I said I loved you, too."

"No, you said there were a lot of things you loved *about* me. Not the same. So let's try this again." He lifts his chin, holding my gaze as he says, "I love you, Wren Wander."

My real last name, the one my birth parents gave me...

It's special that he chose that one. Meaningful. *Perfect.*

I hesitate for a second, but I know what I have to do.

Because he's right. Life isn't about the ending. It's about the love and laughter and every drop of happiness you can soak up or pass on along the way.

So I lean in, press a kiss to his lips, and tease my love with a soft, "I know."

CHAPTER 25

LUKE

I don't expect her to show up, not after what the three of them went through last night. I was so sure she'd be holed up in the camper, sleeping off her vision hangover, that I went ahead and made other plans.

But at nine a.m. on the dot, as I curl up in the middle of sit-up seventy-five, I spot her winding her way through the trees to our sparring spot. There are dark circles under her eyes, her hair is pulled back in a messier-than-usual ponytail, and her arms are crossed so tight across her chest I suspect they're the only things holding her together.

But she's here. Ready to train.

To fight.

Even though, from what I was able to pull out of Dust this morning over breakfast, it doesn't sound like there's much left worth fighting for.

For the hundredth time, I can't decide if she's the

biggest fool in the world or the bravest person I've ever known. Either way, I respect the hell out of her for showing up. She's got more steel in her than I could have imagined the day that skinny girl in an ugly bunny shirt crept down the stairs to my prison in the basement to politely ask if I'd be interested in saving the world.

I wasn't, of course. I'm still not.

But there's a part of me that wants to save something else. Some*one* else. Wants it so much there's a sharp tug in my chest every time I meet her ice blue eyes.

"Hey," Wren says as she comes to a stop on the other side of the clearing. "Mats are out, huh? So what's on the agenda today?"

I'm about to confess that I don't have an agenda and tell her to head back to the cottage to get some rest— she deserves it—when Sierra appears behind her, and an idea snags in my head. The raccoon is shorter than Wren, but she's thicker and stronger, with broad shoulders and a mean right hook I've gotten the worst of a few of the times we've sparred. Even missing half of one arm, she's a force to be reckoned with.

More importantly, she's a woman, and women fight differently. No one seems to know what kind of army Atlas is going to have waiting on his killing fields, but if he's been paying attention all these thousands of years he's been around, he'll have women out there defending him, too.

Male warriors might have superior upper body strength and laser focus in a fight. But women are watching everyone and everything all the time. By the time you figure out their weak spot, they're already three steps ahead, jabbing a knife into the right bottom ribs you keep leaving undefended.

Wren could learn a few things from Sierra. And a day without laying hands on her will do me good. I need to get some fucking distance, to remember how impossible it is for me even to be Wren's friend, let alone anything else.

I rock up to my feet, motioning to the mats behind me. "I was thinking you and Sierra could go a few rounds," I suggest, lifting a hand to the other woman. "That work for you Sierra? Sparring with Wren today?"

Sierra pushes into a jog, trotting the last few yards into the glen. "Sure. If Wren's up for it." She rests light fingers on the taller woman's shoulder. "How you holding up, mama?"

Wren's lips twitch into a weary smile. "Holding. And I'm up."

Sierra's dark eyes tighten sympathetically. "Yeah. Kite was filling me in. It sounds like that was a rough scene. Makes me glad to be out of the loop for once." She shifts her gaze my way. "Bet you're okay with being vision blind this morning, too, huh?"

I grunt noncommittally and jab a thumb toward the crash mats laid out under the trees. "Why don't you two stretch and then we'll go for a run before we start. Lack of sleep is going to make your muscles tighter than usual, and we don't want any injuries. We'll get nice and warm before we start."

The women head for the mats, and the tension in my chest eases. I had no clue that being vision blind was a thing until last night. But apparently it is, and it's a thing "normal" shifters deal with, too. One out of every five or six of them lacks the wiring to communicate telepathically with other shifters.

Which means my secret is safe for another day, but my luck is going to run out sooner or later. It's only a matter of time before they figure out I'm not Lucas Rivera and my shot at a future goes to shit.

I need Wren ready to cross the border ASA-fucking-P.

So why do I find myself looking for excuses to stay here another week? Two? Why do I lay awake at night coming up with new fight moves and combat styles my star pupil absolutely has to add to her arsenal before she'll be ready to face her enemies?

I don't answer that question.

Not even in my own head.

As long as I don't look at any of that too closely, I can keep ignoring it. Keep pretending that she's just a fighter I'm helping prepare for battle, not a lamb to the slaughter or a sweet kid caught up in a game she has no chance of winning or a woman who makes me feel things I haven't felt in so fucking long.

I don't just want to prepare her. I want to stand between her and danger. Better yet, I want to pull her onto the back of my bike, head south, and not stop until we're on the other side of the world from the people who want her dead.

Instead, I push her. Hard.

Hard enough that hopefully it will make a difference between life and death.

"Pick it up, Princess." I clap my hands as I pass her

on the deer trail leading up the mountain, the one we've run so many times the deer are steering clear of its funky human scent by now. "You're here, now it's time to show up."

Wren's jaw clenches and her eyes flash, but she pushes harder, putting on a burst of speed, drawing even with me as we near the top of the rise. I kick it up, pulling ahead, but in a hot second, she's there beside me again, fists pumping hard at her sides. I dig deep, giving the last hundred meters everything I've got, straining until my shoulders ache and my guts cramp in protest.

But she's still there, right beside me when I cross our makeshift finish line, and something hot and fierce explodes in my chest.

Pride, I realize, as I turn to her, breathing hard as I lift a hand for a high five. "Yes, chica! That's what I'm fucking talking about."

"I did it!" she says, pant-laughing as she clasps my hand. "I beat you."

"Tied me," I correct, squeezing her fingers. "But it won't be long. You're an animal, woman. Good work."

She swipes the sweat from her lip with her free hand, expression softening as she nods. "Thanks. That means a lot coming from you."

"Yeah, well…" I swallow. "I'm only hard on you because I want you to be ready."

"So you *do* care if I live or die?" she asks, arching a teasing brow.

"Maybe I do," I say, voice huskier than I would like. "Maybe I care more than I'd like to."

Her lips part as she sways closer to me, and for a

second a crazy voice in my head demands I kiss her. Pull her close, fist my hand in her hair, and kiss her so hard she'll never have to ask me dumb questions like that again.

And then Sierra huffs into the final stretch, and I come to my senses. I drop Wren's hand like it's on fire and turn to watch Sierra with my hands gripping my hips, vowing not to touch Wren again today.

Or maybe ever.

She can practice sparring with one of the others. I've taught her everything I know about fighting dirty, clean, and everything in between. It's time for her to practice what she's learned on fresh opponents, shore up any gaps in her technique, and get in the ring.

"Sorry," Sierra pants, bracing her hand on her knee as she stops beside us, sucking air. "My cardio is for shit right now. I should have been running every morning. Staying fit for the crossing."

"It's not too late," I say. "You'll bounce back fast. A week or two should be plenty of time to get you back where you want to be."

Sierra looks up sharply, her eyes going wide, but it's Wren who says, "A week or two? You think we're that close?"

I let my gaze travel from her sculpted shoulders, down to her tight core and powerful legs and back again before meeting her gaze. "You're strong. You're flexible. You've got solid hand-to-hand technique and firearms and mechanical knowledge from your life fast with the Brit…"

"And you're shifting like a boss," Sierra says, still

breathing hard. "And you've got kin forms for fighting, flying, and fucking up anyone with the nuts to underestimate how dangerous a bunny can be when it's pissed off."

Wren huffs a soft laugh. "Yeah. I think I'll leave the bunny on the backburner for now. Bears and griffins have sharper claws." Her brow furrows as she glances up at me. "You seriously think it's time? You have nothing left for me in your bag of tricks?"

A vivid image of Wren laid out on the grass in front of me while I cradle her ass in my hands and lift her pussy to my mouth, devouring her like she's the sweetest piece of fruit that's ever wet my tongue, flashes on my mental screen. It's so graphic, so fucking real, that I can taste her, smell her salty heat.

I don't even have the chance to fight the effect it has on me. One second, I'm having a rational conversation, the next I'm pitching a tent in my track shorts.

Heart pulsing in my throat—and in other places where it shouldn't be pulsing—I shift to face the view of the Rockies north of our mountain. I lift one arm as I make a subtle adjustment with the other, hoping all those years of playing it cool under pressure won't fail me now.

"I might have one thing." I point toward the tallest peak. "I did some sniffing around yesterday after we finished our morning session. I found traces of wolf scent on every mountain around here except that one."

Sierra hums. "That's weird. With this many packs in the region, you think they'd be strapped for territory. Why avoid an entire mountain?"

"Human settlement would be a good one," I say, "but I didn't find any signs of that. Nothing. Not even old, abandoned trapper stuff like we have here."

"Maybe it's not a smell." Wren lifts her hand to shade her eyes from the sun as she studies the peak. "Maybe it's a sound, something only wolves or other animals with sensitive ears can hear."

"Yeah." Sierra nods my way. "You should check it out while you're furry, man. See what you hear."

I clench my jaw, thoughts racing as I try to think up a reasonable excuse for avoiding furry duty and cursing myself for starting down this fucking road in the first place, when Wren murmurs, "No, it's okay. I'll do it. I can get there faster in griffin form, and I should be able to hear whatever it is, too. I think I might have already heard it. I noticed a weird sound the other day, like feedback almost, but I thought it was just my brain complaining about how hard it is to work a cloaking spell and fly at the same time."

She turns to me, nodding. "But if there's some sort of major electrical line laid through there that's scaring the wolves away, it could be the perfect place to start the crossing." She reaches out, giving my arm a gentle squeeze. "Thanks for the heads-up."

Oh, the head is up, all right. Way up.

What I really need to do is get my other head on straight.

"No problem. Let's start down," I say, backing toward the trail. "Get some sparring in while you're both still warm."

"And then, you should go see Creedence," Sierra

says, falling in beside Wren as she pushes into an easy trot.

"Why? Did his headache come back? He seemed fine this morning."

"He *is* fine. Super fine, and I don't even like boys," Sierra says with a laugh. "That's the point, mama. You need to get that fine-ass man on your team. You're rocking the fight and the furry. Once you've locked down your mates, you'll be unstoppable."

I run faster, hoping to avoid involvement in the conversation, but I should know better. I've only known Sierra a month, but she's proven she isn't the type to mince words.

"You, too, wolf," she calls after me. "You know you want in on the fun."

Wren hisses something under her breath I can't make out, but Sierra's response comes through loud and clear, "Oh, stop. You two have chemistry for days. And trust me, the bigger and badder they think they are, the harder they fall."

I want to tell her to bite her tongue and quit talking about shit she doesn't understand.

But considering I'm still sporting a semi simply from standing close to Wren for too long, I figure I'm the one who should keep my mouth shut.

So, I do.

And I run faster, though I know it's pointless. You can't run away from your heart or your dick. Both come along for the ride, and mine are in way too deep with this girl.

CHAPTER 26
WREN

I approach the sparring session with Sierra with my jaw clenched and my heart racing—yes, she's lost part of her arm, but she's been training with Luke every other afternoon, and she's built for combat. She's short, but powerful, with shoulders so broad I mistook her for a man the first time she threw me over one while helping Kite drag me out my bedroom window.

And she's fierce. And fast.

And she will not cut me any slack because I'm a woman.

Not that Luke cuts me much, but now that I'm more experienced in the ring, there are times I can feel him pull a punch at the last second or slow his pace just enough for me to read where he's going to hit me next.

But Sierra...

She grins, her eyes dancing as we circle each other

on the mats, clearly looking forward to this a lot more than I am. "You going to take it easy on me, mama?"

I snort in response, and she laughs.

"Good. Show me everything you've got." She flexes the fingers on her remaining hand wide before curling them into an easy fist. "Let's see if this wolf has done his job."

"I've done my job. You two should be a good match," Luke says from the sidelines, where he's leaning against a tree, his expression as bored and unreadable as ever. But I felt the pride rolling off him in that unshielded moment up there on the rise. Pride and relief and concern—real concern, the kind you feel when someone who matters to your heart and happiness is in trouble.

He cares about me. And for all his frustrating stubbornness and tendency to lie about almost everything, I care about him, too.

After the visions last night, I know he's coming with us to face Atlas, even if the man himself is still currently in the dark about what his future holds. But I don't know if Luke's coming with us as my mate or just a friend of the cause.

That wasn't clear from what I saw.

A mate-match this soon seems like a long shot, though. Luke still intimidates the hell out of me. He makes me anxious and grateful for my shields and all the other coping mechanisms that keep me from being too vulnerable in his presence. The thought of being intimate with him, every part of me bare and exposed, is scary.

And sexy. So damned sexy... I mean, the man is basically a walking, talking, scowling, brooding testimony to why girls love bad boys.

My gaze slides his way against my will, drawn to those dark eyes I can feel skimming over my body as Sierra and I patiently circle each other, waiting for an opening.

The moment my focus drifts away from the ring, Sierra strikes.

I catch a glimpse of movement in my peripheral vision, and then I'm down on the mat, flat on my back with the wind knocked out of me.

"One to zero," Sierra says cheerfully, ruffling my ponytail as I roll onto my side, coughing and gasping. "You okay there, buttercup?"

"Fine," I choke out, feeling like the lowest form of loser. Worse, like a teenager who walked into the street and got run over while checking a text from her boyfriend.

Only Luke isn't even my boyfriend. Luke is my fight coach, and he is as unimpressed with my performance as I am.

"Come on, Princess. Head in the game. You can think about what color you want to paint your toenails later."

I glare at him as I come to my feet.

Yes, I painted my toenails a few nights back. So what?

"A girl can enjoy feasting upon the blood of her enemies *and* sparkly purple toes, dude," Sierra says, coming to my defense. "Just because you adhere to a model of badassery that has no room for pretty things in it, doesn't mean we have to. Right, mama?"

I cough in agreement, my lungs still reluctant to return to normal function.

"So far I haven't seen this one snacking on the blood of her enemies, let alone feasting," Luke says drily. "You ready to go yet, purple toes? Or do you need to braid Sierra's hair and make sure you guys are still best friends forever before we get back to business?"

"I'm ready," I bite out, hating myself for wasting a single second of my life considering the sex appeal of this man. He is not sexy; he's loathsome.

I *loathe* him. I would like to bite him. Repeatedly. And not in a sexy foreplay kind of way.

"The worst, right?" Sierra murmurs as we resume our positions, facing each other on the mat.

"The very worst," I grumble back.

"But you still want to do him," she whispers, too softly for Luke to hear—I hope.

"I do not. Hush up," I hiss back.

"Do, too." A wicked grin curves her lips. "You want to saddle him up like a pony and ride that big bad wolf all night."

"Less whispering more sparring, ladies," Luke says. "This isn't a sleepover."

"No, I don't," I bite out, fingers curling into my palms.

"High ho, Silver. Ride 'em, cowgirl," Sierra teases beneath her breath.

"Are you trying to make me want to punch you?"

"I don't know, is it working?" she asks, laughing.

I laugh, too, and then I lunge for her. This time, I take her down, but just barely, and we end up on the mat, giggling and fake-punching each other until we're out of breath.

Clearly, neither of us has our heart in this today.

I'm flat on my back, breathing hard and fighting another giggle fit when Luke's face appears above me, silhouetted against the storm clouds rolling in from the west. I can tell he's trying to make his angry face, but he's not pulling it off, and the sight of his forced scowl makes me start laughing again.

Sierra giggles beside me. "Relax, Wolf Boy. We sparred. We learned things. Now we need to laugh. Haven't you ever heard that laughter is the best medicine?"

Luke shakes his head slowly, like Sierra and I are the saddest excuses for warriors he's ever seen in his life, and I laugh so hard tears leak from the corners of my eyes.

"Luke can't," I wheeze between giggles. "He's vision-blind and laugh-blind."

His mouth twitches at the edges.

I gasp and point at his face. "Wait! Look! It's happening! He's going to do it. He's going to break."

"I'm not going to break," Luke says, but his lips are already curving.

"You are!" I clutch my stomach. "Stand back, Sierra, he's gonna blow!"

"Take cover!" she gasps beside me as Luke's shoulders begin to shake.

A second later, all his pearly whites are out for

show-and-tell, and his Adam's apple is bobbing lightly in his throat as he laughs. He laughs and for a moment I can see who he might have been if he'd had a different life, one filled with love and laughter instead of terror and violence, and it makes me sad.

Breathlessly sad.

My giggle fit ends as abruptly as it began, leaving me heavy on the mat.

Joy and sadness. They come so close on the heels of each other these days, like a snake eating its own tail. No matter how fast I run toward the light, the darkness is always there, clinging tight.

"You two finally pull yourselves together?" Luke asks, his smile fading.

"Laughter looks good on you," I say, folding my hands over my laugh-sore belly.

"It does," Sierra agrees. "You should laugh more often."

"Yeah, well... Not much to laugh about these days, is there?" He runs a hand over his closely cropped hair.

He gave himself a buzz cut last week, shearing away all his gorgeous glossy hair, but he's still handsome without it. He's just more...haunted looking, like a tree without its leaves, bare against a winter sky.

"I'll work on my stand-up," Sierra says. "I used to be funny. Back in the day. Before..."

She doesn't have to say before what. We all have a before, a life that was ripped out from under us. That, even if it wasn't the best life, was familiar and our own.

Now, we can't afford to take anything for granted.

"It's going to rain." Luke glances up at the sky. "You two should head back, get some rest."

"Be there in a minute," I say, not moving a muscle. "I want to watch the clouds for a little while."

Luke nods. "Don't stay too long. It could be a big one."

"It won't be." I inhale, drawing the scent of the storm into my lungs. "It's a baby storm. I can smell it."

Sierra sits up beside me, tilting her head back to drink in the dark sky. "I want to learn how to do that. Smell the size of a storm. Kite tried to teach me once, but I didn't have the patience for his long-ass explanations."

I smile because I love those long-ass explanations. They're one of the things that make Kite, Kite. "Stay. I'll give you the cliff notes version." I turn my attention to Luke. "You can stay, too, if you want."

He shakes his head. "Thanks, but I'm going to grab some lunch. The run made me hungry. You two psychos look out for each other. Stay together."

"Will do," I promise, while Sierra assures him, "I'll keep a close eye on your star pupil, coach."

He waves and lopes away through the woods at an easy jog.

I stay on my back, but I can't help rolling my head to the side to watch him go.

"Admiring the view from behind?" Sierra asks.

"Shut up," I say good-naturedly.

She laughs. "No shame in it. That ass is almost enough to make me consider giving men another try."

I arch a brow as I shift my gaze back to her flushed face. "You used to like men?"

"Um, no. I used to sleep with men. Back when I was a teenager who was scared shitless of being gay. Didn't say I liked them."

I frown. "Why were you scared? Family? Church?"

She rolls her eyes. "Both. My mom is old-world Catholic, and the nuns at school made it pretty clear where girls who liked to kiss other girls ended up."

"Roasting in eternal hellfire?" I ask, my nose wrinkling sympathetically as she confirms my suspicion with a click of her tongue and a finger-pistol fired in my direction. "My church was more subtle about the hellfire stuff," I say, "but there was still plenty of guilt to go around. We were supposed to stay virgins until marriage, only sleep with our husband or wife, and avoid being gay if at all possible."

Sierra snorts. "And if it wasn't possible?"

"Then you were supposed to keep it a shameful little secret. They used to say 'love the sinner, hate the sin,' all the time when LGBTQ issues came up in meetings for the shelter."

"Hate the sin of what? Loving someone a bunch of assholes don't think you should love?"

I nod. "Pretty much. I kept at the elders until I was able to give queer kids the same services as the straight kids. Back then I didn't have the strength to fight for more than that." I study her profile, which is uncharacteristically sober. "I'm sorry."

She turns, meeting my gaze. "Why are you sorry?"

"I could have been a better ally."

"You did what you could," she says with a shrug. "That's all any of us can do. And it sounds like it won't matter in the end. We're all going down together, gay, straight, and everything in between." Her eyes narrow. "It was bad, wasn't it? What you saw last night? Dust gave me the heavily edited version, and even that sounded like a fucking shit show."

I sigh. 'Yeah. It's bad."

"How bad?" she asks, sitting up.

I sit beside her, bracing my arms on my bent knees, taking a breath as I try to think of the best way to break this kind of news. I don't want to send Sierra spiraling into the same despair pit I barely crawled out of this morning, but I don't want to lie to her, either. She isn't a child. She's a member of this mission who is putting her life on the line for the future, just like the rest of us.

She deserves to know exactly what she's fighting for.

"Because here's the thing," she says, breaking the silence before I can put my thoughts together, "when it comes to suffering, I have some pretty strong opinions. I've had them for a while. Even before this." She holds up her stump, sending that familiar pang of guilt flashing through my chest.

It's not my fault that she was tortured and maimed. But it *feels* like it is.

Maybe if I hadn't fought her that night, if we'd gotten away from my house even a few minutes sooner, we could have made it to safety. Maybe Atlas wouldn't have pulled her out of the river, and she wouldn't have such brutally informed opinions on suffering.

But "could have been" is always a losing game. I should know that by now.

"Tell me." I turn on the mat to face her, wrapping my arms around my shins and hugging my legs to my chest.

"It should have an end in sight," she says, her expression as serious as I've ever seen it, even on the morning she first showed up at the hotel with Leda. "Suffering is a part of life. None of us can escape it, no matter how rich or powerful or pretty or lucky we are." She pauses, tapping a measured finger on the sock covering her still-sensitive stump. "But it shouldn't be something that goes on forever, you know?"

I nod, my throat going tight. "I hear you."

"Do you?" Sierra's brow furrows. "'Cause I don't think Dust heard me this morning. He kept talking about salvaging what can be salvaged, but…" She shakes her head. "That sounds like a bunch of cruel bullshit to me. Not to mention elitist as fuck. I mean, he can fly away to higher ground, no matter how high the sea rises. He can swoop his griffin ass off to the artic when the mosquito plagues start killing off everything south of the Rockies and the storms get so bad the tropics aren't fit to live in. But what about the rest of us?"

"We're going to help everyone we can, Sierra. I promise you, I will do everything in my power to—"

"But is that going to be enough?" she cuts in. "Even if you manage to take the throne from this monster, you're not going to be a god for real, Wren. You'll be a super-powerful supernatural, one with a sweet soul instead of a bag of dicks for a heart. But so what?" She lifts her hand, fingers spread wide. "No offense, but no matter how sweet and powerful you are, you won't be able to save everyone. You won't be able to save *half* of everyone. There won't be enough inhabitable planet or enough resources, those are the cold hard facts of where we're headed. Even if we win, and we both know what a big fucking *if* that is."

I press my lips together, fighting the despair pressing on my heart.

"So maybe it would better to just...stop," Sierra says, a hitch in her voice. "Just lay down our weapons, take an honest look at the big picture, and find a gentler way to end the human experiment."

"You don't really believe that."

She meets my gaze, the clear, calm of her brown eyes saying she's never been more serious. About anything.

"You believe in kindness above all else," she says. "All I'm asking is that you look at this with your heart, without letting cultural shit or some deep-seated belief in the sanctity of human life get in the way." She opens her hand, holding her palm out between us. "Or maybe you *should* take that last part into account. Because there is nothing holy about living out the rest of your days sick and starving and scared out of your mind, without even the relief of knowing there's a chance things will get better. For millions of people, there will be no chance, Wren. No hope, nothing but suffering, world without end, amen."

Before I can respond, before I can argue that there has always been suffering, but there will always be hope as long as we refuse to let the light go out in our hearts, a fat raindrop plops into the center of Sierra's hand.

Her lips quirk. "I smell rain now, too."

A beat later, the sky opens up, the clouds releasing the burden they've carried over the mountains from far away, pelting us with raindrops that used to be oceans and lakes and tears rolling down cheeks to evaporate into the air.

In seconds, I'm soaked to the skin, and the mat beneath us is sliding sideways as the ground beneath turns to mud. Squinting into the assault, Sierra and I scramble off the mat, prop it against two trees to be rinsed off in the rain, and start back toward camp in silence.

The smack-patter of the rain against summer leaves is too loud to talk without shouting, and I suddenly find I don't have much to say.

I could argue my side, but I'm not sure it really is my side. This morning, cradled in Creedence's arms, even a flash of light in the darkness seemed worth fighting for.

But now...

Now there's a dragging feeling inside my brain and a weight on my heart and leviathan-size questions I don't have any clue how to answer.

I glance over at Sierra to find her already watching me through the veil of rain. She reaches out, taking my hand and giving it a hard squeeze. "I'll be there, though, mama. Count on it. If you're going in, I'm going in with you. Okay? No doubt about that, sister."

I return the squeeze as I nod.

I know she'll be there. I saw her in my visions last night. In every single version of the future I glimpsed— even the ones where I was missing from the final line up—she made it across the killing fields. Sierra was the only constant in all the shifting sand.

I would say she was born under a lucky star, but there's nothing lucky about being on the front lines of a fight as ugly as this one, and she's already lost so much.

We all have, and the losing isn't over, I'm afraid.

Not by a long shot.

CHAPTER 27
DR. MARTIN HIGHBORN

It's been over a month since we lost Subject 7.

Thirty-two days, to be exact.

Long enough that the tension has begun to seep from my shoulders. That I walk the halls of the institute without slowing before every turn, wary of what might be waiting around the corner. Long enough that, just this morning, I gave my new operations manager orders to transition half of our shifter force into remission.

Keeping a genetic modification that severe in active shift mode is hard on the human parts of the organism's body. If they aren't going to be deployed on a moment's notice, it's better for the long-term health of our warriors to be allowed rest and a more traditional training regimen.

I convince myself that's what Atlas would want if he were available for consultation. I convince myself the monster's attention is required elsewhere, and that he will be pleased with the way I've tended to his interests in his absence.

When I arrive home late one afternoon to find the front door standing open and the flower pots on the porch overturned—Bea's pansies strewn across the brick steps like soldiers fallen on a black, potting-soil battlefield—I realize the error of my ways.

I drop my briefcase on the lawn.

My keys fall next.

I break into a run, heart in my throat, blood rushing in my ears. The sound reminds me of a seashell, and how on our last visit to the Natural History Museum, Wendy begged for a souvenir from the gift shop—a conch that when held to your ear, sounded like the sea. I explained there were no waves inside, but Wendy didn't care.

It's been decades since the beach was safe to wander looking for shells, and even longer since mollusks were wiped out by algae plagues. It was a valuable artifact, but not worth what the museum was asking.

But I should have bought the damned shell.

I wish, now, that I'd given her the magic, because inside the house, the destruction continues.

Glassware on the entry table smashed. Potpourri Bea made herself scattered, the dried flowers from our garden like the brittle shells of beetles bursting beneath my feet as I stumble to the kitchen.

Pop, pop, pop...

"Bea? Wendy?" I know they won't answer. The house is too quiet, the kind of quiet that means empty.

Or dead.

Empty or dead, empty or dead... The words repeat on a gut-wrenching loop as I careen into the den, the study, the playroom where Wendy keeps her toys in such meticulous order.

She was such a sweet girl, just like her mother.

I'm already there—at *was*, at past tense, at the worst-case scenario, teetering on despair—when something outside catches my eye. I look up through the large picture window with the built-in seat where Wendy and Bea love to read on chilly autumn afternoons. But for now, it's sunny and warm outside, the leaves are bright green, and the pool is filled with peaceful blue water.

Water, where someone floats...

Face down.

My heart stops.

Just...stops.

Pressure builds in my chest, shoving up into my throat, blurring my vision, making me wonder if I'm having a heart attack. But after a moment, my heart jerks into motion again, throwing off the first rush of shock as it races faster, faster, until I feel like I've run a marathon to get here.

To this place.

To what was once my home, but never will be again.

Because the woman who made it home is dead.

As I stumble outside, I drag my phone from my pocket with trembling hands and dial 911, but I already know it's too late. Bea is too still, too pale, her arms limp in the water and her soaked dress dragging at her lower body, threatening to pull her down to the bottom, even farther away from me.

She's already too far. Gone. My Bea, my beautiful brave Bea.

My heart is destroyed. Ripped away. Torn out through my throat. I taste blood with every breath.

"911, what's your emergency?" The voice sounds like it's coming from a million miles away, and I suddenly can't imagine how to communicate with it. How to tell a stranger that my world is gone, my love is dead, my sweet Bea has been murdered and I am nothing without her?

And then I see the words spelled out in a mass of twitching ants on the concrete near the water—*Make it right. Kill the mates or Wendy is next.*

I hit the end button, hanging up on the voice pricking at my ear.

Make it right... It will never be *right*, but I'll kill Wren Frame's lovers if that's what it takes. Anything the monster wants to convince him to cough up the last bit of goodness left in the world.

My granddaughter. She's still alive.

"I'll get her back, Bea." I fall to my knees by the pool, fingers dipping into the too-warm water a foot from her hand. She always liked the water bathtub hot, my Bea. She got cold.

Now she'll never be cold again.

"I'll get her back," I swear, tears filling my eyes. "I promise, sweetheart. On my life. On her life."

Something tickles the back of my hand, and I flinch, looking down to see the ants have formed a new message—*Now.*

"Absolutely," I say, my voice hollow. "Right away."

And then I open my hand and bring it down in the center of the word, smashing dozens of ants beneath my palm and spread fingers, hoping it hurts him, at least a little bit, to have this tiny piece of him destroyed.

Though I know he will never hurt the way I hurt.

And that the chances of getting Wendy back alive are slim to none.

But I'm going to try. Because that's what people do—we keep fighting, even when the predators roaming the darkness beyond our campfire outmatch us in every way.

Still, we take up our spear and go to face the darkness.

The monsters.

The monster.

I dial the phone again. Gareth picks up on the first ring, "Mobilize all forces. We move tonight, as soon as we can get everyone on board the plane."

CHAPTER 28

CREEDENCE

Luke shows up just as the sky lets loose, trotting up the steps to the cabin where Kite is making chili for lunch. For once, Wren isn't trailing beside him.

I'm about to head over to ask where she is—nicely, because I'm trying to give the cranky bastard the benefit of the doubt—when I spot two soggy heads in the distance, and my heart leaps into my throat.

There she is.

My woman.

She isn't *mine* officially, yet, but maybe in a few hours...

All we have is today. Right now. Last night highlighted that for me. Highlighted, underlined, and set up flashing yellow arrows that said to quit sitting on my hands, worrying about things that might never happen, when I could be using those hands for better things.

Like making Wren come for me. Showing her what

she means to me, how she's changed me, how she makes me want to come home to someone for the first time in so long.

Maybe in my entire damned life.

My parents loved both their kids. They loved us in a fucked-up, unpredictable, major-strings-attached kind of way, but it was still love. I grew up knowing I was worthy of affection and respect, if not always where I was going to sleep at night or what alias I'd be using in the next town. But there was never anything that felt like home. We were a band of drifters held together by greed, necessity, and codependence, and the place we laid our head was just a box to hide our crazy from the world for a little while.

It was easy to breeze out of there as a teenager. It didn't even feel like running away from home. You can't run away from something you never had.

My van became my crash pad, followed by a string of studio apartments and the occasional remote mountain cabin rental. But those weren't homes, either. They were shelter and privacy. It takes more than a messy bachelor holed up in a room with his camera collection and a fridge full of beer and mustard to make a home.

Home is something you create with someone else.

Just like family.

These psychos are my family. All of them—Wren, Dust, Kite, even Luke and Sierra, to a certain extent— but Wren is where home comes from. She's the one who took a hammer to my cynicism, smashing every window in that tired old shack and sending fresh, sweet air rushing in. She's the one who makes me want to be a better person, a kinder, braver man. The kind of who can be trusted with fierce and delicate things like my woman's heart.

I've never loved anything or anyone the way I love the girl lifting her hand to wave at me through the pouring rain, her lips curving into a sad smile.

She's sad again, but that doesn't stop me. I flip up the hood of my raincoat and descend the camper's creaky steps, my mind and heart made up and my mission clear.

First, I'm going to put a happy smile on that pretty face.

Then I'm going to show her why, once you go lynx, you never go back.

CHAPTER 29

WREN

"You want me to crawl inside that? In there?" I prop one hand on my hip and swipe rain from my forehead with the other, dubiously surveying the two-foot by two-foot crevice at the base of the hillside.

"No, I want *us* to crawl in there," Creedence corrects. "I'll go first, you pop in behind me. It gets tight about fifteen feet in, but after that, it's all doable on hands and knees."

My brows shoot up. "How tight is tight?"

"A little belly crawl never hurt anybody." He laughs and tugs the bottom of my T-shirt. "Relax, Slim. If I can make it through, you won't have any trouble. Where's your sense of adventure?"

I wrinkle my nose, my feet squirming in my soggy shoes. "Couldn't we go sit by the fireplace instead? Fires are adventurous, and you don't have to squeeze through any dark, tight places to get to them."

"I'm going to warm you up, I promise." He takes my hand, threading his fingers through mine, sending a current of electricity prickling across my damp skin. "Have I ever taken you on a bad date?"

My mouth twitches. "You've never taken me on *a* date. Period."

"Well, then, it's high time I start." He motions toward the crevice. "Your first date awaits, gorgeous."

I hedge, but this time it's guilt, not fear of enclosed spaces, that makes me hesitate. "I really shouldn't, Cree. Luke might have found a good place to start our crossing." I briefly explain the absence of wolves on the mountain and the humming sound. "I would love to go on a date with you, but it would probably be a better use of my time to grab Dust and have him fly over with me to check things out. We'll be heading north soon, and I know we'll all feel less anxious once we've got our course charted."

"The mountain will be there tonight, after the rain has stopped, and you deserve a break." Creedence puts a finger to my lips when I start to protest. "And this isn't going to be a waste of your time, Slim. I spent the morning in lockdown meditation. Boxing up my kin gift nice and tight. It won't be coming out to play any time soon."

I blink, too distracted by the feel of his finger, rough and sexy on my mouth, to put the pieces together right away. When I do, my body heats up, going from damp and chilly to blazing hot in seconds flat.

"So, we'll be safe?" I ask, lips moving against his finger. "Safe to…"

Holding my gaze, he shifts his hand, curling it around the back of my neck in a way that makes my blood rush. "Yeah. We'll be safe. And we're going to do everything that just danced behind your eyes, baby. Then I'm going to teach you some new things your other mates haven't gotten around to yet."

I arch a brow. "Oh yeah? How can you be so sure? I'm wild these days, pretty kitty. Might even have a few tricks up my sleeve for you."

"Oh, I hope so." He growls as he pulls me close, kissing me with a smile on his full lips before he says, "But I don't think you've quite caught up to me yet, sweetheart. Now get your fine ass on your hands and knees and follow me into that cave where we can get out of the damned rain."

"I know all about hands and knees, for example," I tease, nipping at the sides of his waist with my fingers. "I know I like to be on them with someone I love behind me with his fist in my hair, for example."

Creedence growls again. "Which of those crazy kids worked up the balls to put a fist in your hair?"

"I don't kiss and tell," I say, the ache low in my body spreading as Creedence grips my ass tight in both hands. And then he swats my bottom—hard enough to sting—making me gasp-laugh as I pinch him again, under the tee this time.

"What about that?" He slaps my ass again, the second time even more sizzling than the first. "Either of the boys in your bed given you the spanking you're practically begging for?"

"I don't. Kiss. And tell." I bite his bottom lip hard enough to summon a soft groan from deep in his chest.

"Fine," he says, his voice husky. "Keep your secrets, baby. But someday soon, I'm going to know all about the way those boys fuck you. Because I'm going to be there, helping get you off while we take turns inside you."

His words send a nuclear rush across my skin, making my nipples pull tight and wetness soak my panties.

"Yeah, I saw that last night," he murmurs, his hands drifting under my shirt to tease up and down the valley of my spine. "There was a lot of bad shit, but there was also you and me... Naked... And not so alone..."

I shiver. "Not in all versions of the future."

"We're not living those versions, Slim. We're going to live the best version, the one where you get fucked well and often by all four of your mates. And when you want us all in your bed, you only have to crook your finger, and we'll come running."

My cheeks blaze at the thought. I've come so far, but *that* level of sexual confidence still seems ridiculously out of reach.

But Cree's words do make me wonder...

"So, you would be okay with that?" My pulse throbs faster as he finds the elastic band at the bottom of my sports bra and nudges it higher. "With...sharing. Like that. At the same time?"

"Well, I'm not going to blow another guy or even jerk him off... Especially none of these idiots," Creedence says good-naturedly. "But if his balls and my balls happen to make each other's intimate acquaintance while I'm taking your pussy and he's fucking your ass, then I'm all right with that." He pushes my bra even higher, making my breath catch. "I'm okay with just about anything that gets me in your pussy. Or pussy adjacent. Or even in your mouth while someone else is fucking you. Or sucking your tits while—"

I cut him off with a nervous laugh and fingers pressed to his lips. "Okay, I get it."

"Do you really, Slim?" he murmurs seriously, the humor fading from his beautiful eyes. "I'm here because of you. I will work for you, sacrifice for you, fight for you, even die for you if it comes down to that."

I nod, tears pressing against the backs of my eyes, overwhelmed by the emotion in his.

He cups my now-bare breast in his hand. "Getting naked with the other people you love is nothing compared to all that. Especially when I know how good we can make you feel together." His thumb brushes across my tight tip, building the ache already twisting low in my body. "I can't wait to make you feel good, baby. And make you mine. So, if you're up for that…"

I swallow hard, knowing he means more than just sex, that he means he's ready to be mine for keeps. For life.

And I am absolutely up for that. No doubt in my mind.

"Inside," I whisper, pressing a quick kiss to his lips. "I'll go first."

"Perfect. I'll stare at your ass while you crawl."

I smile. "I wouldn't expect anything less."

I drop to my hands and knees and start into the murky passage. As expected, Creedence waits until I'm almost all the way in before delivering a sharp swat to each butt cheek.

"I knew you were going to do that!" I laugh, even as a sharp wave of arousal courses through me, making my already damp panties even wetter.

"What about this?" A beat later I feel his breath warm on my thigh and then teeth dragging over my skin just below the cuff of my shorts, and my eyes shutter closed.

"No, I wasn't expecting that," I murmur, every nerve in my body pulsing electric as Creedence cups my pussy through my clothes.

"And this?" His fingers somehow find their way under my shorts and panties to press into where I ache.

"Oh, God…" I push back against him, moaning as his fingers glide inside me. In and out, in and out, until I'm trembling all over. "N-no. Not that, either."

"Keep crawling, Slim." He kisses the back of my other thigh as he gently pulls his fingers away. "I've got more surprises for you. Just head for the light at the end of the tunnel."

He's my light. And by the end of this afternoon, it's going to be official.

Anticipation warm and thick in my veins, I start forward on my hands and knees, moving through the darkness toward the warm flicker of flame.

CHAPTER 30
CREEDENCE

I've fucked up a lot of things in my life.

I've hung back when I should have reached out. I've let go when I should have held on. I've locked my jaw and swallowed 'I love you' more times than I should have, so afraid of wrecking a woman's life the way my father and my grandfather did before me that I drove relationships onto the rocks before they could get out of the harbor.

But all that ends today.

Right now.

Maybe I just needed time to realize that sitting on the sidelines is a cowardly way to waste a life. Or maybe some part of me was waiting for her, this beautiful, headstrong, sweet as hell woman who I always sensed was out there somewhere, waiting to turn my world upside down.

"Oh my goodness." Wren's hands come to cover her mouth as she sees her surprise, waiting by the edge of the steaming pool I discovered last week and have been keeping in my back pocket, a secret just for her and me. She glances over her shoulder, her eyes shining. "What is this place? It's incredible."

"Natural hot spring." I slide up behind her, wrapping my arms around her waist as I point up at the oval of sky at the top of the cave. "With natural light and ventilation and guaranteed privacy."

"And snacks." She laughs as she snuggles closer, the curve of her ass brushing against where I'm already hard, where I've been hard on and off since we came together in the woods. "How did you manage to sneak a picnic in here without anyone noticing?"

"I have my ways," I say, kissing her neck. "I smuggled in a bottle of champagne, too. Stole it from Dust's secret stash in the camper. Did you know he had a secret stash?"

She brushes her nose against mine. "No, I didn't. So he's been holding out on us, huh?"

"Oh yeah. He's got liquor in there, cash, even a hard salami."

"Hmmm," Wren hums, rocking back against my hard-on. "A hard salami. I could go for one of those."

I grin and kiss her. "Good. Because I stole that, too."

"I wasn't really talking about salami," she says, shifting in my arms, her palms coming to rest on my chest, where my heart is already beating on the door, dying to come in out of the cold for good.

"I know, Slim." I cup her face, dragging the pad of my thumb lightly over her bottom lip.

I hold her gaze for a long beat, until her smile softens and she asks, "Is everything all right?"

"Everything's perfect. I was just thinking... Until I met you, I almost never saw myself in the future. I'd see visions, but I wasn't a key player." I cock my head. "Which is pretty normal. Most of us with sight don't see ourselves that often. Our mind protecting us from the gift, maybe. But now..."

"But now you do," Wren says, sadness creeping into her eyes. "I'm sorry."

"Don't be. I like seeing my future. Myself. Happy. With you."

Her brow furrows. "Even though that's the one-in-a-million long shot?"

I shake my head. "Not one in a million. A thousand, maybe. Not a million."

"Still... It might never happen. Those things we saw, those..." She trails off, but I know exactly what she's thinking.

"Oh, the kids are going to happen," I say, sending a mixture of anticipation and anxiety flickering across her face. "Especially that little girl. I'm already in love with that little girl."

Our little girl. With her mother's blue eyes and my shaggy hair and her own one-of-a-kind gap-toothed smile.

"Me, too," Wren whispers. "I want that life with you. And her. With all of them."

"And we're going to have it, baby," I swear to her. "They're going to have to tear it out of my cold dead hands."

"I love you," Wren says, tears filling her eyes.

"I love you, too," I say, heart beating in my throat.

"And I don't want snacks."

"Me, either. Fuck snacks. I want you. Naked and under me," I say, crushing my lips to hers as I add between kisses, "Let's get these damned clothes off."

"Yes, please," Wren agrees.

And so, we do. She tears at my T-shirt, and I rip hers over her head. We unbuckle and unzip, stealing kisses as we back toward the blanket by the water. And then she's naked and so am I and I'm finally where I've been dying to be.

Well…almost.

"Inside me," Wren begs after only a few minutes, long before I've explored as much of her as I would like.

"Not yet," I grit through clenched teeth, even though there's no place I would rather be.

But I don't want to rush our first time. I need to take her somewhere she's never been before, to show her that when it comes to her pleasure, I'm a man of my word.

I reach down, gathering some of her delicious wetness on my fingers and guiding it back to the tight hole behind her pussy. Immediately, she tenses, confirming that her other mates are as vanilla as I've assumed.

"You're going to like it." My tongue flicks over her nipple before I add, "I promise."

"And if I d-don't?" She arches beneath me, her breath catching as I nip her other nipple before sucking it into my mouth.

"Then I'll stop." I circle her rear entrance with my fingers, teasing her with the barest bit of pressure. "But I don't think that's going to be our problem."

Her breath coming fast, she asks. "What's going to be our problem?"

"How much you're going to love it," I whisper in her ear, cock jerking as she shudders beneath me. "And how soon you're going to be begging for two of us inside of you at the same time. I know you've been dreaming about it, Slim, Dust in your pussy while I take you here." I glide one finger inside her ass as my thumb dips into her pussy, and she catches fire, the way I knew she would.

She moans, clinging tight to my shoulders as she rocks into my hand. "Oh my God, Cree. Oh my God…"

"Yes, beautiful," I groan into her neck as I find the rhythm she likes and fresh heat rushes from her pussy to coat my hand. "I can't wait to see you come again. Come for me, baby. Come so fucking hard for me."

She shakes her head and bites down on her bottom lip, clearly fighting the release on the verge of sweeping her away. "I want you inside me. Please, Cree. Let me love you. Let me feel it."

I'm sure there are men out there who can resist a request like that, but I'm not one of them. Keeping my finger in her ass, I replace my thumb with my cock, easing into her inch by inch, staring deep into her eyes as two become one and I sign my heart over to her.

Right on the dotted line. Without a second's hesitation.

The mate bond flows between us, through us,

binding us together tighter than needle and thread as I make love to her, taking her higher, until she comes hard. Her muscles clench tight around my cock and fingers, and I have no choice but to fall. Apart. To pieces. My balls clutch and release until I am wrecked by the beauty of being this close to my mate. My woman. My reason, the one that once seemed so elusive and is now so incredibly clear.

"You're all I want," I say as we're soaking in the hot pool after, stealing kisses in between bites of fresh strawberries I picked this morning, and generally feeling delighted to be alive. "This is it, Slim. I want you and that house in the orchard and that crazy pack of kids. That's the dream for me."

"Me, too," she says, kissing my cheek. "But let's not tell the others yet, okay? I don't want them to be sad if…"

If we don't all make it. If some of the kids we saw in our vision don't end up being born because their daddy is killed before we can take out Atlas.

I'm about to assure her that I won't tell anyone but that I'm for damned sure keeping every one of those faces in my heart, when Wren winces and her hands fly to clutch her chest.

"What is it?" I ask. "What's wrong?"

"Kite," she says, fighting for a breath. "He's in trouble. Under attack. They all are. He's found us, Cree." Her eyes go wide and fill with terror. "Highborn. He's here."

CHAPTER 31

WREN

In seconds, I'm a griffin, claws and feathers rippling across my skin so fast it burns.

But will it be fast enough?

Or am I already too late?

I turn in the now cramped space to find Creedence furry and leaping up the rock formation beside me in his kin form. Without any telepathy, I know where he's headed and lower my right wing, clearing the way for him to jump onto my back. He lands, the faint sting of his claws on my thick hide assuring me he's holding on for the ride, and I launch myself like a bat out of hell at the circle of sky above us.

The hole is too small, but I don't hesitate. I fly harder, faster, reaching top speed just as my head shoots through into the cooler air. My shoulders force their way out next, the momentum and mass too much for the rocks surrounding the moss-covered opening.

Creedence and I soar out into the late afternoon sky,

sending boulders rolling down the rock face in our wake.

The moment we're clear, I scream out a warning, a high-pitched half eagle cry, half lion's roar that I know will carry, and pump hard toward camp. Below me, colors no mortal eyes will ever see swirl and pulse beneath the canopy. In my griffin shape, I can see body heat. I mark every spark and flash of life, from the rabbits and squirrels fleeing the shouts and gunfire coming from our glen, to the men closing in on the cabin.

No, not men....

They're moving too fast.

I fly low, belly nearly brushing the treetops, but a part of me knows what I'm going to see even before I catch my first glimpse of fur. It's them—the Gen Mods, the monsters. And they've already got us surrounded.

Heart surging into my throat, I cry out again, relief rushing through me as a matching cry echoes from beneath the trees by the homestead. It's Dust, in griffin form, holding his own against the monsters swarming around him, battling with claws, beak, and the deadly whip of his tail. Kite is on his right, in bear form, wrestling with a Gen Mod who's already bleeding from a wound at his throat. And not far away, crouched behind a rock formation, Luke is armed and dangerous, firing at the line of armored Hummers parked at the top of the ridge beside the flaming remains of our camper.

No...he's not firing at the vehicles. He's shooting the men in SWAT gear streaming down the hillside with their own much larger, much more serious guns drawn. We are seriously outmatched.

As Sierra bursts from the cabin with our fireplace axe in hand, seconds before a missile hits the already rickety structure, sending it exploding into flame, I put together the pieces and conclude we're never going to make it out of here alive.

We're outnumbered and out-armored. We need more firepower, but my Wren-size column of flame won't even come close to cutting it. I might be able to save myself that way, but it won't do shit for the people I love.

I need something bigger.

Something that doesn't just channel fire, but wields it.

As if my father is suddenly there with me, a voice whispers through my mind, reminding me that I come from a long line of dragons. A line of *fire-breathing* dragons, the kind the ice dragons ran out of Europe hundreds of years ago because they were afraid of how much damage we could cause if we ever decided to break the treaty we'd signed, vowing never to use our flames on other shifters.

But those men with guns aren't shifters, and the creatures attacking us aren't, either. They're robots, machines controlled by the man standing up there on the hill, far from the line of fire. The man in the suit, who set all this misery in motion.

Dr. Highborn. *He* did this. And I will make damned sure he pays for it.

I land in the only space near the cabin large enough

to accommodate a form even larger than a griffin, and I dip a wing. The moment Cree bounds off my back, leaping at the closest Gen Mod with his claws bared, I reach down into the heart of me, down to the place where memories of my father and the secrets of the dragons who raised him are hidden away, and I curl my fingers around that buried treasure, drawing it fast toward the surface of my skin.

Just like the griffin, this form comes easily, a gift from someone who loves me, sending me the knowledge I need, even though he's far away, reminding me that none of us are ever truly alone.

Dragon scales ripple across my even larger, more powerful body, cooling my skin even as a molten heat coils in my core. I'm nearly there, griffin claws transforming to razor-sharp dragon talons, when I hear a shot and see feathers and fur fly into the air. A beat later, Dust falls to the ground in his human form, and horror—cold and shocking—dumps into my blood.

Luke fires, and two of Highborn's soldiers—the ones closest to his location, the ones who must have shot Dust—jerk and crumple, tumbling to the ground to lie still.

Instantly, Kite is between Dust and danger, battling another Gen Mod as Luke hurries to Dust's side. Gratitude explodes in my heart as I realize that Dust is moving, talking to Luke.

He's still alive, and I intend to keep him that way.

Connecting to the heat in my belly, I drop my jaw and rain fire on these people who have dared to threaten what's mine.

CHAPTER 32
LUKE

Sweating in the heat of the fires breaking out all around us, I shove my gun into the back of my jeans and haul a protesting Dust into a fireman's carry. With one last glance over my shoulder, ensuring Kite has my back and the Gen Mod situation under control—for now—I take off through the pockets of flame, bound for where Wren is blasting the freaks swarming around her.

But there are too many of them, and our enemies have her hemmed in, pinned between the advancing force and the bluffs behind her. Even with fire on our side, we're no match for their numbers, or their firepower. I'm almost out of ammo, and there's no way I'm getting back into the cabin to reload.

The cabin is toast. So is the camper. And if we don't get out of here, we'll be dead before sundown.

Dust probably sooner. He needs medical attention, ten fucking minutes ago.

"Leave me," he moans again, more hot blood rushing onto my shirt as he tries to give me the suit coat he snatched from the ground as I lifted him. "Take this and get her out of here."

"Not a chance, man," I growl, cutting right to avoid a Gen Mod on fire, its fur going slick and pink as it—he—comes back into his human form screaming in agony.

Several of our attackers are on human legs now, reeling in pain and confusion, but Wren doesn't let up. She keeps laying down rows of fire, lighting up the underbrush between her and the armored hummers idling by what's left of our camper.

She's a pacifist, but she's no fool.

And she wants all of us out of here alive, a fact she's proven by digging in and fighting her ass off when it would have been far easier—and probably smarter—to take to the sky with Kite and Creedence and leave the rest of us here to save our own asses.

Or to die.

Like Dust is always saying—we're replaceable; she's not.

But she clearly doesn't see things that way. That's why she's still here, waiting for Sierra to fight her way through the swarm of monsters between the cabin and Wren's position. The axe in the one-armed shifter's hand flashes like sunlight on water as she cuts a blood-soaked path to Wren and then holds the line near her left flank, keeping the way clear as I race through the gathering smoke with a bleeding man across my back.

Fifty feet away, I skid in the mud and nearly go down—the forest floor is still slick, though the rain has finally stopped—but I find my feet and push hard for the finish line, trying not to think too much about the fact that Wren's the only one left with functional wings. Dust's too injured to shift, let alone fly himself or anyone else off the mountain. There's a chance Wren will be able to carry us all. Her dragon is even larger than her griffin, with broad, scaled wings and a neck so long it would extend above the treetops if she lifted her chin to the sky.

But her shoulders aren't that wide—Creedence is already up there in lynx form, taking up a decent chunk of real estate—and between the five of us, she's looking at close to a thousand extra pounds.

Someone might have to stay.

You, my inner voice decrees with a finality that leaves no room for argument. The other three men are Wren's mates—they give her strength and the kin gifts she'll need to survive—and Sierra is the only one who can open the path to Atlas.

I am the only expendable guest at this party.

I don't want to die, but the thought of being left behind doesn't tear a hole in my gut the way I expect it to. Somewhere between that day in the basement and the moment the first gunshots rang out this afternoon, I drank the Kool-Aid. Maybe it was all the time spent training her, or maybe it was the hours looking into her eyes and seeing nothing but heart and a driving need to set things right. Maybe it's something closer to home, closer to the muscle that jerks hard in my chest every time I catch sight of her after time apart, but I'm Team Princess now.

Team *Wren*.

And I want my team to win, even if I'm not around to see it.

I reach her back leg, where her dead-serious claws are digging into the damp ground for traction as the force of her own flame threatens to send her skidding backward, and I shift my grip on Dust. Curling one hand under his armpit and the other around his hip, I overhead press him with a groan. He's lean but tall, at least one-seventy, and a hell of a lot more unwieldy than a barbell. And he's bleeding, hot liquid oozing over my right hand, making my grip way too slippery.

I call out for help, but Creedence is already there, grabbing Dust around the ribs with one furred arm, dragging the other man up and over the curve of Wren's rear haunches.

As soon as they're up, I turn, shouting to Sierra, who has just dispatched a saber tooth Gen Mod, and Kite, who's shifted back into his human form and is running —buck naked—toward me, "Load up! You've got to get out of here. She can't hold them off much longer."

Tossing her axe to the ground, Sierra shouts, "Leg up!" Without missing a beat, I squat low, forming a basket with my hands. Sierra's small, booted foot lands in it a beat later. I shove hard up and over, sending her sailing onto Wren's back, where she scrambles up and out of sight.

I have no idea how much room is left up there, but Kite is going next. After that…

After that, we'll see.

I squat back down, threading my fingers together

again, but Kite just claps me on the chest on his way by, and calls, "Follow me. She'll help us out."

And as if by magic, she does. A second before Kite reaches her foot, she extends her back leg, making a ramp for the two of us. Kite run-scrambles up, and I follow, wondering if I'm ever going to get used to catching an eyeful of another man's balls during a fight.

One part of my brain observes that Kite has some seriously large, weirdly hairless gonads, while another part celebrates the amount of space still left on Wren's back, and a third warns that something's changed, something's coming, and we're not close to out of the woods yet.

"Helicopters!" I shout as the *whump-whump* sound fires the appropriate synapses.

"Go, Wren," Sierra shouts. "Now! They've got artillery on those fuckers. We've got to get out of range."

"Everyone hold on." Kite grabs handfuls of the surprisingly silky-looking mane that forms a comb down Wren's neck to tuft around her shoulders like a golden mink stole. Sierra and I follow suit, and Creedence, still in lynx form, wraps a furry arm around Dust, holding him close as he grabs a mouthful of mane. "We're out of here," Kite warns. "She's going in three, two, one!"

I'm braced for lift-off—or I think I am—but I'm not anticipating anything like this. Wren shoots into the sky like a missile headed for the moon, leaving my stomach dragging against my spine as it fights to keep up with the rest of my body's momentum. The G-force pulls at my face, and my shoulder sockets hum in protest, but my fingers stay locked tight in Wren's baby-fuzz soft hair.

Fingers know when to shut up and do their job. And their job right now is holding the fuck on so I don't go careening into a free fall while my woman is trying to keep the pack of us from getting shot.

My woman...

But she's never going to be *my* anything. I don't belong here. I have nothing to give her. I'm a fraud, and as soon as we're out of harm's way, I have to tell her the truth.

Fuck getting over the border. Fuck my fresh start.

Wren is what matters, and the best thing I can do for her is get real and get out, before I put her in more danger than I have already.

CHAPTER 33
DUST

I can feel her trying to wrap a cloaking spell around us, but it isn't working.

The magic flickers and sparks but refuses to take hold.

The dragon form is too new to her, and she's too exhausted.

I can feel it, through the bond where Wren and I are connected. When I swallow, my throat is raw and dry, ravaged by fire that came too hot, too fast, and for far too long. My muscles are burning, and I can sense her faltering, slowing, as the places where her wings meet her body scream for relief.

There's too much extra weight, and she's moving too fast.

But she can't ease off. The choppers are locked on our tail, just barely out of firing range. If she slows down, they're going to get close enough to take her down. And when she falls, we'll all fall with her.

I can feel that, too, how it's killing her to know we might not make it. She might not be able to get us all to safety, especially...

Especially *me*.

She knows I've been shot, she can feel the way my heart stutters as blood continues to seep from my wound. The flow has slowed since the initial rush, but not enough.

If I don't get medical attention soon...

I refuse to finish the thought, but I know where it leads. The world is spinning, my limbs have gone cold, and if it weren't for the arm Creedence has locked tight around me, I wouldn't be here. I would have slid off Wren's back during take-off.

And if it weren't for Luke, you wouldn't have been up here in the first place.

I open my eyes, pulling the wolf into focus. He's clinging to Wren's mane between Sierra and Kite, blood staining the top of his gray tee and streaks of red smeared across his forehead.

I made a mess of him, but he didn't hesitate to help me.

He's part of this, now. Part of *us*, whether he realizes it or not. And he'll be good for Wren. He risked his life for a man he barely tolerates; he won't hesitate to give it for her.

He loves her, it's written all over his face, humming, warm and steady, in his energy. Before bonding with Wren, I didn't have much talent for reading people. Now, there are times when Kite's kin gift wafts through me, like smoke carrying the scent of whatever's cooking inside a person's heart.

Luke is hers, now, and he'll bust his ass to take up the slack I'll leave behind. And there are other beasts of antiquity who bear the mark. My cousin, for one. Or one of the ice dragons, though they won't be happy about this new form of hers.

But there are options.

Options that make my heart feel like it's twisting in the wind.

I want to stay with her so badly it burns inside me, causing a pain keener than the bullet lodged in my chest. But if she makes it out of here alive, she'll have a chance without me.

Getting her to safety is the first, the *only* priority.

There's only one choice to be made. I know it even before a rocket whizzes past overhead, getting so close that when it explodes beneath us, I feel a burst of heat on my skin.

It's time. I have to give what I have left to give and hope like hell it's enough.

Turning to press my face into the whisper softness of Wren's dragon's mane, I funnel everything I've got into a cloaking spell. Almost immediately, my wound starts to bleed faster, but I don't stop. I open my mouth and breathe magic into the air, pouring it out like a bucket flipped upside down, and we wink out of sight.

Through the milky haze of the spell, I can still make out the dim outlines of the others, but our enemies won't be able to see a damned thing, a fact proven when Wren cuts sharply to the right, heading north over the mountains, while the choppers whizz due west on a trail they have no idea has gone cold.

Ice cold.

Like what's left of the blood in my veins...

By the time we reach the border crossing fifty miles from our camp, I'm shivering so hard Creedence has to dig his claws lightly into my arm to keep me from shaking my way off Wren's shoulders. But I don't back off the spell. We're traveling at the speed of dragon, the fastest fliers the world has ever known. If I can hold on to the spell a few minutes longer, we'll be able to land far enough away from the border guards to be safe.

Or at least, the others will be safe.

"The passports, the money," I mumble, my lips as frozen as the rest of me. "In the lining of my...coat."

I figured there was a reason you were rocking a suit coat in the middle of the woods, Creedence replies telepathically, *aside from your commitment to stuffy asshole fashion. Good thinking. We'll need that passport to get you checked into a hospital.*

There's a hospital in Lethbridge, Kite pipes up. *Wren's headed there now. We're going to touch down just outside of town and—*

"No," I whisper. "They'll know. They'll be looking for gunshot victims. They'll find us. Stay out of the cities. Find..." I try to suck in a breath, but my lungs refuse to respond. They sip the air, leaving me just enough to wheeze, "Hide... Promise..."

Wren flies faster in response, making me wonder how sensitive her hearing is in this form. Pretty damned keen, I'm guessing, and she's apparently communicating telepathically with Kite, which is huge. That was a problem for her, even a few days ago.

She's come so far so fast. She's going to make it all the way.

She's going to rip that old man off his throne and burn it all down. Every mess he's made, every prison he's built, every war he's helped start and lie he's fostered, it's all going up in flames.

I swear I can see it, that bright future, flickering behind my eyes as they slide closed. It's like when I touched Creedence in the glen—a vision, a prophecy—but so beautiful and full of hope. I want to share it with Wren. I want to tell her that we were wrong, that it isn't too late, but my lips refuse to move.

And then my heart refuses to beat.

It goes still in my chest and pressure builds behind my ribs. It swells, bigger and heavier, until I'm pinned beneath a thousand-pound boulder, but still, I hold on to the spell, keeping us out of sight until Wren touches down in a field between two mountains.

Only then do I let go, gasping for air like a landed fish.

I force my eyes open, drinking in the sight of a meadow filled with flowers—delicate alpine flowers that would be just as at home in the mountains of France. It reminds me of where my parents celebrate summer solstice, hiking deep into the mountains outside Annecy to meet with ogre friends and dance until the sun sets in the middle of the night.

I'm suddenly possessed by homesickness, by a

longing to see my parents, even the twisted halls of Meadwood Castle, one last time.

But this is beautiful, too. As last looks go, it could be so much worse.

Wren is safe. And I got to love and be loved by her.

I'm a lucky man.

It's my last thought.

My last—

CHAPTER 34
WREN

I come out of my dragon skin screaming and clawing at my bare chest. My heart is being torn apart, shredded, hacked to pieces by a butcher who doesn't care how much it hurts. The pain is unlike anything I've ever known—physical, yes, but psychic, too. Mental and emotional and magical and so terrible I fall to my hands and knees in the grass, sobbing so hard I make myself sick.

I bring up cheese and crackers and chunks of something charred I don't recognize and continue to wretch long after I'm empty and my fire-ravaged throat is begging for relief.

But there is no relief.

There is no way out, no way back.

Dust is dead. Dust has been carved out of me, and this aching emptiness in my soul will never heal. I will walk wounded the rest of my life, carrying the memory of the love stolen from me like a piece of shrapnel lodged in my heart.

"No, no, no," I sob.

I become aware of hands on my back and a soothing voice whispering, "Sorry, baby, I'm so sorry," but I don't want to hear "sorry."

I shrug off the hands and stagger to my feet, swiping my arm across my mouth as I search the grass around me. I see him almost instantly. There. *Dust.* Just a few feet away, curled on his side, not moving, not breathing.

Dead.

And no one is doing anything about it. They're all just standing there, staring at me, looking sad when sad isn't going to do jack shit to make this better.

"We have to fix it," I shout, anger flaring so hot my palms burst into flames. "Help me fix it!" I flap my hands, swiftly putting out the fire before curling my fingers into fists. "Come on! We have to get him to the hospital. Now!"

Kite shakes his head, tears shining in his eyes. "He's gone, baby. We can't bring him back." He reaches for me, but I shake my head.

"No!" I shout, my entire body trembling as I stagger back. "It's only been a few minutes. And he's strong. He's not human. He's Dust."

"He didn't want to be taken to the hospital." Creedence, fresh out of his lynx form, sinks wearily to his knees in the grass. "He made us promise not to take him. He knew they'd be looking for us there."

I shake my head. "No. This isn't happening. This isn't happening." I rake clawed hands through my hair, thoughts racing. There has to be a way. There has to be a way to turn back time, to get him help faster than we're thinking possible, to crawl inside him and stitch him back together with my bare hands, to pour my life into his body.

"That's it." I motion to Kite, pulse spiking as I kneel on the grass beside Dust, grateful, for once, that we come out of our kin forms naked and there's nothing between his skin and mine. "My blood! It can help. Make him stronger. Like when we were kids."

"No," Kite says, fear leaping into his eyes. "You can't, Wren. Blood magic is forbidden. It could wreck you, even kill you if—"

"It's dangerous, but she's right," Creedence interrupts, appearing beside me on the grass, one finger already curled into a lynx claw. "It could work."

"He could also kill her," Kite says, "and come back as something fucked up and unnatural."

Creedence shakes his head. "Not if we stop him before he takes too much. Give me your wrist, Wren. You'll need to hold it to his mouth. Smearing blood on his skin isn't going to be enough for something like this."

"Get close." Kite gestures to Luke and Sierra, clearly not thrilled about this decision, but ready to help since I refuse to be stopped. "It might take all of us to pull him off her. If it works."

I hold out my arm. "Yes. Do it. Now." I'm so high on fear and adrenaline that I barely feel the sting as Cree rakes his claw across my wrist, going just deep enough to bring blood pooling slowly into the cut.

I'm about to insist he deepen the wound, to make sure Dust has enough, when he brings my wrist to Dust's mouth, cupping the back of the other man's head to press them closer together.

Almost instantly, I feel a spark, a sizzle, a wild cry echoing through my bones. A moment later, Dust's lips part, the small sign of life enough to make my heart thrash like it's going to beat right out of my chest. And then Dust's breath rushes across my skin, making my wrist pulse and sting, and his mouth closes around the wound.

The suction is faint at first, but as the color begins to seep back into his cheeks, he drags harder, deeper, until my head begins to spin. I try to pull away, but Dust's hands shoot up, gripping my arm and holding on with surprising strength, giving me a good idea why blood magic is forbidden.

"Now! Get him off her now!" Kite calls, prying at Dust's fingers.

Dust, who is still unconscious but clearly prepared to claw his way out of the grave by any means necessary, with no clue he might be killing me in the process.

It takes Creedence, Kite, Luke, and Sierra, all fighting like hell to separate us. By the time they do, I'm gasping for breath, and my heart is racing like I've just sprinted a mile uphill. I'm trembling, pulse jerking hard in my throat, stomach pitching, my entire body sending out a red alert that I'm headed toward the dangerous side of empty.

But I don't care how close we cut it, or how easily this could have gone wrong.

All I care about is Dust opening his eyes. Coming back to me. Stitching up the empty place in my soul only he will ever be able to fill.

I huddle, shivering in the grass as Dust lies quietly on the ground. Sierra takes her hands off his legs, Kite releases his torso, and finally, Creedence and Luke loosen their grip on his arms. Luke stands, taking a cautious step back, clearly ready to rush in and pin him again, but Dust doesn't move.

He doesn't move for a minute that feels like a breathless, terror-filled eternity before his lashes finally flutter. And then his lips part, and he sighs in a weary voice, "Don't ever do that again, Snow," and I burst into tears.

I sob so hard my vision blurs, and I can barely see Kite's face as he scoops me into his arms, cradling me close. He carries me to Dust, and I throw my arms around him, fighting not to squeeze too tight, "No, don't *you* ever do that again," I whisper, pressing my damp cheek to his. "You are not replaceable. Not to me. Not ever."

He wraps a weak arm around me, "I'll argue with you later. Right now, I just…love you."

"I love you, too." I sob harder, unable to stop now that the dam has burst. I'm just so relieved. "We're all okay. We made it."

"Not quite yet," Sierra says, running back across the field. I've been so out of it, I didn't even see her leave. "Border agents. On the road headed this way. I don't know if they saw us or this is just part of their usual patrol, but I suggest we don't stick around to find out."

Nodding fast, I smear the tears from my cheeks and take a quick glance around. "Let's divvy up clothes, get those of us without anything to wear covered as best we can and head into the woods toward Lethbridge. I'm tapped out right now, but hopefully, by the time we get to civilization, I'll have enough juice to work a cloaking spell on those of us who are going to attract too much attention. Then we'll figure out who we have to rob to get enough money for a hotel room."

"Dust has money is his coat," Creedence says, holding up the suit jacket. "And passports. We didn't come out of there empty handed."

My shoulders sag with relief as I slip on the white wife-beater Sierra offers me from beneath her flannel. "Good. Then we'll get a cheap room, send someone out for supplies, and see where we go from there."

We head for the woods, a ragged group of battered people with Luke and Kite carrying Dust in a cradle hold between them and most of us dressed like mental patients escaped from the psych ward, but I can't help feeling like we've won.

Our enemies ambushed us. We were surprised, outnumbered, and laughably under-armored. But we're all here. Alive and almost whole and north of the border —one step closer to Atlas.

Maybe it's the blood loss, but for the first time, I feel like we have a real shot of taking him down. Maybe even a good one.

"You ready for this, mama?" Sierra asks as we crouch in an overgrown ditch at the edge of the city an hour later, waiting for a bus to pull in at the stop across the street so we can hopefully scramble quickly on board without attracting too much attention.

My shielding is going to have to be in top form to conceal the more naked among us, but I'm not scared.

"I'm ready," I assure her, adding silently, *So fucking ready.*

CHAPTER 35

WREN

We're in a motel room again, but not in the middle of nowhere this time. We're in the heart of southern Alberta's largest city, sharing two adjoining rooms in the kind of place that takes cash and doesn't ask questions.

I'm not sure they clean the sheets, either, but Dust's wound is wrapped up tight in bandages Creedence stole from an urgent care facility a few blocks over—crawling in a back window after it closed for the night and crawling back out with bandages, drugs, and bags of various blood types he assured me would all be fine for Dust and me.

The blood of the beasts of antiquity isn't particular, apparently. It will mix and match with anything human without putting up a fight. I took one bag of AB negative, but I'm not sure I really needed it. I recover so fast these days. By the time we checked into the hotel, I felt good as new.

Almost as good as new…

I won't be fully whole until I know Dust is out of the woods. He passed out as soon as we laid him down and has been sleeping like a rock ever since, not even Cree cleaning and dressing his wound enough to wake him.

"It's going to be okay, you're going to be fine," I murmur, smoothing a hand over Dust's forehead, brushing his hair away from his face. He's still too pale, but his skin is warm to the touch, and sometimes his lids flutter when I talk.

"You're going to wake up tomorrow feeling so much better," I promise. "We'll find a place to lay low until you get your strength back, and then we'll finish what we started. All five of us. Together."

And in the meantime, I'm going to find a way to shut Highborn down. He's done enough damage. It's time he, and his institute, become a thing of the past. I won't let him hurt the people I love. Not ever again.

I'll kill him if I must.

I've killed lots of people, now.

I close my eyes, willing away mental images of the creatures I set on fire, screaming and writhing as they burned. The death toll makes me physically ill, but I had no choice. No more than they did. Highborn took all our choices away, forced us to do terrible things to each other.

It's past time for him to have a taste of his own medicine.

"Wren? Can I talk to you for a second?"

I glance up to see Sierra standing in the doorway

leading to the adjoining room, where the others are finishing dinner.

I should eat something, too, but my stomach is still full of smoke and rocks. I almost lost a piece of myself today—did lose him for a little while. That horrible knowledge is taking up all the room in my belly where food used to fit.

How can I eat dinner and go about business as usual when I know exactly what it will be like when the man I love is lost to me forever? When I know that it's worse than dying?

So much worse...

"Yeah, sure." I lay a gentle hand on Dust's cheek. "I'll be back." His lids don't flutter this time, but I know he's okay. He's getting better with every passing minute. I can feel the strength pumping back into his body, knitting his soul tight to his flesh and bones.

Still, it takes willpower to force myself out of the chair beside his bed and cross to meet Sierra as she opens the door leading onto our cramped balcony. I don't want to leave him for a second. And though it's nice to escape the sour-bedding-and-moldy-carpet smell of our room, the view outside definitely leaves something to be desired.

The building directly across the alley from ours is condemned, a sagging heap of metal and cinder block with smashed windows and graffiti-streaked walls that hint at habitation by local homeless. Now, floodlights blast the structure from the sidewalk below, a deterrent to future squatters that casts the graffiti in pools of light, like works of art spotlighted at a gallery.

Fuck all sluts dead scrawled in red beneath a swirled gang tag is especially attention-grabbing, making me sigh.

"Charming, huh?" Sierra grunts. "Seems like men would have more appreciation for sluts. That's what they want, right? Willing women on their backs for them, taking dick without putting up a fight?"

"I don't know," I say, voice still rough from all the dragon fire. "I don't think men know what they want. Women, either. I think a lot of people are just...confused."

"Asleep," Sierra says. "They're asleep at the wheel, getting jerked around by unconscious shit that makes them miserable to co-exist with, and the rest of us pay the price for it." She leans against the spindly balcony railing, facing me. "That's what I wanted to talk to you about. Unconscious shit. Things people around here might be doing without knowing they're doing it."

I frown. "What do you mean?"

"Luke," she says, gaze flicking to the door behind us before returning to my face. "I'm pretty sure he's lab-made. I didn't want to say anything until I was—"

"It's okay. I know. *We* know," I correct, too tired to worry about Sierra feeling left out of the loop. "Not one-hundred percent certain, but we've strongly suspected for a while."

Sierra sucks her bottom lip into her mouth, chewing as she nods. "Okay... And he's still here because...?"

"He's still here because he bears the mark and hasn't done anything to prove he isn't on our side."

Her eyes widen. "Seriously?"

"Seriously."

She rocks back on her heels. "Listen, I'm all for protecting the rights of lab-made shifters. I've risked my life for the cause more than once, but this isn't..." She trails off with a rough sigh, her brows furrowing into a squiggle of worry. "He could be one of High-born's, Wren. He could have been the one who led them to our camp. Maybe not on purpose, but if he's a Gen Mod they could have tech in him that—"

"Creedence scanned him for tech when the L.A. pack dropped him off. He came up clean. And he saved Dust's life," I remind her. "He risked his life to save my mate, when that was never what he signed up for. He didn't have to be a hero, but he was."

Her gaze softens. "Yes, he was a hero today, but that doesn't mean he isn't also a spy. Maybe a spy without even knowing it if they've got a DNA protocol rigged to run in him when they pull a trigger."

"He was made at least fifteen years ago," I say. "They didn't have those kinds of protocols back then."

Sierra shrugs. "Doesn't mean he couldn't have been modified since."

"If he was going to kill us, don't you think he would have done it by now?"

"No. Not if he's the failsafe, the last trigger to pull if all their other plans go to shit."

I drive a hand through my nearly dry hair with a sigh. Even after my shower, it smells like smoke. Ash. With an undernote of charred flesh that makes me want to get back in the shower and scrub and scrub until the reminder of how much blood is on my hands is gone.

But it will never be gone. The fact that I killed in self-defense may keep my soul clean, but my heart will never be the same. Something died in me tonight, something innocent and hopeful that I'll never get back again.

"I want to know how they found us as much as you do," I say. "Believe me, I do. But I'm not going to rush into laying blame where it doesn't belong. Luke's done everything in his power to prepare me to fight our enemies, and we were there for over a month before we were discovered. That makes me think it must have been something else. Maybe Highborn caught us on a satellite feed or—"

"I respect your sense of fairness, mama." Sierra shakes her head. "But this isn't the time for it. It's time to take extreme measures to keep you and your mates safe and apologize for hurting people's feelings later. Pardon my French, but seriously, it's time to grow the fuck up, Wren," Sierra says, knocking the breath out of me.

I barely bite back the "fuck you," on the tip of my tongue.

"I'm working on it, Sierra, believe me," I say instead, forcing the words through a clenched jaw. Two people lashing out from fear and anger won't make this better. Still, my tone isn't gentle. "There are other factors aside from immediate safety. I need four mates to have a real shot at taking down Atlas. There's a whisper-thin chance I might pull it off with three, but blasting through a few hundred versions of the future showed me how highly unlikely that is. I need Luke."

Her lips part on another argument—the cold fire in her eyes leaves no doubt it's going to be another argument—when the screech of the window opening in the adjoining room makes us both flinch.

A beat later, Kite sticks his head out into the night air and motions us in. "Hey, you two. Get in here. You should see this. It's all over the news."

"Be right there," Sierra says, before adding to me in a whisper. "We'll talk more later. I'm not going to let you Pollyanna anyone into an early grave, especially yourself."

Before I can respond, she spins on her heel, heading back inside.

Taking a moment to unclench my fists and jaw, I follow her, emerging into the adjoining room as Creedence kicks up the volume on the ancient television chained to the wall.

An aerial shot of a forest on fire—our forest—fills the screen.

CHAPTER 36
WREN

"I s it about us?" My fingers curl around the neck of the scratchy black T-shirt Creedence brought back for me to put on after my shower. "Have they shown photos?"

If our pictures are on the air, we need to get out of the city, to a place where there are fewer people to report they've spotted the motley crew the authorities are looking for.

"No," Kite says. My shoulders relax away from my ears, only to shoot back up again as he adds, "It's Highborn. Looks like he cracked."

Before I can ask for clarification, a female newscaster's disembodied voice speaks over the footage of trees collapsing in a shower of sparks. "According to official statements from the U.S. government the forest fire raging just south of the border is being blamed on a drug enforcement agency mission gone awry. But sources close to Dr. Highborn, the controversial head of the Elysium Institute, infamous for their aggressive treatment of Meltdown viruses in children, say otherwise."

Eyes wide, I turn back to Kite, but he just motions to the screen. Apparently, he's heard this part of the story before. I wonder how many stations are covering the fire.

And if Atlas watches the news...

"Just minutes after the fire outside of Columbia Falls, Montana was reported to the authorities," the newscaster continues, "two doctors with ties to Dr. Highborn received phone calls from the physician, who alleged to be on the mountain when the fire broke out. Dr. Highborn accused the U.S. government of an elaborate conspiracy to conceal the existence of supernatural creatures, alleges to have received taxpayer money to fund illegal and unethical experiments on U.S. citizens without their consent, and insists he's being targeted by a supernatural being of, quote, 'unimaginable power, who will kill us all,' end quote."

This time my "what the hell?" glance lands on Creedence, who responds with an "I know, right? What the fuck?" arch of his brows. When I glance back at the screen, the view of burning trees has been replaced by a photograph of Dr. Highborn, wearing a suit and looking benignly dignified, that quickly crossfades to a picture of a fifty-something woman with pretty, gray-blond curls and a warm smile.

"These calls came only hours after the body of Dr. Highborn's wife of thirty years, Beatrice Highborn, was discovered in the family pool," the anchor continues, sending a flash of pain through my chest. "It appears to have been a suicide, but the authorities haven't ruled out foul play. We can only speculate as to how the death of his wife contributed to the doctor's mental state tonight."

The camera cuts to a shot of a twenty-something Latina reporter in a brown sock cap and a red windbreaker, backlit by the flickering forest behind her.

She presses a hand to her ear, nodding as she maintains eye contact with the camera. "Looks like we've received audio of Dr. Highborn's phone call to Dr. Lillian Craven of Mount Sinai Hospital in New York City." She nods again, buying time as she processes whatever the voices in her earbud are telling her. "We'll play that for you now."

The camera lingers on the woman's tense features for another beat before the screen is filled with a graphic whipped up for the occasion. On one side of the screen are photos of Dr. Highborn and Dr. Craven, a tiny woman with gray hair and thick glasses, who is at least eighty if she's a day.

But when she speaks, her voice is surprisingly youthful, easily understood without following the transcript scrolling up the screen.

Highborn: Are you recording? Are we good?

Craven: Yes, I'm recording, Martin, but I beg you to slow down and think about what you're doing. There are some things you can't take back, no matter how hard you try. And you never know who's listening. You know that better than anyone.

Highborn: That's why I called you, Lili. I remembered

what you said, about being too old to be afraid. Do you remember?

Craven: *Of course, but that doesn't mean I—*

Highborn: *Beatrice is dead. By now, Wendy, too, I'm sure.*

Craven: *Oh, no...*soft choked sound* Oh, Martin, I'm so sorry. So terribly sorry.*

Highborn: *I failed the test. Lost the game. That's all it is to him, a game. Murdering the people I loved was just...entertainment, a way to break the monotony. *sobbing sounds**

Craven: **unintelligible words* *hushing sounds**

Highborn: *And now I have no reason to be afraid, either. There's nothing worth fighting for. I sent the happily ever after package. Just now. From my email.*

Craven: *Of course you did. That's what that monster doesn't understand. We need more than the blood pumping through our veins, we need a reason for our hearts to keep beating.*

Highborn: **choked sound* I don't. Not anymore. There were both so good. So innocent. I loved them so much.*

Craven: *And they loved you, Martin. Go in peace, friend. I'll do what I can to make sure this isn't buried.*

Highborn: *I sent the package to everyone, Lili. Half the Pentagon is getting an in-depth briefing on everything we know about Atlas. Every colleague in my contacts list, all my friends overseas. There's not a blanket big enough to cover it up. The truth is coming out. By the end of the week, the entire world will know what they're up against.*

Craven: *I hope so. I've always thought, if we could all just stand together...*

Highborn: *They're here. I have to go. Happily ever after, Lili. I'm going.*

Craven: I know.

The call cuts off, and the anchor reappears, her haunted expression sending a chill down my spine even before she says, "A body believed to be that of Dr. Highborn was discovered earlier this evening as firefighters brought the worst of the Columbia Fall's peak fire under control. The doctor appears to have died from a self-inflicted gunshot wound to the head."

My heart jerks hard in my chest.

He's dead. The man who nearly killed Dust, destroyed Carrie Ann, and hurt so many people—human and shifter, alike—is gone. Forever.

So why am I more frightened than I was five minutes ago?

The woman on the screen lifts her chin as if bracing herself for what's coming next. "The recording you just heard was turned over to the FBI by Dr. Craven, who also emailed the file to news outlets across the United States, Canada, and Europe." Her throat works above the zipper of her windbreaker. "And we... Just minutes ago, we received word that Dr. Craven's body was discovered at eight-thirty-eight eastern time on the sidewalk outside her Madison Avenue apartment building, an apparent victim of suicide after a leap from her twenty-fifth story window."

Kite curses beneath his breath, and Creedence mutters, "Suicide, my ass."

"Stay tuned for developments in this story, as well as a list of road closures caused by the peak fire," the anchor continues, recovering her composure. "Despite heavy rains earlier today, flames continue to spread east, and the fire department warns of possible evacuation orders for citizens of both Columbia Falls and Kalispell."

Kite mutes the television and turns to lean against the wall beside it. "He's gone. Why don't I feel better?"

"I was just thinking the same thing," I murmur, nibbling the pad of my thumb. "Why turn on Highborn? I agree that Atlas seems to enjoy hurting people for sport, but why take out an ally? Highborn got close to killing us. Twice."

"Maybe close isn't good enough for Atlas," Creedence offers.

"Maybe he's crazy." Luke, who's been even more stoic than usual since we checked into our rooms, motions toward the screen from his seat at the foot of the sagging bed. "Maybe he lashed out in anger, killing the guy's family before he thought it through."

I shake my head. "That doesn't feel right. I mean, yes, from what I know about his history, I'd say Atlas is out of his mind, but he's not impulsive. And he wants us dead. That's his first priority, so why would he—"

"But what if it's not?" Luke asks. "At least, not killing all of us. That night on the reservation, and tonight on the compound, no one was shooting at you, Wren."

I blink, surprised to be "Wren" not "Princess," but try not to show it.

"He's right," Creedence offers. "At least tonight. I wasn't with you when the fighting started in the lodge."

"Maybe he's right about the shooting, but the Gen Mods weren't pulling any punches," I say. "They were swarming me tonight. And one almost ripped my throat out at the lodge. He would have if I hadn't caught fire and forced him to back off."

"But we can withstand a lot of damage from each other," Kite says. "That's why my mom and all the other old timers were so upset when the Rule of Tooth and Claw went out the window. Silver bullets have a way higher mortality rate than even the most brutal hand-to-hand injuries." He motions toward the other room. "Like with Dust. If he'd taken claws in the gut, he'd already be up and about right now."

"I am up…" The soft voice from the doorway sends my heart pinging around in my chest like a freshly launched pinball.

I turn, hurrying to where Dust is leaning weakly against the doorframe. "What are you doing? You shouldn't be out of bed. You'll reopen the wound." I reach for him, intending to wrap an arm around his waist and help him back to the other room, but he captures my hand, holding it with surprising strength.

"I'm fine. Thanks to you," he says, holding my gaze as a wave of love and gratitude washes over me, bringing tears to my eyes.

"No thanks needed," I whisper. "I love you so much, and I'm so glad to see you awake again, but I need you to lie down. Okay? I won't risk losing you because you're too stubborn to give yourself time to heal."

"I don't need time. I need that file Highborn sent to his friends," Dust says, the jut of his jaw making it clear that getting him back in bed isn't going to be easy. "I have a contact in the Pentagon. I need to get to a secure computer and reach out, see if he has access."

"Agreed." Creedence bounces up from his chair. "And I can help. I picked up a surprise for you while I was at urgent care. A little something I thought we might need before you're back in fighting shape." He opens the closet door and pulls out a folded wheelchair he pops open with a jerk of his arms. "There." He grins. "Ready to roll when you are, Captain."

"I get to be captain again?" Dust asks with a wry twist of his lips.

"You do," Creedence says. "Almost dying comes with certain privileges. At least until you piss me off again." He nods toward the door. "Should we head out? Or do you want to get pretty first?"

Dust grins. "Just let me put my suit coat on over my sweatpants."

"No," I protest. "Even with the wheelchair, it's too soon. You should rest. At least for the night."

"We might not have the night," Sierra says, speaking up for the first time since the newscast ended. "There's another option no one's mentioned. What if Atlas took out Highborn because he doesn't need him anymore?" Her gaze shifts to me, landing with an almost audible snap. "Because he's already got us exactly where he wants us?"

"Doubtful," Dust says, before Sierra's 'Luke is a traitor' argument can become a matter of public discussion. "Highborn wouldn't have attacked us without Atlas's approval. Atlas wanted us dead before we could cross the border, not safe on the other side, making plans to get even closer to his stronghold."

"Agreed again," Creedence says. "We're under the

radar now, and the dirt in the file might help us stay that way. Ready to roll, Dust?"

"Fine. Then I'm coming with you." I grab my new jean jacket off the back of the chair across from Sierra's at the small dining table.

"Me, too," Luke says, surprising me again. He grabs his gun off the bedside table, tucking it into the back of his pants.

I cut a quick glance Sierra's way, but she isn't looking at me. She's staring out the window at the building across the street with a brooding expression. But she's keeping her mouth shut, which is good. I'm not ready to confront Luke yet, not when Dust is too weak to walk, and we don't have our next move sorted out.

I toss a "we'll be back ASAP; meet at the bus stop where we came out of the woods if we get separated," reminder in Sierra's direction, kiss Kite goodbye, and hurry out the door behind the other men, crossing my fingers that there's a secret weapon waiting for us somewhere in cyberspace.

CHAPTER 37
LUKE

P romises are important.

Even the ones no one else knows you've made.

My parents taught me early on how shitty life can get when you refuse to hold yourself accountable. They were the inspiration for the first vow I ever made—that I wasn't going to grow up to be anything like them. It's a promise I've never broken, not even when I was in prison, where lying to myself and letting accountability get flushed away along with my privacy and autonomy, would have been so much fucking easier.

So as soon as Creedence, Dust, Wren, and I are inside the basement of a creepy old office building, where the resistance evidently has a secure computer stashed away behind a derelict mailroom, I decide it's time to keep my promise.

"Can I have a second?" I ask once Dust is seated at a

grimy-looking desk, waiting for a computer older than Wren to hum to life. "There's something I need to get off my chest."

Dust nods, Creedence arches a brow, and Wren turns to me, surprise in her eyes. "Um, yeah. Sure." She leans back against the edge of the desk. "What's on your mind?"

"There's no easy way to say this, so I'll just spit it out." I take a breath and uncross my arms, wanting it to be clear that I have nothing to hide from them. Not anymore. "I'm not Lucas Rivera. I'm Luke Barajas. I don't know if the L.A. pack kidnapped the wrong wolf by accident, or what, but I'm not the guy who's supposed to be here. I clocked onto that pretty fast, but I kept up the act so I could get papers, a fresh start. I figured you owed it to me after ruining my parole, but…" I shake my head, my jaw working back and forth as I search for the right words. "But I don't feel that way anymore. And I don't want to put any of you in danger by being the wrong guy when you need the right one. So I'm just… I'm sorry."

Wren makes a relieved sound that's confusing as hell until I take a closer look at her eyes.

What I see there makes my breath rush out and shame rush in.

"You already knew." My gaze darts to Dust and then Creedence, seeing confirmation in their not-the-least-fucking-bit-surprised expressions. "All of you knew. So, Kite too? Sierra?"

"Kite, too," Wren confirms. "Sierra wasn't kept in the loop, but she has some… Some other suspicions."

"Like what?" I ask, throat tightening as I answer my own question, "That I'm lab-made, not Kin Born?"

Wren nods. "Yes. She shared that with me earlier tonight and got angry when she realized we'd kept you around for so long after we knew the truth."

"Part of the truth," Dust adds. "I can't get the L.A. pack to return my calls, and Lucas Rivera has conveniently disappeared, making it difficult to determine why you were offered in his place."

"Any ideas on that, Slick?" Creedence asks. "Now that you've decided to let Jesus take the wheel?"

My jaw clenches as I shake my head. "None. I'm not tight with the L.A. pack, but I've been careful not to make enemies there. All of us were. We knew we were one wrong move away from getting our throats slit just for existing."

"All of who?" Creedence cocks his head.

"Lab-made shifters," I say. "There were a bunch of us, all close to my age, all from fucked up, low-income families south of L.A. Whoever did this to us was careful to pick kids no one was going to care too much about."

"You don't know who made you?" Dust's gaze is fixed on the computer screen as he taps at the keyboard, but I know better than to think it's an idle question.

"No, I don't." I stuff my hands into the pockets of my jeans. "I don't remember who took me when I was a kid, what they did to me the year I was missing, or most of the year after I was dumped back at my mom's in the middle of the night. I wasn't..." I shrug. "I wasn't okay. Even after I started talking again and eventually went back to school, there are gaps in time... Missing pieces. It wasn't until high school, when I figured out how to control the shifts, that it stopped."

"I'm so sorry that happened to you." The empathy in Wren's voice pricks at the shields I'm fighting so hard to keep in place. "I have so many questions, but I know this must be hard."

"It's not hard. It's the past. It has no power." I nod her way. "Ask."

Her forehead wrinkles. "That's not how I experience the past, but all right. How old were you when you were taken?"

"Seven. I turned eight while I was gone."

"So about..." Creedence taps his fingers to his thumb one by one. "Twenty-two years ago?"

I nod, forehead furrowing as I realize... "Almost twenty-three. I think it's my birthday in a few days. Is it July third yet?"

Wren smiles. "Tomorrow is the first. I had to check the newspaper at the front desk. We lost a lot of time out there in the woods."

"It wasn't lost. It was well spent," I say, continuing in a tone that feels uncomfortably earnest, but true. Real. "For what it's worth, I did everything I could to get you ready to fight this monster. None of that was a lie. And if I..." I scrub a hand over my face, fighting an unexpected rush of emotion. When I'm sure my voice won't crack, I continue, "If I could be what you needed, I'd try."

"So you've decided you'd like to save the world?" Creedence asks.

"Something like that," I say, but I don't look at him. I hold Wren's gaze, staring deep into those heartbreaker blue eyes, hoping she can see what I really mean. That it's *her* I want to save, to protect, to pull into my arms and hold so close she'll know that I'm never going to let her go. Not without one hell of a fight.

"What if we can be what *you* need?" she finally asks, the words pure temptation.

But as much as I want an excuse to get her in my bed, to solidify a connection to this woman who's locked down my heart in a way I wasn't sure was possible, I can't lie to her. Not anymore.

Throat tight, I shake my head. "I'm not your wolf, Princess. You need the real deal."

"You have the mark," she says. "That's real."

"I haven't shifted in almost a decade," I find myself confessing. "I lose my fucking mind when I do. I'm pure rage, all animal, nothing human in there at all."

Dust makes a concerned sound, and Creedence says, "That's a problem, man. You've got to shift. The longer you deny that part of yourself, the angrier your kin form is going to get at being forced underground."

I give another tight shake of my head. "Not happening. I've hurt people. People who didn't deserve to be hurt. Next time it could be something worse."

Wren's eyes tighten. "Or it could be better than you ever imagined. If you let us help you. You've seen how strong we are together. It's at least worth a shot, right? Wouldn't it be nice to dump a few of those demons that've been following you around?"

Jaw working, I shift my gaze to Creedence and then

to Dust, who's rising unsteadily from the desk chair, looking about as ready to banish demons as he does to run a marathon.

"Give me a day to recover. Maybe two," he says, making me wonder when I got so damned easy to read. "And then I think she's right. I think we can help you shift safely. And in the meantime, you can help us."

Wren nods, hope flickering in her eyes. "When my mother came to me in my dream, she told me one of my four had the secret to finding my sister locked inside of him. That he would need my help to set it free." She motions to the men now standing on either side of her. "I know it isn't Dust, Cree, or Kite. That leaves you."

"Leaves Lucas Rivera, you mean," I remind her.

"No," Wren says, lifting that stubborn chin of hers. "I don't know why the L.A. pack did what they did, but you're the one who's meant to be here. I've seen it. And this…" She motions between us. "Me and you. It's felt right to me. From the very start, even when I was so pissed at you I didn't want to admit it, I wanted you to stick around."

I huff softly, the laugh loosening some of the tension fisting in my chest.

"And I think…" She tilts her head, blinking in that unconsciously sexy way that drives me crazy. "I think you've felt it, too."

I clear my throat, but I don't speak. I don't confirm or deny. I stand there, torn between the ugly lessons of the past and an oh-so-tempting hope in the future, so close I can almost taste it.

But I've fallen for hope before. I've reached for that

shiny red apple only to have it turn to ash in my mouth. There are places in my soul scarred so thick that I'll never feel anything there again.

No seed will take root; nothing will grow. Nothing sweet or innocent could ever survive there. I'm half a man, at best, and Wren deserves so much more.

"You're missing a year of your childhood," Dust adds, filling the uncomfortable silence. "As well as those other gaps you mentioned. That creates a lot of space for secrets to hide."

"And if we went into your past, it wouldn't just be to help me find my sister," Wren says. "It would be for you, too. Wouldn't you like to have that time back? To be able to fill in some of the blanks?"

I cross my arms. "I don't know." Honesty still makes me skittish, but it's also the only way through this mine-field. "Some things are better forgotten. Like finding my kid brother and his girlfriend torn apart. If I could wipe that from my head, I'd do it in a heartbeat."

"Understandable," Wren says, wincing.

"But..." I take a deep breath and let it out slowly. "I'm willing to try." My heart beats faster at the thought of wading into the shadowy recesses of my childhood. I held on to enough from those early years, before I was old enough to get out of the house, into the streets where I could breathe, to know I won't be uncovering any golden memories.

There's no hidden treasure there for me, but there might be for Wren.

"We appreciate it. But it's only going to be possible if we establish a secure link." Dust arches a meaningful brow. "With you being vision blind, the only way for the rest of us to gain access to your memories will be by accessing them via your connection with someone else."

I frown, but before I can ask what he means, Creedence makes it plain, "You and Wren. Mate bond. Tonight. Now, would also be good. Dust and I can step outside, give you two some space if you'd like." He glances at the barren, dusty, beige and despair-colored office. "I mean, it's pretty fucking romantic in here, right?"

Something happens to my face. My cheeks go hot, and my neck starts to itch, and Wren laughs.

She laughs high and sweet and easy, her eyes dancing as she beams up at me. "You're blushing. You! I never thought I would see the day."

"I'm not blushing," I grumble, fighting a smile. Because...fuck. I *am* blushing. I'm standing here, thinking about getting shifter-married to a girl, and blushing about it like a twelve-year-old passing love notes in math class.

"I like blushing Luke," Wren says, her grin softening. "I like honest Luke even more. Thank you for trusting us and for believing in me." She sighs. "And I would like to say that there's no rush to move forward, that we could take that next step when or if it felt right. You know, after we've had time to go on a date or two, see if the occasional urge to strangle each other ever fully goes away..."

I smile, falling deeper in love with her on the spot. "I hope not. I kind of enjoy fighting with you, Princess. You're sexy when you're mad."

Now it's her turn to blush, and she's cute as hell while she does it. Her pale skin goes pink, and her eyes roll self-consciously as she mutters, "Yeah, you're okay, too, I guess."

My grin widens. "Yeah? Okay? You wouldn't kick me out of bed for eating crackers?"

"Okay, lovebirds," Creedence says, clapping his hands. "You two are nauseating, and we should get going. This place is giving me the creeps. I keep hearing rats in the vents." He heads for the door, grabbing the handles of the wheelchair and rolling it back to the desk.

"And I have reading to do." Dust settles into the wheelchair without putting up a fight, making me think this outing has been more draining than he's let on. "My source sent the file, and I forwarded it securely to my private email. If we pick up a burner phone on the way back to the hotel, I can read it tonight and debrief everyone in the morning."

"You need to sleep," Wren chides, brushing his hair tenderly from his forehead.

Dust looks up at her, love so clear in his eyes it makes my chest tight.

What would it be like? To be that sure? That unafraid to let your heart out of its cage?

"I will sleep," he promises, taking her hand and giving it a squeeze. "But I'll sleep easier with a little privacy. We don't have enough beds for everyone without sharing. I think when we get back, you and Luke should get your own room."

"On a different floor," Creedence adds, pushing Dust

toward the door with Wren trailing close behind. "So we don't have to listen to the frenemy sex."

Wren makes a startled-embarrassed sound. "Stop it, Creedence."

"I won't," he says, his amber eyes sparkling at her over his shoulder. "Until there's a chance of getting in on the action, I don't want to listen to other guys make you come. Sometimes a man just has to take a stand. Right, Dust?"

"I want Wren safe. That's all I care about," Dust says.

"Liar," Creedence mutters. "But you're right. I'll sleep easier once Wolf Boy is on board for keeps." He bobs his brows. "Aren't you excited, Luke? We're going to be family. You'll get to enjoy the pleasure of my company for the rest of our lives. Maybe even raise a few kittens together someday. Because they will be kittens. Right, Wren? Because you want our babies to be beautiful, intelligent, and loyal, with dazzling personalities and—"

"Hush, Creedence," Wren says as we head down the litter-strewn hallway toward the back of the building.

"It's a fact, Slim. Kittens are superior to all other shifter babies. And they tend to have a lower human weight at birth. Better for your figure."

"Not the time," she insists.

"Not that I won't love you if you get all fat with a giant bear baby," he prattles on, clearly enjoying himself, "or whatever weirdness a griffin would work on your fine ass, but—"

"Creedence." Dust glares at the other man, but the cat is on a roll.

"Because I will always love you, Slim." He jabs a

thumb at me. "Even after you're mate-bonded to this cranky bastard who smells like wet dog every time he gets out of the shower."

Bubbles swell and pop in my chest, and before I know it, laughter bursts from my lips. From the look on their faces, Dust and Creedence are as surprised by it as I am.

But Wren just smiles and slows her pace, falling back to walk beside me.

And then she holds out her hand, palm up, fingers soft.

It's a simple gesture.

A little thing.

And it lights up my insides like the Fourth of July.

I take her hand and hold tight. I'm not sure what I'm getting myself into, but as long as I'm with her, I'm down. She's my ride-or-die, this girl, and by the end of the night, she'll be...my wife.

Mine.

For keeps.

We get a room on the tenth floor, high enough to see over the faded building next door to the rest of the city, rolling across the hills with the Rockies standing guard in the darkness beyond.

Luke opens the door and stands back, letting me lead the way inside.

It's not much different than the rooms downstairs. Still dingy and worn, with depressing paintings of circus performers that make me wonder if the decorator was deliberately trying to underline the hopeless vibe of the Seventh Avenue Grand.

But it is also strangely…perfect.

It's a room where Luke and I can be alone with no secrets or lies or potential betrayal lingering between us. It's just him and me, and a choice we're making not just to save the world, but to save ourselves.

I need him, I realize, as I turn and open my arms, heart twisting as he comes to me without a beat of hesitation, drawing me close and cupping my face in his big hand, sending an electric ache pulsing across my skin.

Dust gives me solid ground to stand on, Creedence brings mischief, laughs, and perspective into my life, Kite is my unconditional, meant-to-be love with bear hugs on top, but with Luke...

With Luke, I can face the demons.

Not just his, but mine.

We grew up thousands of miles apart in families that couldn't have been more different, but the places where he hurts are the places where I hurt. The bruised regions of my soul ache with recognition every time we touch. We were both stolen away from our homes, robbed of our innocence and our free will, battered and betrayed and denied our humanity by people who had none of their own.

But we are also survivors, and stronger than all the people who hurt us rolled into one. And together, we're going to be even stronger.

"You've got that look in your eyes again," he murmurs, his mouth so close I can feel his breath warm on my lips.

"What look?" I ask, my pulse dancing with anticipation. I can't wait to kiss him, to taste him, to explore all the undiscovered country waiting on the other side of this choice.

"Like you're going to save the world," he says. "Or maybe just a man."

"Only if you save me, too, Wolf Boy," I whisper,

nipples pulling tight beneath my tee as his eyes go dark.

"That's why I'm here, Princess." The tenderness in his voice transforms the taunt into something heart-breakingly sweet. "That's the only reason I'm here."

And then he kisses me, and every nerve in my body lights up. Flashes of light dance behind my closed eyes as his tongue strokes into my mouth and I taste him for the first time. He tastes like salt and pain, loneliness and regret, but also like the first berry plucked from a wild vine, tart but sweet and full of promise. We could have chosen to tear each other apart, but instead, we're here, patching each other back together. Healing the hurt. Saving what was so close to being lost.

"So damned sweet," he murmurs against my lips as he guides me toward the bed, his hands smoothing under my shirt to curl around my waist. The feel of his bare skin on mine is enough to make my head spin.

"You, too." I sigh into his mouth, pulse spiking as the backs of my knees hit the mattress.

"I'm the farthest thing from sweet there is, Princess."

"I'll be the judge of that." I grip the bottom of his shirt, drawing it up and over his head, baring his incredible chest. Heart in my throat, I trace a finger down between his pecs to the thick ridges of his abdominal muscles. "You look pretty sweet to me."

His lips quirk. "Yeah? You into muscles and scars?"

I nod, lifting my gaze to his. "But mostly into you."

An unspoken question flickers behind his eyes. I bring my hand to his face, fingers playing across the strong line of his jaw. "What?" I ask.

His fingers curl around my wrist, squeezing hard

enough to send a jolt of awareness spiraling into my core. "I don't love like the rest of them, Wren. It's not going to be easy. *I'm* not easy."

"I don't want easy." My heart hammers faster as he grips my other wrist, holding me captive. "I want you. I want you so much it's hard to breathe. And I don't just mean this. Tonight."

"Just the sex?" He guides me back onto the bed, lengthening himself over me as he pins my hands to the mattress over my head.

"No, I don't mean just sex. I mean everything. Every piece of you. Even the broken ones." He nudges my thighs apart, settling between them, making my breath shudder out as I feel how hard he is behind the fly of his jeans.

"But you're okay with the sex part?" he asks, a teasing lilt in his voice as he presses a kiss to my throat, where my pulse is fluttering like a butterfly on speed.

"I am *so* okay with that part." I lift my hips, rocking against his thickness. "I'm sort of desperate for that part, actually."

"You don't know what desperate is, baby." He strokes one hand down my arm to my ribs, my waist, to the curve of my hip, where he squeezes tight. "It's been so fucking long for me, Princess. I'm going to be lucky to last five minutes."

"Quality not quantity," I say, my head spinning as he pops the button on my jeans and draws the zipper down. "And it won't take me five minutes to get there. I'm already so wet."

"Yeah?" He slips a hand down the front of my jeans,

into my panties, groaning as he glides two fingers inside where I ache. "Damn, baby. I want my mouth on you so bad." He drives his fingers deeper, the friction so delicious my eyes roll back in my head. "I want to get drunk on your pussy."

Before I can express my enthusiasm for this plan, he's already ripping my jeans and panties down my thighs. I claw off my T-shirt and sports bra and reach for him, gasping against his lips as he kisses me hard and deep while he touches me everywhere.

Absolutely everywhere.

I swear he must have three hands, four. He's plucking my nipples, stroking my clit, squeezing my thigh, threading his fingers through mine—all at once. And then he's sucking my nipples while he rocks the heel of his hand against the top of where I'm so wet, and suddenly I'm flying, falling, calling out his name as his mouth replaces his hand and he teaches me how fast I can recover. How fast I can soar off the edge of the world all over again, this time with his fingers pinching my nipples while he moans his appreciation and encouragement against my swollen flesh, making me feel like a hero for coming twice.

He does it again. And then again, and just when I'm sure my body can't handle any more, he assures me that it can. I can.

We can.

"Look at me." He pauses, the tip of his cock pressed lightly against my entrance. "Watch my eyes, Princess. I want you with me for this."

"Yes," I whisper, gazing into him as he sinks oh-so-slowly into me, each inch a revelation, a miracle, a gift I had no idea I was about to receive.

He is so open. So real. So completely here with me as we begin to rock together that tears sting into my eyes. "I love you." I cling to his shoulders as he glides deeper, erasing every barrier between us.

"My life." He threads his fingers through mine, holding on tight. "It's yours, Princess. I belong to you, baby. God, I fucking belong to you. Can you feel it?"

I suck in a ragged breath, tears spilling down my cheeks as the mate bond folds over us like a blanket, wrapping us in love and belonging. "Yes. And I to you. Oh God, yes. Luke. Please. Come with me. I'm going to come, I'm—"

My release twists inside of me, clutching so hard that it hurts. But the hurt is sweet, as sweet as the shattered-by-pleasure expression on Luke's face as his cock jerks against my inner walls. I cling to him and him to me, both of us riding out the bliss together until we lie —heavy and spent—in each other's arms.

We're quiet for a long time, so long I'm on the verge of drifting off when Luke whispers, "That was the best thing that's ever happened to me."

I smile, my eyes fluttering open. "And we get to do it again. Whenever we want. How cool is that?"

"So fucking cool." He rolls on top of me with a grin that makes me laugh. He laughs, too, a beautiful, hopeful sound that lights up every corner of my soul, and then he makes me cry again.

Because it's just *that* good.

Him. Me. No clothes. All heart. All good.

We don't sleep for hours.

Hours and hours and hours…and it's absolutely fucking perfect.

CHAPTER 39
LUKE

I wake up to a prickling feeling on my lids. It reminds me of being back in prison, when I'd open my eyes to find my first roommate, Bart, a dude as sweet as he was occasionally dangerously violent, perched on a stool by my bottom bunk, watching me sleep.

He said that I looked peaceful and it reminded him of watching his kids sleep.

It was still creepy as fuck.

But this? Opening my eyes to find a gorgeous woman propped up on one arm, smiling down at me like I fished the sun out from behind the mountains this morning, is pure sweetness. When I realize she's still naked, I'm pretty sure I can't get any happier.

"Good morning, sexy," I murmur, keeping my mouth turned away from her out of respect for my possible morning breath even as I urge her on top of me.

"It *is* a good morning," she says, summoning a groan

302

from low in my throat as she straddles my hips. I can feel how hot she is against my already hard cock, even through my boxer briefs. I silently curse myself for pulling them on before I drifted off last night as she continues in a giddy whisper, "As long as I was touching you, I didn't dream at all. Not a single thing. It's like someone yanked the electrical cord out of the wall. My brain was a big blank, all night long."

I arch a brow. "That doesn't sound all that nice, but you sure look happy."

"Oh, I *am* happy." She leans down, pressing a kiss to my cheek before she whispers in my ear, "I'm in love with your vision-killing superpowers."

I laugh. "I think the word you're looking for is handicap."

"No, it's super." She rocks against my erection, making me groan again. God, I want to be inside her ten minutes ago. "I feel so rested and amazing and—"

"Horny?" I ask, sucking in a shaky breath. "Please say horny."

She hums seductively. "Yes. That. And wet. Just smelling you makes me wet."

Cursing softly, I roll over, pinning her beneath me, concerns about morning breath and anything else going up in a puff of smoke as she shoves my boxers down my thighs and fits me against her. And then my cock is gliding into her molten heat and her long legs are tight around my hips, and her eyes are sliding closed with a blissed-out cry that goes straight to my heart.

"Fuck, Wren, you drive me crazy," I murmur, fingers digging into her fine ass as we begin to writhe together, going from sleepy good morning to hot, desperate, frantic fucking in seconds flat.

But that's how it is with us. We're fire and a room full of matches. The chemistry is fierce and wild, and I wouldn't have it any other way.

"I want to make you scream," I say against her lips as we push harder, faster, slamming into each other with soft gasps and grunts. "I want to make you come so hard you can't hold it in."

"Yes. Oh God, yes." Her lips part, and her features twist in prelude to release, and I lose the last of my thinly held control.

With a growl, I hook her knees over my elbows, spreading her legs even wider as I pump fast and deep, balls leaden weights dragging at my body until I feel her pussy lock tight around me. The second she comes—screaming my name loud enough to wake the entire hotel—I spin out. I bury myself to the hilt in her pulsing sheath, spilling every piece of my soul into her. My balls throb in the seam of her ass, and still, I want to be deeper, closer. I want to rip open my chest and pull her inside, keep her safe in the shelter of my skin and bones, where no one can ever hurt her again.

The mate bond isn't anything like I imagined it would be. I was thinking sparks and fire, magic that would leave me feeling different than I had before.

Instead, I feel like...myself. My true self, the one I've had to keep hidden for so long just to stay safe and alive. But with Wren, I don't have to hide. She sees me—every angry, wounded, sad, bitter, and secretly hopeful part—

and she loves me. Not despite my scars, but because of them.

Because when she looks into my eyes, she knows that she isn't alone. I've been where she's been. I've known that kind of pain, and I know we can get past it.

Together.

"I love your nipples," I say as she lies on the bed beside me, her chest rising and falling as she catches her breath. "I want to bite them."

She turns to me, her lids drooping as she says, "Then bite them."

I arch a brow. "Yeah? Right now?"

"If you're ready for round two, I am. I haven't had nearly enough of you." She cups her breasts in her hands, plumping them together in a way that makes my cock suddenly capable of Herculean feats of recovery and stamina.

I suck her tits, bite them, pinch them as I take her from behind with her fingers wrapped around the rickety spindles of the headboard.

We break three of them before we're finished.

By the time Dust knocks on the door a little after eight a.m., we've already worked up a sweat. Three times. But there's no time for a shower.

"We've got news and food and coffee downstairs," Dust says, smiling over Wren's shoulder at me when she opens the door. "And it looks like you're ready to jump into some memory recovery this morning."

"Whatever it takes," I say, squeezing Wren's hip. It's still a little weird to me—that Dust doesn't seem to care that we're going to be sharing Wren.

It's even weirder that it doesn't bother *me*. In the past, I've been possessive with the women in my life. I didn't want another man looking at them too hard, let alone putting his hands all over what was mine.

But with Wren...

She's mine, but she's also *ours*, and as crazy as it sounds, it feels right. Good. Like this is the way it was always meant to be.

So I don't mind tugging on my shoes, grabbing our small bag of overnight things, and following Dust out the door and down the hall. There will be more time for Wren and me to be alone. Soon. But for now, we've got to work together to keep her safe.

And maybe pull the world back from the brink while we're at it.

CHAPTER 40

DUST

W e're finally here, right where we need to be. A complete set, a Fata Morgana in full power, supported by her four mates.

It's evident the moment that Luke, Wren, and I step back into the room where the rest of the crew are waiting for us. The energy sizzles with possibilities, like a wave about to crash against the shore—inevitable, beautiful, and dangerous.

"Wow." Sierra's eyebrows shoot up over the edge of her breakfast sandwich. "You guys…. Good luck blending in walking around like that."

"Like what?" Wren grabs an egg and cheese sandwich from the pile on the bureau.

Sierra shakes her head, chewing thoughtfully. "Like…rock stars. Movie stars. Superheroes from another planet. Something like that. The kind of people who attract a lot of fucking attention."

"She could have a point." Kite wraps his arms around

Wren from behind, cuddling her close, clearly glad to have her back with us. "I didn't realize it would be this intense. I feel like I could run a marathon or something, and I haven't even had any coffee yet."

"I feel like I could eat two of those." Luke motions toward the pile of sandwiches. "Is that cool? It looks like there are extra."

"Go for it. I bought three more than usual," Sierra says. "I figured you and Wren would be starving after the, um...workout. Sorry about being suspicious of your ass, by the way." She shrugs. "I can admit when I'm wrong, and I was wrong."

Luke nods as he unwraps a bagel with extra egg and cheese. "It's cool. And who knows, you could still be right. Like I told them yesterday, I don't remember what happened to me when I was a kid, or who was responsible. It could have been Highborn who turned me, I don't know for sure."

"Well...even if it was, it doesn't matter now." Sierra wads her empty wrapper into a ball. "He's dead, and his institute is under investigation. It was on the news this morning. Sometime overnight, his Happily Ever After file was posted on Encyclo.com, and now everyone is losing their shit."

"So much for the secure computer trip," Creedence says with a grunt.

"Oh, and it gets better." Sierra tosses her foil ball into the trash, sinking it clean. "The FBI stormed the Elysium Institute in the middle of the night, arrested eight of Highborn's doctors, and started seizing shit. Either they didn't know that the Department of Homeland Defense was in bed with Highborn, or they're pretending they didn't in hopes it will slow down some of that crazy."

She motions toward the muted television behind me, where shots of protestors filling the streets in L.A. carrying "Shifters are citizens too!" and "We Welcome Supernatural Diversity" signs contrast sharply with chilling footage of a group of Doomsday Preppers on a farm in Wyoming. They've declared their property "Demon Beast Free" and are offering sanctuary for humans who need it and a chest full of bullets for any shifter who sets foot in firing range.

"It's not only in the States, either." I curl my fingers around my coffee, soaking in the last of the warmth. "There are protests popping up all over the world. Highborn's file didn't just leak the medical records of the shifters he'd tortured and the intelligence his people had gathered on Atlas. It also listed over a hundred high-ranking global power players he believed to be shifters, names he added to a hit list that started circulating the dark web a few years ago. In the time since his original post, sixteen of those people were murdered or mysteriously disappeared."

"He was out of his mind," Wren murmurs.

"Completely," I say. "And now, for better or worse, the entire world knows it. They also know about *us* in numbers we've never faced before."

"A lot of people won't believe it," Creedence says.

"But a lot of people will. The fall out is going to be… massive." Kite blows out a slow breath, shaking his head. "There are enough people in our own community who've been frustrated by being forced to keep our powers secret. Once you get enough of those coming out of the shadows, showing the world what they can do..."

"We're going to have a hundred new Highborns on our hands," Luke prophesizes darkly. "A thousand."

He's a pessimist, that one.

He's also most likely right.

"Which means we're probably not going to find a better time to make our move. The chaos is going to get worse before it gets better." I draw out the map of Banff I liberated from the brochure stand downstairs and spread it open on the table beside Sierra. "Looking through the files last night, I noticed a pattern. Dr. Highborn's people have been tracking Atlas for years, following his comings and goings, trying to locate his compound."

"So they could bomb the shit out of it and not have to play his reindeer games anymore," Creedence helpfully supplies, standing back to make room for Wren and Luke to stand on either side of me.

"Most likely," I agree. "Though, it would have been difficult getting the Canadian government on board with a mission like that. Especially since it looks like Atlas is holed up somewhere in the middle of Banff National Park. He was tracked to these locations before the people following him lost his trail." I point to the longitude and latitude points I marked on the map in red pen. "We're thinking they're portals to his realm."

"Or damned close to one." Sierra taps a finger on the

mark nearest the highway. "This one is especially interesting. Atlas kept me on a leash outside his study for a while, back when I was too weak from the torture to be a flight risk. Sometimes he would go inside for hours and come out smelling like he'd been sitting in a restaurant. One time he even brought back a plate of this fancy ass poutine with a little egg on the side. At the time, I thought he must have a dumbwaiter or a secret passage or something in there. Because I knew I hadn't seen any of his slaves coming or going while I was sitting outside. But look at this…" She waves my direction. "Show them, Dust."

I pluck the burner phone from the table and pull up the menu we found last night before handing the phone over to Wren.

She squints at the tiny letters for a moment before her brows lift suddenly. "Beef Brisket poutine with quail egg." She looks up, her gaze finding mine. "Where is this?"

"The restaurant at the Fairmont Banff Springs. The most exclusive resort in the area. It looks like Atlas has a portal somewhere on the property."

"A portal that might still be guarded," Sierra adds. "But it won't be spelled against outsiders the way the others are, so you won't need me to open it."

Wren's forehead wrinkles. "Why not?"

"It can't be," I explain. "Not with that many people coming and going in the surrounding area. Privacy spells, even the strongest ones, are only reliable in remote locations, where there isn't a lot of human traffic to begin with. Which is probably why Atlas has the portal behind a locked door, where possibly his own people don't even know about it."

"So you won't be walking in through his front door," Sierra says, excitement dancing in her dark eyes. "Or even one of the side doors. You'll be coming in his private entrance, and I seriously doubt even *he'll* be expecting that."

"If we're lucky, the door could open right into his study," Kite says, floating the best-case-scenario we're all hoping proves true. "Which means we bypass the army on his killing fields and the guards surrounding the castle completely."

Wren nibbles at her thumb. "I don't want to get my hopes up too high on that, but..." She makes a fist, thumping it on the table. "But let's do it. It's worth a try, and it sounds like the best shot we've got."

"We thought you'd think so," I say. "So we went ahead and made a few arrangements."

"Sierra's heading out tomorrow morning." Kite crosses to rest a hand on the back of her chair. "We won't need her to lead us to Atlas, and since this was never meant to be her fight, we thought you'd agree it's best to send her out of harm's way."

Wren nods firmly. "Absolutely."

"Not that I'm not willing to stay if you need me." Sierra lifts her arms, the fingers on her remaining hand spread wide, a vivid reminder of just how evil our enemy truly is. "Just let me know. Whatever you think is best, mama. You're the head cheese around here, and don't you let these boys forget it, all right?"

"No, you're out of here," Wren says, lips curving.

"They're right. This is our fight, and I'll feel so much better knowing that you're safe."

"Me, too," Kite agrees. "You've given enough. More than enough."

Sierra shrugs, clearly uncomfortable. "It's not enough until that fucker is dead. But there's nothing in the books about a Fata Morgana facing Atlas with the help of her four mates and a random lesbian who's along for the ride. And I don't want to get in the way, so..." She shifts her gaze my way. "But if the fancy hotel portal doesn't pan out, I'll be back before you can say 'Atlas sucks ass.' Like I told you last night, I'm ninety percent sure the portal I went through was over here." She points to a star near an isolated portion of Lake Louise. "I smelled water, and this is the only one close enough to the lake to make that possible."

"Thank you," I say, nodding as I promise. "We'll call you if we need you."

But hopefully, we won't. Sierra's right. Every prophecy regarding the downfall of Atlas is firm about a rival Fata Morgana facing Atlas alone, with only his or her mates. No army, no spies, no secret weapons, and no tricks.

And Kite is right—Sierra has already lost more than any of us. Getting her out of the line of fire now that she isn't necessary to gaining entrance to Atlas's kingdom is the decent thing to do.

"So how are things going with reservations?" I ask Creedence.

The cat lifts both thumbs. "We're ready to rock. I've already booked two rooms using a gift card I bought with a reloadable debit card that I bought with Mr. Sam Thompson's considerable credit, so our trail shouldn't be easy to trace." Creedence tosses the card onto the table beside the map. "I saw Mr. Thompson dump hot coffee on a homeless kid on his way into the office this morning. Footing our bill is the least Sam can do by way of karmic retribution."

"Be nice, Sam," Wren murmurs, drumming her fingers thoughtfully on the table. "Kindness doesn't cost a thing."

My heart twists. She's changed so much in the past few weeks, but she's also still the same. Still Wren, still kind to the center of her bones, the polar opposite of the man she'll face on the battlefield far too soon. Her gentle spirit used to worry me, but the closer I get to my mate and her beautiful soul, the more I think it's her greatest strength. She has a power Atlas will never possess, and I pray every damn day it will see her through.

See us all through.

I'm not ready to go out yet. I want more time, more memories, more of the woman I love.

As if sensing the emotion rushing me, Wren shifts closer, sliding her arm around my waist and lifting her chin. "I like seeing you so much better this morning."

"I like seeing you all the time." I lean down, pressing a kiss to her sweet mouth.

She hums against my lips. "You taste like Dust again," she says as we pull back.

I arch a brow. "As opposed to?"

"Dust with a side of death." Worry creeps in to

tighten her features. "But you're not in fighting shape. Not yet. Tonight feels too soon."

"Our reservation doesn't start for two days," Creedence assures her before I can ask what dates he was able to secure. "The captain will be good as new by then. And that gives us time to find out what Luke has locked in the cranky head of his." Cree nods toward the other room. "You kids ready to get to work on that? I don't know about you, but I figure the sooner we know the rest of Tall, Dark, and Scary's backstory, the better. Wren's sister's life could depend on it."

"I'm ready," Luke says, before adding with an openness that's as unfamiliar as it is refreshing, "I guess I am, anyway. I have no idea how any of this works. You'll have to show me what to do."

"Don't worry, buddy," Creedence says in a faux seductive voice. "We'll be gentle."

Surprisingly, Luke grins. "Nah, that's okay. I like it rough."

"That's a true story." Wren steals Kite's coffee, grinning wickedly as she takes a sip, making Creedence laugh.

"Oh, Slim, look at you. Making sex jokes in front of everyone." He presses a hand to his heart with one hand as he wipes an imaginary tear from his cheek with the other. "I'm so proud."

Wren narrows her eyes, slapping him on the chest but grinning wider as he pulls her into his arms. "Hush, you mess. Someday you won't be able to embarrass me this easily, you know?"

Creedence clucks his tongue and kisses her cheek.

"Yes, I will. I'm always going to be ahead of that curve, baby. I love making you blush too much."

And I love her—every gorgeous, brave, and determined inch of her.

"Let's do this." I start toward the other room, Luke close behind me and Creedence, Wren, and Kite trailing after. An army of five might not seem like much to most people, but this morning it feels like...everything.

All we need and more.

CHAPTER 41
WREN

We settle into a circle cross-legged on the floor around the same coin Dust and I used to life fast. It's bent and worn from the last time we let it ground us in this time and place while we visited another, but Dust assures us that it still has enough juice left to keep us safe.

Now, all we have to do is link up and tap into Luke.

"Ready?" Dust rests a hand on my lower back, right next to Cree's and below Kite's warm palms, which are pressed lightly against my shoulders.

I take a deep breath, fingers flexing and releasing. "Ready." I peek at Luke. "You ready?"

He sits up straighter, fists propped on his knees. "As I'll ever be."

"Then close your eyes and concentrate on your breath," Dust says. "Wren is going to put her hands lightly on your chest, and we'll let whatever comes come. Don't worry about trying to direct your memories, Luke, and don't fight too hard to find Scarlett, Wren. You're the only one touching Luke, so the energy we're summoning is automatically going to seek out the places where you're connected. We're just here to give you the boost you need to find things buried so deep in Luke's subconscious mind that he doesn't remember them."

I nod. "Got it. Here we go." I hold Luke's gaze, waiting until his eyes slide closed before I reach out, gently flattening my palms on his powerful chest.

For a long moment, there's nothing but the sound of light rain falling outside and the creaking of the old building settling in the morning chill, but as soon as my eyes close, the movie starts.

That's what it feels like, sitting in a darkened theater, watching a story play out.

But this isn't fiction.

This is real life, and everything I'm seeing happened.

Those kids—dozens of them, filthy and freezing and scared to death—really were herded into a stall in a barn somewhere in what looks like the Pacific Northwest. That little girl, so tiny she can't be more than four or five years old, really was knocked flat in the rush as their captors goaded the children forward with cattle prods, her nose bloodied so badly she looks like she's grown a beard of flaking red.

She's crouched in a corner, weeping and calling for her sissy, when a dark-haired boy of maybe nine or ten offers her the bottom of his flannel shirt. He's dipped it in one of the buckets of water left for the children to drink from, making it easier to mop up her tiny face.

"Your sister's okay," he says, his voice gentle, but strong. "She's in the pen across from ours. Right over there, see? Her name is Scarlett, right?"

My heart jerks hard in my chest as the little girl—me, all those years ago, in this terrible place I can't remember—nods, her blue eyes wide. Little me grabs a handful of the boy's jeans and holds on tight. "Yes. Scaw-wett," I whisper, because I couldn't pronounce my Rs or my Ls until I was in second grade. "My name is Wen."

"I'm Luke," the little boy says, though I already know. He's so much smaller, but those dark, fearless eyes are just the same. "We're going to be okay. I promise. You don't have to be scared anymore, all right?"

Little me nods, and the memory dissolves, summoning a shaky sigh from Kite and a hum from Dust that assures me they're seeing all this, too. It's only poor Luke who has no idea what's going on. My lips part to tell him that we met before, but the movie is already flickering to life again, sucking me into a new chapter in the story.

Our story.

Now Luke is older, almost a man, but with that softness to his cheeks so many teenagers carry into their early twenties. He's on an abandoned airfield, in a place where palm trees whip back and forth in the evening breeze, watching the horizon as he directs a group of weary-looking people into a plane that's clearly seen better days.

"Only three more," an older man barks from behind him, pointing at the redhead—Scarlett!—standing with the cluster of remaining refugees. "The girl and two more small ones. Keep the weight down, or we won't make it across the ocean."

Scarlett moves forward, and I watch with my heart in my throat, praying this is the moment my mother was talking about, the memory that will lead me to my sister.

Luke extends his hand, and she takes it, shivering as they touch.

A beat later, Scarlett's chin jerks up, and she pins him with wide green eyes. "You're going to meet some-one," she says, her voice hoarse as if she's fighting off a cold. "An amazing girl. The best person I've ever met. You're going to think you hate her at first, but she's going to save your life."

Luke frowns and tries to pull his hand away, but Scarlett clings tight. "Believe me. It's my kin gift. I know love. I see it. It's coming to you, but not before a lot of pain. A lot of loss. It's not going to be easy, but she's worth it." Her throat works, and tears rise in her eyes. "She's so worth it. So, take care of her, okay?"

"Right, sure," Luke says, not unkindly, before motioning toward the steps to the plane. "But you should board. I don't know when the next plane will be able to take off. Might not be for days, and it's not headed to Thailand."

"Neither am I," Scarlett says, her gaze sharpening as she adds in a firmer tone. "I'm going to Germany. Bavaria. Near Neuschwanstein castle. The Fey have a secret fortress there. Don't tell anyone but her. The girl I told you about. Okay?"

Brow furrowed, Luke nods as he squirms his fingers free. "Got it."

He clearly thinks Scarlett is out of her damned mind, but she wasn't.

She *isn't*, and now I know where she is!

I also know that Luke being here isn't a fluke or a mistake, after all. It's what was always meant to be. He was meant to be mine, and I was meant to be his, and Scarlett saw it all.

The knowledge is a bright, beautiful light shining inside of me, filling me with joy and gratitude as the screen goes dark.

CHAPTER 42
WREN

I come out of the vision with tears streaming from my still closed eyes, my heart full and every cell in my body dying to get even closer to the four incredible men in my life.

Just sitting here with their hands on me, and my hands on Luke, is one of the most amazing things I've ever experienced.

There is so much love here.

Love for me, yes. But also love for each other, a bond of friendship and loyalty that grows stronger every day. I know some of them aren't ready to fess up to those feelings just yet, but they're there, and they make me so happy it's hard to pull in a full breath. Even with so much darkness hovering just around the corner, I feel like the luckiest woman in the world.

I have four brave, smart, funny, good-hearted, kick-ass men on my side, and my sister is out there across the ocean, alive and well and rooting for me.

For *us*, our circle of five, which Luke was always destined to be a part of.

I need to tell him, I realize, since he won't have seen it himself.

When I blink open my eyes, more tears slip down my cheeks, but I'm smiling as I meet Luke's worried gaze.

"What happened?" he asks tightly. "You guys aren't going for my throat, so I'm assuming it's not that bad."

"It's all good, bro," Creedence says, affection in his voice. "You're in the clear. And you're one of us. No doubt about that now."

"And we know where Scarlett is," I say, my smile stretching wider. "We can get her a message, warn her about Atlas. You did it. You saved my sister."

Dust raps on the wooden post at the end of the bed. "Don't jinx it, Snow. We've got to get word to her, first." He rises to his feet, tugging at the hem of his coat. "I'll go now. Reach out to my parents and have them spread the word to their connections in Germany. If all goes well, Scarlett should get a message by tonight."

"I'll go with you," Kite says. "Watch your back." With a final squeeze of my hand and a soft kiss on my cheek, he stands, as well. "Fill Luke in, baby. And then try to get some rest, okay?"

"I'm not tired," I lie, wrinkling my nose at Kite's dubious look, though, I should know better than to try to fool a man who literally knows what I'm feeling almost every second of the day. "Okay, so I am tired, but I'm too excited to sleep. Make sure to tell Scarlett how much I love her, Dust. That I love her, and that I can't wait to see her. As soon as this is over."

Dust nods, the faith in his eyes making me believe we're going to get there, to the other side of the night-mare, where everything will be okay. He and Kite head for the door as Sierra pops her head in from the other room.

"I heard voices," she says. "Does that mean I can come in and hear the news?"

I glance at Luke, silently asking his permission, which he grants with a quirk of his lips and a wave of his arm. "Come in, but come quick. The suspense is fucking killing me."

Creedence and I spend the next thirty minutes filling Luke in on everything he missed out on by being vision blind. He doesn't remember our meeting when we were little any more than I do, but the second we start into the account of his run-in with Scarlett, his eyes light up.

"Shit," he murmurs. "I do remember that, now that you mention it. I thought she was crazy, but..." He pauses, his throat working before he adds, "I also wanted to believe her. To believe some amazing girl was waiting for me out there, at the end of the shit show." He takes my hand, threading his fingers slowly through mine. "Glad she knew what she was talking about."

My heart swells until it feels like it's going to explode, and suddenly everything feels possible. Maybe it's because we've found Scarlett, and I'm one step closer to having my sister back in my life. Or maybe it's that secret passage hidden in a beautiful hotel in Alberta, the one just waiting to give up Atlas's secrets and usher in a new world order.

I *will* have to fight him. There's no doubt in my mind about that. I may have to kill him. But I'm ready to do what must be done, and to do it all with this love overflowing inside of me, so warm and right that even if I have to destroy someone in its name, I'll survive it. It won't mark me or ruin me or turn me into someone I can't face in the mirror in the morning.

"Fuck me," Sierra finally says, startling me out of my rosy haze with a laugh.

"Pretty crazy, right?" I squeeze Luke's hand. "How people can come in and out of your life without you even knowing it."

She nods. "For real. And your sister hiding in some enchanted fairy castle. That's wild. I mean, I knew fairies existed at one point, but no one's seen or heard from them in so long. Millenia, you know? I kind of thought they were all dead." She snorts. "And I was pretty sure they hated shifters."

"Because everyone hates shifters?" Luke arches a wry brow.

Sierra laughs as she slaps his arm. "Right? Vamps, fairies, merfolk. Even shifters hate shifters. We're the worst, dude. Why can't we just get the fuck along?"

"We will," I say, feeling the truth of it with everything in me. "What's that they say? The fish rots from the head down?"

Sierra's eyes narrow. "Yeah. So once you get rid of Atlas…"

I shrug. "Once there's love on the shifter throne, I

think we'll see more love in the shifter world. The whole world in general." I glance over to Luke before turning to meet Cree's warm gaze. "At least, I hope so."

"Know it." Creedence rests a hand on my back that sends a fresh wave of goodness coursing across my skin. "I do."

"Me, too," Luke seconds.

Sierra nods. "One of the books I read while I was in training said something like that. It also said the Fata Morgana throne has so much power because that's where all the other supernaturals came from. Once, a long-ass time ago, one of the first Fatas split into pieces when she died, forming all the others. Vampires, water folk, shifters…" She waves a hand. "Except fairies. They were around before anything else. Even the dinosaurs." Her eyes narrow. "I should have known they were still around. Probably will be here after all the rest of us are dead, and the world is ruled by raccoons. Real raccoons, not shifters."

"Why's that?" I ask. "I'm betting on cockroaches, personally. Or ants. Some sort of insect. They've got serious staying power."

"Nah." Sierra pulls a face. "Raccoons, woman. Real raccoons are the fastest adaptors on the planet. They're omnivore scavengers in charge of finding their own food, just like humans. Their brains are getting good nutrition *and* practice being clever enough to survive in a rapidly changing habitat. Someday they will be our mischievous overlords, mark my words."

"Why not shifter raccoons, too?" Creedence asks, playing along. "Too human on the inside?"

"Yep," Sierra confirms. "We can go kin, but we'll never *be* kin. Not unless we give up the fight and go furry." She winces, glancing my way. "Shit. Sorry, Wren. I didn't mean that."

I shake my head. "It's okay. I know you weren't talking about Carrie Ann."

"Not even a little bit," she confirms. "That girl went furry a hero. No doubt."

The mention of Carrie Ann dulls the happy love buzz, making my eyes feel heavy. But I refuse to nap when there's still so much left to be done.

"So, who's coming shopping with me?" I slap my palms to my thighs, making my way off the floor. "Because nothing any of us are wearing right now is going to cut it at a fancy hotel."

Creedence claps his hands, playing up his excitement as he leaps to his feet. "Oh, me! I love shopping. And I'm really good at picking pockets so we'll be able to afford something other than the Goodwill."

"Or we could shoplift," Sierra says. "Not to brag, but I'm pretty good at it. Until the resistance gave me a reason to turn my life around, I was a full-time juvenile delinquent. And if we steal directly from our corporate overlords, we'll know we're lifting shit from a big bad company with insurance." She points a finger my way, pulling the trigger. "Because you know Princess doesn't like stealing from random, possibly innocent people."

I press my lips together. "This is true. I'd rather not shoplift, either, but desperate times call for desperate measures."

"But they might not be desperate for too much

longer." Luke stands, jabbing a thumb toward the other room. "Anyone mind if I grab a nap while the shopping is going down? Not to be a wimp, but that was weirdly draining."

"Not at all, friend, you can trust me to pick you out something nice," Creedence says. "In mustard yellow, I'm thinking."

"Yellow makes me look like I have jaundice, man," Luke says.

Creedence winks. "I know. Can't have you looking too pretty, Wolf Boy." He grins as he grabs an unfamiliar wallet from the bedside table. He was busy while I was gone claiming my final mate.

Which reminds me…

"We haven't talked about what happens to Atlas's mates if I have to kill him," I say, casting a glance at the door, though I'm sure Dust and Kite won't be back for a while. "Remind me to have a sit down about that as soon as we're back together tonight. I want to set them free if we can. They were forced into the mate bond. They aren't his allies or his wives in any real sense of the word. They're his prisoners."

"Totally," Sierra agrees, shrugging into her jacket, a nod to the cool morning. "Those poor women have been through enough. The last thing they deserve is to become collateral damage in a war they never wanted to fight in the first place."

"And how many mates does he have now?" Creedence asks, shoving his hands in the pockets of his jeans. "Forty or fifty still living?"

Sierra nods. "Something like that."

Creedence huffs. "No wonder. Even Fatas weren't made to have that many bonds. That's probably one of the things making Atlas crazier than a box of dildos."

A laugh bursts from my lips unexpectedly. "Really?" I arch a brow. "I didn't realize dildos were that crazy."

Cree wraps an arm around me, pulling me close. "They aren't. I just figured that would make you smile, gorgeous. Now come on, let's get you something to wear other than this hideous T-shirt. I'm starting to forget how beautiful you really are."

Sierra snorts as she starts toward the door ahead of us. "Yeah, right. That's why you can't keep your hands off her, kitty cat."

"I resemble that remark," Creedence says, copping a feel of my ass as we follow her.

I laugh as I wave goodbye to Luke, who's watching from the doorway leading into the adjoining room. "You okay here by yourself?"

"I'll be fine," he says indulgently.

"Lock the doors behind us," I say. "I've got a key."

"Will do," he promises. "Love you."

"I love you, too." I slip out the door, that happy glow cozying to life inside of me again.

And it stays there, burning warm and constant, making it so easy to believe that everything is going to go as planned. Even as Creedence threads his fingers through mine and his kin gift sparks to life inside me, filling my head with a vision that threatens to shatter my heart into tiny pieces, I hold tight to the balloon of hope lifting me high into the air.

I glance up at Cree, but he doesn't seem to see it, the

dark story playing out on one side of the street as we walk down the other. But I do. I see, and I know now without a doubt that Dust was right.

Things are going to get worse before they get better.

They're going to get so bad I might not survive to see the sun rise again. But there's a chance I'll win, too, and Atlas knows it. He's running scared, which is right where I want him.

He thinks I don't see him coming, but I do.

I do, Atlas, I whisper quietly inside my heart, where I have everything I need to face this monster. *I see you. And I'm ready.*

CHAPTER 43

CREEDENCE

My hopes are up. Way up. For the first time since I found out I was chosen for this job, I feel like I might actually survive to witness the aftermath.

Though, of course, it doesn't feel like a job now.

It's a calling. A reason for living.

And she's all I want to do.

Even with the scent of wolf clinging to her, it's all I can do not to drag Wren into the first dark alcove we pass on the street and ravage her mouth with mine. I'm addicted to her, constantly starved for a taste of her skin, the feel of her arms wrapped tight around me.

Even with Sierra bopping along in front of us, promising she knows a store that's "super mob douchey and deserves to be robbed blind," I consider it. A stolen kiss behind the newspaper stand at the end of the block, or even right in the middle of the damned sidewalk, where everyone walking by can stop, stare, and get properly jealous that they aren't the one kissing this fine ass woman.

She's glowing this morning, so beautiful I can't keep my eyes off her.

It's still hard to believe she's mine. Even harder to believe that seeing how much her other mates love her doesn't make me jealous.

It actually makes me feel...safe. If something happens to me, if I die in this fight, she has three other people there to pick up the slack. People to protect her, to adore her, and to make sure she never doubts that she can rise to this and any other challenge life throws in her path.

I'm so deep in sappy contemplation, I don't realize we've arrived at our destination until Wren stops abruptly beside me, her brows furrowing. "This is it?"

Sierra nods toward *Gio's High Fashions*, a hole-in-the-wall wedged between a cheap shoe store and a wholesale shop selling garishly bright purses, with a faded gold sign and a sagging rack of raincoats sitting on the walk outside the door.

"I know. It doesn't look like much, but trust me— they've got tons of high dollar stolen shit in the back. I spotted it yesterday when I was scoping out the neighborhood." She bobs her head back and forth. "They've got a big guy guarding the front door, too, but no cameras and only little old ladies manning the floor. Just signal what you want, and I'll stuff it down my empty sleeve. But go for something slinky, Wren. It'll look great on you and be small enough to fit a shirt or two for the boys in there while we're at it. Then we can buy something small to throw them off the scent and head over to the department store near the conference center for more casual stuff."

The back of my neck prickles, and I turn, surveying the sidewalk behind us.

But there's no one there. The entire block is deserted, in fact, which is...strange.

The area around the hotel was crowded, and just two minutes ago I was dodging pedestrians in order to keep my arm around Wren's waist. I glance at the other side of the busy street and at the block we left behind on the other side of the crosswalk. Both have a decent amount of foot traffic.

So why not here? Why are we suddenly all alone?

"I don't like it," I say beneath my breath, but loud enough for Sierra and Wren to hear. "Something smells off. Let's go straight to the department store. I'll buy a cheap jacket, and we can both get to sleeve stuffing."

Wren steps toward me, but Sierra stops her with a hand on her arm. "Come on, guys. Seriously. This place is going to be a breeze. We'll be in and out in five minutes. Trust me."

Trust her...

Do I trust her? Earlier this morning, the answer would have been a fairly easy yes, but I spent too many years hustling with my parents not to sense when someone's trying to play me.

Sierra wants this too much. There's no reason this hole in the wall should be so important to her, no reason she should want us to follow her inside so badly her fingertips are going white as she grips Wren's arm.

I open my mouth to tell Wren to run, but something happens to the words between my brain and my mouth. "Sure, let's go," I hear myself saying, my tongue flopping in my mouth like someone shoved a hand up inside me like a sock-puppet.

And then my feet are moving toward the door, ignoring my every cue to stop, drop, run, shout, throw Wren to the ground and hurl my body on top of her to protect her from whatever is waiting behind those mirrored doors.

I fight with everything in me, my voice screaming inside my head, but my body keeps plodding forward, zombie-style. I spot myself in the reflective entrance, a shell with a slack jaw and someone else calling the shots, and I panic.

I'm desperately trying to think of something I can do to warn Wren when she stops beside me, turning to study my profile.

"Cree, are you okay?" she asks.

"Just fine, baby." My lips curve into a smile so hideous I silently beg Wren to look up. *Look at the reflection! Get an eyeful of this fucking weird grimace on my face and run, Slim. Run!*

But she only frowns and follows Sierra inside. I'm at the back of the line, the last to shuffle in and see...a room full of cheap clothes.

There are circular racks at the front, a few large bins overflowing with tennis shoes that smell like they've been dipped in oil, and a tower of suitcases in the far-left corner. In the right corner are racks spaced farther apart, holding goods of a much higher quality. Even from across the room, I can spot real leather, Egyptian cotton, and suits cut to flatter a man with the money to afford the very best.

It's just like Sierra said, but I know better than to think everything is going to be okay. I'm someone's goddamned puppet, and as Sierra guides Wren in front of her, headed for the good stuff, she looks way too pleased with herself.

And then her dark eyes shift to catch mine, and her face...ripples. Like water disturbed by a handful of stones.

For a moment, she's not Sierra—she's a hundred different things, zipping by at light speed in a kaleidoscope of horror—and I know that it's over.

Wren isn't going to live to face Atlas at his stronghold.

Wren is going to die.

Right now.

Right in front of me, while I'm being mentally held prisoner by a monster with the power to turn people into playthings and the patience to hide in plain sight until presented with the perfect moment to strike.

Sierra's face reassembles itself, and she turns, trailing after Wren in slow motion.

My hope swirls down the drain, and a howl of despair echoes through my brain. If I had control of my arms and legs, I would throw myself at Atlas-Sierra's back, try to hold him-her down long enough for Wren to get away, but my body doesn't belong to me anymore.

I'm a pawn, shuffling into place by a row of dress

shirts, my chin tipping down toward my chest. To the casual observer, I must seem to be checking out the selection of linen button-downs. But if they looked closer, they would see my eyes shifted sharply in their sockets, glued to Wren as she selects a white sundress with spaghetti straps that she holds up to the light, pretending to examine the fabric as she passes a sleek navy dress to Sierra behind her back.

"Yeah, that's cute, but you should try it on, mama," Sierra says, stuffing the other dress into her sleeve. "Make sure it's not see-through, or you'll have to buy a slip."

Wren glances at the shorter woman over her shoulder, hesitating a beat before she nods. "Okay. Do they have changing rooms?"

"Yeah. They must." Sierra lifts an arm, signaling to the older woman standing by the vat of shoes.

She starts toward them, a smile on her wrinkled face. "Can I help you girls?"

"My friend wants to try on the white dress," Sierra says, an eager smile curving her lips.

"Of course." The woman reaches for a key ring clipped to her belt loop. "That's a pretty one. Might be a little short, though. You're so tall, like a model. And so beautiful! What lovely skin."

"Thank you," Wren says, fidgeting with the strap of the dress.

"You should let me bring you a few other options," the sales attendant continues, crossing to the line of dressing rooms on the back wall. "We got a new shipment last night. Lots of things in your size."

"That would be great," Sierra says, as the woman unlocks the room on the far right. "Something in black, maybe? We've got a fancy dinner coming up. A real special event."

The woman nods excitedly. "Oh, yes. I have just the thing. I'll be right back." As she shuffles away, Wren moves toward the door Sierra is holding open, and my soul rips down the center, sending out a warning cry I already know Wren won't hear.

But surprisingly, she glances over her shoulder, lifting her fingers to her lips and blowing me a kiss. As her hand drops to her side, I watch her eyes go dark with the same knowledge that's been scalding through my nerve endings since we got to this fucking place.

My heart lurches as she drops the dress, spinning to grab Sierra around the shoulders, and tackling her to the floor of the dressing room.

They both vanish before they hit the floor.

We fall for what feels like ages and no time at all, eternity and a single blinding second, tangled together and tied up with a scalding hot bow.

It's boiling in this place, wherever *this place* is. Sweat rolls down my spine and my skin goes slick, but I don't let Sierra go, no matter how hard she struggles.

Because she isn't Sierra. She hasn't been Sierra for a long time. I know that even before we hit bottom and the smell of death floods into my nose, making me gag.

My arms spasm—tight then loose—and the wriggling thing in my arms slithers free. A giant pool of what looks like liquid mercury oozes away across the hard earth as I fall to my hands and knees, coughing hard, fighting the urge to vomit as I see what's causing the smell.

It's Sierra, propped against the earthen wall beside a rough wooden door.

The corpse is rotted, sagging, and toothless, black with some kind of creeping growth, but I recognize the spiky hair and combat boots. Tears rush into my eyes as I press a hand to my mouth, but there isn't time to cry.

Atlas is already finding another form, this one also upsettingly familiar.

"What's wrong, Wren? Are you feeling okay, honey?" He's wearing my adopted mother's face and blond bob this time, reaching for me with those familiar arms.

I scramble backward until I hit another cold dirt wall and rise to my feet. "Stop it. I know who you are. You can't trick me anymore."

"It was never a trick, child," he says, still in my mother's voice, in her body. "It was a test. And you did so well."

I shake my head. "I didn't sign up for any test."

Atlas curves my mother's lips into an indulgent grin. "But you were always good at them. Even when you were a sick, sad little girl. But now you're so smart, so strong and kind. You're exactly what I've been waiting for."

"Oh yeah?" I arch a brow as my fingers curl into fists at my sides, ready to defend myself the second he makes a move. "How's that?"

"I never wanted to kill them," Atlas-mom says. "The others like us. But they couldn't see what you see, Wren. They didn't have your good heart. They were going to force humanity to endure hundreds of years of suffering, all for nothing." He-she takes a step toward me. "But our talk in the clearing that day touched you. I could see it. You have the capacity to think clearly, to understand the big picture. To realize the kindest thing we can do for the people of this planet is to make it quick. Painless. Together, we could make that happen. Almost instantly." His stolen eyes twinkle. "No one's ever told you what two Fata Morganas can accomplish together, have they? They want you to believe it's you or me. One or the other."

"It *is* one or the other." I flatten my hands against the wall behind me, feeling my way along as I ease to the right, into the shadows. The only light in this hole or cave or whatever it is comes from an ancient orange bulb above the primitive door. I have no idea what's lurking in the darkness, but I already know it can't be worse than the creature closing in on me wearing my mother's skin.

"I'm not going to help you destroy everyone on the planet," I continue, wiping sweat from my forehead before it can drip into my eyes, and fighting another wave of nausea as the smell of decomposing flesh hits me all over again. "I don't want a part in anything you have planned. I've seen you in action. I've seen the things you've done, all the innocent people you've destroyed. You don't care about humanity or anything else."

My mother's features tighten with regret. "I admit it's hard to take them seriously. From where I sit, they're already so damaged, so wounded. Is it monstrous to put a suffering animal out of its misery, sweetheart? Or is it kindness?"

"Don't call me sweetheart," I snap, cursing to myself as I reach the place where the wall curves back toward the door. This antechamber is even smaller than I thought. And damper. I glance down long enough to see black gunk stuck to my fingers then shift my attention quickly back to Atlas as I brush it off onto my jeans. "You're not my mother. Show your real face."

"This could be my real face. Reality is ninety-five percent what we choose to believe. So, what would you choose, Wren? This? Or this, maybe." My mother's face ripples and stretches, smoothing into darker skin with high cheekbones and melted-chocolate brown eyes.

"You're not Kite," I say, my chest tight. "You're not any of the people I love, and I'm never going to believe you are." I stand up straighter, nails digging into my palms. "And I won't help you. You have two choices— step down peacefully and let me try to fix the mess you've made, or we fight for the throne. Your call."

Kite-Atlas arches a brow. "Threats of violence so soon? I expected better from you, Bird Girl."

"Stop." The backs of my eyes begin to sting. His voice sounds so much like Kite's, and I want so badly not to be alone here in the guts of the earth with a monster. But he's not Kite, and I can't forget that for a second, no matter how hot it is down here or how my head is swimming. "You started the violence. You killed Sierra."

"And Carrie Ann," he says pleasantly. "I found her in the woods, that night after she went furry and ran away. Ripped her head from her body."

A wounded sound escapes my scratchy throat.

"I didn't want to." He moves slowly closer, making my heart race. "But Highborn was watching, and I couldn't resist playing with him a little." He smiles, a mad smile I've never seen on the real Kite's face. "You're right, I do like to play with them. You'd enjoy it, too, if you let yourself. Take a step back and you'll see, Wren. They're ants. Maggots. Dim-witted, short-lived beasts who will ruin Earth for all of us if we let them. And there isn't another inhabitable planet close enough for us to reach, not even in spore form. Believe me, I've tried."

I shake my head, fighting for breath as my pulse races and my face flames so hot it feels like my eyes might bulge out of their sockets. But clearly Atlas isn't feeling the heat the way I am, so there must be a way around it.

Swiping at my sweat-covered face again, I reach down, finding my flame form and turning it inside out, pulling ice to the surface of my skin, instead. Almost instantly I'm cooler, calmer, able to think more clearly.

And to realize the door behind Atlas is my only way out.

If I have to face him alone, I will. But if there's any chance I can run, escape, find my way back to my mates, I have to try. I need them, now, more than ever.

I fix the door in my peripheral vision, refusing to look directly at it again for fear of tipping Atlas off to my intention. "I won't enjoy hurting people." I shift ever so slightly to the left. "Hurting anything. Ever. But if I have to, I will."

Kite-Atlas crosses his arms at his chest. "If you have to hurt me, you mean? Well, if that comes to pass..." He smiles. Widely. Nightmarishly. "But you have other demons to battle first."

I glare at him, fighting to swallow past the lump swelling in my throat. "Like what?"

"You know, little girl," he whispers. "That part of you that wants to run home. To run away and wake up in your childhood bed, too sick to be expected to grow up and take care of yourself like all the other girls. Admit it, lovely, you liked being sick. Being weak. Leaving the hard decisions to the grownups while you felt noble and special for accomplishing nothing with your life except managing not to die."

I shiver, suddenly too cold. Almost frozen. But I can't seem to thaw the ice oozing through my blood

Atlas winks. "I have a Creedence of my own. Her name is Desdemona, and she's shown me every possible consequence of this choice. In most of the possible futures, you don't make it out of here alive. And when you do, you almost always choose to join me. To help me." He extends a hand, his fingers suddenly only inches from my face, though I can't remember seeing him move. "You even come to love me. I can be everything you need, Wren. I can make you believe they're still here with you, all the people you love, every single one."

His skin ripples again, shifting from Creedence to Luke to Dust and back to Kite again, sending tears spilling down my cheeks as I realize I may never see them again.

But then again, I might...

"There's also a v-version where I w-win," I stammer,

my teeth chattering from the chill I can't throw off, no matter how hard I try. "I've seen it."

Atlas-Kite cocks his head. "Yes. A slight chance. Worth the risk, I think, for an opportunity to wipe the slate clean. I have so many lovely things waiting in the wings, pretty girl." He smooths a hand over my hair as I sag against the wall, my knees liquid but the rest of me ice. "Terrible, beautiful things. I can't wait to show you. You'll come to love them, I think. As much as I do." His bends low, keeping his face even with mine as I slide to the floor. "But if I never see you again, I've enjoyed this. You're magnificent. The best challenger to come around in ages. You could complete me, Wren, and I you." He leans in, kissing my forehead, making me shudder with disgust.

"Sweet dreams, darling." He stands, backing away. "The black under your fingernails is a fungal parasite, similar to Ophiocordyceps unilateralis. It's extinct on Earth, but still alive and well here in my realm. It's one of the so-called zombie parasites. The priests and priestesses of my boyhood used it to test the worthiness of their devotees."

He reaches for the doorknob, and I try to stand, but my body refuses to respond. I'm frozen solid now, locked in the fetal position against the fungus-infested wall.

"If you're very strong and very lucky," he continues, "you'll fight your way free of its control and come find me on the other side. If not, you'll go gently, surrounded by all the things that make you truly happy."

"N-no," I stutter, my voice thin as smoke.

"It can only use what it finds inside you." Atlas-Kite grins. "We carry the seeds of our own destruction, lovely, and the fungus knows it. Good luck tending your garden."

I blink, frozen lids dragging down and back up again, and he's gone, vanished through the door or into thin air, leaving me alone with Sierra's rotted corpse and the parasite burrowing inside, already making it hard to remember how I got here.

To this place.

To this toxic womb somewhere between the real world and a monster's forbidden kingdom.

To being so alone when I had so much, so many...

When I had love.

Love. I hold tight to the thought, wrapping my arms around it and squeezing with all my might as my eyes close and my brain goes cold, colder, frozen so solid my thoughts are trapped beneath the surface, giving the darkness within a smooth place to travel.

It glides closer, coming to teach me. To test me. Maybe even to kill me.

But I will love my way through it. All of it.

Because we don't just carry the seeds of our own destruction inside of us—we carry the seeds of our salvation, too. And mine lies in the bonds I've formed with the men I love, the men who love me, the four irreplaceable people who are out there somewhere, waiting for me to find my way home.

To be concluded in

Unbroken
Dark Moon Shifters Book 3
Keep reading for a sneak peek of Chapter One!

Subscribe to Bella's newsletter to receive
an email when book three is released!
https://www.subscribepage.com/q9t2v1

SNEAK PEEK ONE

Please enjoy this sneak peek of PUSH UP BRAWL, the
start of the sexy new Supernatural in Seattle series. Set
in the world of Unleashed and Untamed, each
Standalone story ends with its own happily ever after
and features cameos from characters you've met
before...

About Push Up Brawl

**One beauty-queen-turned-shifter out to squash her
evil ex boyfriend.**

**Two vampires looking for a one-of-a-kind girl to
help reclaim their stolen throne.**

And a sexy bargain that's triple the fun...

The only thing worse than dating a mad scientist who couldn't keep his swizzle stick out of other women's beakers? Discovering he secretly revenge-altered your DNA while you were sleeping.

Now, I'm the world's only rhino shifter.

That's right. A rhinoceros.

I went from second-runner-up at the Miss U.S. pageant, spending hours perfecting my ballet routine, spray tanning, and selecting the perfect push-up bra, to rolling in the mud to keep the ticks away and wondering what I'll do if militant shifters determined to kill lab mad freaks like me catch up with me before I'm able to stay human full time.

Enter two stupidly hot vampires who say they can give me what I need.

All night long...

Okay, so they don't say the second part flat-out, but it's all sorts of implied. I scratch their backs, they'll scratch mine, and we'll all part ways with multiple O's, no regrets, and no one's head on a pike outside the Kin Born Shifter headquarters.

But what happens when I fall in love? With both of them?

And when I decide being one-of-a-kind isn't so bad, after all?

Can rhinos live happily ever after?

Subscribe to Bella's newsletter to receive an email when Push Up Brawl is released!
https://www.subscribepage.com/q9t2v1

Wren...

I wake from the strangest dream.

The strangest, wildest dream... There were monsters and mad scientists and secrets and sadness and four amazing men and love, unlike anything I've ever known. God, there was so much love, a shameless abundance, spilling over the edges of my cup, making me feel like anything was possible.

I try to hold on to their faces, their names, but it's all slipping away, the way dreams almost always do.

Slippery dreams, as slippery as that thing...

At the end of the dream, there had been something horrible oozing across the floor. Something I'm not going to regret forgetting.

My eyes creak open, letting in the sunlight, banishing the last of the nightmare shivers. My room is brighter than usual, making me wonder if I've slept through my alarm and whether I'm going to be late to the shelter.

But then Mom calls out from down the hall, "You want waffles or pancakes, Wren?" and I remember that it's Saturday.

"Waffles, please. Be there in a second," I call back, bringing a hand to rest on my belly beneath the covers. My stomach is a little unsettled, but the nausea isn't nearly as bad this morning as it has been the past few months. Maybe the doctors have found the right cocktail again, the mix of drugs that will hold the Devour Virus at bay for a few more months, maybe a few years, if I'm lucky.

The thought is logical, but it feels...off. Wrong, somehow.

I sit up, hugging the covers to my chest as I scan the room, plagued by the terrible feeling that I'm forgetting something more important than a dream. My gaze flicks from my books on the shelves, to the papers strewn across my desk, to the bureau with the big mirror where the pill bottles sit all in a row, waiting to be tipped out, one at a time, and gulped with the glass of water I keep by my bed.

I tip my chin down to see the big pink Tupperware bowl in its usual place, as well. But I don't need it this morning. I'm not so sick that I won't be able to make it to the bathroom in time.

I'm not that sick at all, in fact.

The slight nausea fades as I swing my legs out from under the covers and start toward the bathroom, rubbing the sleep from my eyes, wishing I could remember the dream.

Or that thing bigger than the dream...

But I can't remember going to bed last night or what my parents and I ate for dinner. It's all a blur.

"The meds," I grumble as I use the bathroom and wash my hands, meeting my own weary gaze in the mirror. It's happened before—the meds that make me feel the best physically aren't always the best for maintaining prime mental function.

It comes down to a choice: feel shitty or think shitty.

Usually, I choose the former—my brain is too important to my work to risk making one of my kids feel bad because I can't remember what we talked about the day before or, God forbid, their name—but I can't deny it's nice to omit vomiting from my morning activities. My shower is equally pleasant. I don't have to use my sit stool a single time, and I even have the energy to brush on a little blush and mascara after I get dressed.

Mom will like that. Not that she cares whether or not I wear makeup, but she gets so excited when I look healthy. Even if it's a lie.

We all know the virus is winning.

No, it's not. You're not sick. Wake up, Wren! Please!

I blink at the voice drifting through my head. It's my voice, but...*not* mine, too. It feels like it's coming from somewhere far away, another place and time, a place I instinctively know I *don't* want to be. It's a cold, frightened voice, a voice that's running out of hope and options, the voice of someone who's left behind all comforts of home and is alone in the wilderness.

Not alone. You're not alone you have... So much...

I shake my head, squeezing my eyes shut until the nagging tug at the back of my thoughts fades away.

Auditory hallucinations. I make a note to mention them to my doctor at my next check-up and pad down the hall toward the heavenly smell of crispy waffles and warm maple syrup. I turn the corner into the kitchen to find Mom setting the table and Dad just in from the garden, a huge bouquet of roses in his arms, and my throat goes tight.

God, it's so good to see them...

So good. Like I haven't seen them in ages, like a part of me expected never to see them again.

"Grab forks will you, Wren?" Mom asks, her smile fading as she sets the creamer down and glances up to find me standing frozen in the archway. "What is it, baby?" She hurries around the table, reaching for me. "Are you okay? Are you feeling worse? Did the pain in your hips come back?"

I shake my head, swallowing past the lump in my throat as I struggle not to cry. "No, I'm just... I just love you so much." I fall into her open arms with a laugh that turns into a sob against my will.

"Oh, honey, I love you, too." Mom wraps me up tight, the way she's done ever since I was a little girl. "More than the sun and the moon and the stars in the sky."

"Me, too. I don't know what I'd do without my girls." Dad appears, enfolding us both in his even bigger arms, cradling us close to his chest. He smells like the garden —sunshine and herbs and freshly cut flowers—and I pull in a deeper breath, wanting to suck the comforting smell down into my soul.

This. Home. Family. Safety. Acceptance. Love without fear that it's all going to be ripped away.

How did I ever take it for granted?

It's so precious. The most precious thing in the world.

"I'm just so glad to be here," I say, swiping at the tears on my cheeks as I pull back with an easier laugh. "Sorry to be so emotional."

"Stop it." Mom takes my hand, giving it a firm squeeze. "I love your big heart. I wouldn't trade it for a mountain of pancakes."

"What about waffles?" I narrow my eyes, and Mom laughs, the way I knew she would. She's been through so much hell in her life that she's always ready to grab at a piece of heaven.

And what's more heavenly than laughing with someone you love?

"Well, waffles are another story." She winks as she motions toward the table. "You sit down, baby. I'll grab the forks. I can't wait for you to try the new recipe. These are sweet potato waffles. With honey butter to melt on top and caramelized walnuts, whipped cream, and warm syrup for toppings."

My stomach growls, and we both laugh again. "That sounds amazing." I settle in, sighing happily as Dad arranges the roses in the vase in the middle of the table. "And those are so beautiful."

"It's a perfect day out there, too," Dad says, his eyes crinkling at the edges.

I glance over my shoulder at the garden, where the morning sun is kissing every fruit, vegetable, and tightly curled flower bud, coaxing life out of the ground. "It is. We should go for a walk after breakfast. I have extra energy this morning."

"Well, of course, you do." Mom clucks as she sets a fork by my plate and slides into her seat next to me. "It's the new medicine. Working like a charm."

"Won't be long now," Dad agrees. "And you'll be good as new."

"Healthy and strong and able to live the life you've always dreamed of," Mom says, beaming at me. "And then it will be like this every day. Perfect and happy and safe."

"No more scary things. No more death waiting around the corner," Dad says, his words sending a shiver up my spine. "Not ever again."

Death. Around the corner. Waiting. To spring a trap.

I blink, and visions of a cramped cave and a corpse flash on my closed lids, making my drink of orange juice go rancid on my tongue.

"All our prayers are finally being answered." Mom sighs, eyes shining as she reaches for the syrup. "We should celebrate. It's almost your birthday, Wren. What would you like to do? A day trip to the mountains? Tea at the botanical gardens?"

A garden. There's something there.

A reminder that I have business that needs tending. My thoughts lunge toward a connection, but they're a puppy on slick tile, unable to gain traction, spinning out on unsteady paws.

"Wren?" Mom prods when I take too long to respond.

"The mountains," I say, forcing a smile. "Or we could just stay here. Have a barbeque, maybe? It's been so long since we've had friends over."

"Perfect." Mom claps her hands. "You can invite Carrie Ann and your friends from work, and we'll ask a few couples from church."

Carrie Ann. Church. The words unlock a door deep inside me, sending heat rushing out. My skin goes hot, and my hands ball into fists.

Carrie Ann is dead, and the Church of Humanity is a lie. This is all a lie.

The me-not-me voice is back, louder now, and when I look at my curled fingers, I'm struck by the sudden certainty that I know what to do with these hands.

These fists.

That I know how to fight, even if I'm too sick to cause much damage.

You're not sick, but you're in trouble. It's time to fight, the voice insists, growing so loud I can barely hear my father as he asks, "Everything okay, button?"

It's not okay.

And that's not Dad.

Subscribe to Bella's newsletter to receive an email when book three is released!

https://www.subscribepage.com/q9t2v1

ABOUT THE AUTHOR

Bella Jacobs loves pulse-pounding action, fantasy, and supernaturally high stakes, mixed with swoon-worthy romance and unforgettable heroes. She's been a full time writer for over a decade and is deeply grateful for the chance to play pretend for a living.

She writes as Bella for her trips to the dark side and can't wait to take you on her next adventure.

Visit her at www.bellajacobsbooks.com

Made in the USA
Monee, IL
18 January 2020